praise for *everyman*

"A bold and colorful exploration of personal and communal history...Fueled by intellectual inquiry and steeped in history, this book is personal and political, an unapologetic engagement of the heart and the mind."

SHEREE L. GREER,
author of *A Return to Arms*

"History owns every page of this beautifully intimate novel, residing as willfully as the fictional world Conner creates. With writing that is both smart and unapologetically edifying, Conner depicts a human experience with totality that is strikingly small, made so by the binds that tie us in our infinite search for understanding. A powerful read."

EDWARD A. FARMER,
author of *Pale: A Novel*

"Utterly compelling. It's a deep exploration into who we are in the fabric of our souls and the deep and complex power of womanhood; what makes us, what we need to know about who we are, and when we can and should just accept with love and without condition, not only those closest to us, but ourselves."

NATASHA BOYD,
author of *The Indigo Girl*

"*everyman* is a vivid and winding tale of self-discovery that I was quite happy to trail along after. With a cast of fascinating characters, each one lovingly drawn, Conner's debut is captivating, smart, and beautifully written."

SHARON LYNN FISHER,
award-winning author of *The Absinthe Earl*

everyman

everyman

A NOVEL

M SHELLY CONNER

**BLACK
STONE**
PUBLISHING

Printed in the United States of America

First edition: 2021
ISBN 978-1-0940-0620-8
Fiction / Historical / General

1 3 5 7 9 10 8 6 4 2

CIP data for this book is available
from the Library of Congress

Blackstone Publishing
31 Mistletoe Rd.
Ashland, OR 97520

www.BlackstonePublishing.com

For my mother, Jerri,
a librarian who raised me in a literal universe of books,
and my brother Marcus,
who read first and wrote first,
paving the way for his little sister.

small southern spaces

The truth about any subject only comes when
all the sides of the story are put together.
—Alice Walker, *In Search of Our Mothers' Gardens*

Small southern towns change slowly. Perhaps it's just the natural pace of southern spaces unencumbered by city-slick speed. It's best represented by the southern drawl, like golden honey dripped onto biscuits. Larger northern cities are au jus, but small southern towns are thick sausage gravy. Everything is thicker in the South. The air is thickened by the blossoms of various trees. Speech is thick on the tongues of its inhabitants. Thick-hipped women embrace their curves in the South. And southern men boast of other thicknesses. The South is syrup, and small southern towns are sorghum molasses, the long *ee* pronunciation of *pee-can*, and restaurants with sweet tea on their menus. It's the birthplace of the blues, the music that became its soundtrack, and the deep-wood shacks that played it on juke machines or, better still, with in-house bands. Language meanders like the Mississippi River, and *y'all* is directed at both singular and plural subjects.

The South cultivated its reputation for being dirty in a bad-means-good sort of way. The dirty South breeds excess and private debauchery behind the closed doors of southern sensibilities. Its dry counties and refusal to sell liquor on Sundays belied by moonshine stills and Saturday night jukes.

Small southern towns don't embrace change. Ideal, Georgia, noted only two major ones—when the Railroad married it and when the Railroad divorced it. Ideal preferred age over distinction and still boldly declared itself to be "the only ideal city in Georgia," as a painted slogan beckoning from the town's water tower proclaimed. There was a police station, a small windowless brick building with a front door on one side of the facade and a garage on the other. Next to it was a small storefront post office. Three churches—a Baptist, a Methodist, and a Church of God in Christ—flanked one gun store. Located in the curve of the Bible Belt, Ideal was protected by God and guns—often the latter before the former.

Of the two schools, the one high on the hill overlooking the town served the minority white population. Down the hill and around the bend, hidden in the hindquarters of Ideal, a small brick structure held the responsibility of educating Black youths. Still, Ideal was one of those towns where children seemed to be rare, and eventually small-town self-segregation would disappear. Time would bring the decaying of the "Black school" just as it had crept into the bones of the train depot once the Railroad ceased to stop there.

By 1972 most of the town's residents could recite only the conclusion of its name-story: that the Atlanta, Birmingham, and Atlantic Railroad had deemed their 1.2-square-mile patch of land as being "an ideal place." Adding nuance to the meaning of Ideal were the various pronunciations of the word as it was transformed through the southern dialect of the majority African American township. Ideal became "I-deal," as in to distribute, manage, or handle; "Idle," as in inactive or at leisure; "Idea," as in a thought; and sometimes "I'da," the bastardized contraction of "I would have."

The AB&A's name stuck even though the Railroad did not. The tracks remained. The 1907 Victorian depot—complete with turret, clapboard siding, and portico—remained. And the trains continued to ride the rails, but in 1972 they no longer stopped in Ideal; rather, they rushed past it on their way to places that had become "more ideal"—cities that were large enough to be called by their names instead of lumped into one collective county. Ideal had lost its trains and much of its identity. Residents traveling outside its borders told people they were from Macon County, Georgia— as did the citizens of the other two small towns that constituted the county. Two years later, the brown Victorian depot would be painted blue and donated to the town as a community center.

And so in the autumn of 1972, Eve Mann did not arrive in Ideal by rail but, rather, bumbled across the Georgia clay in a Greyhound bus that deposited her at a shared station for Macon County—if the two-pump filling station with an unevenly laid wooden-plank walkway could be classified as a bus station. It was little more than the city bus stops Eve was accustomed to from Chicago, which would have also appeared as portals to nowhere without the thriving metropolis enfolding them.

Ideal was a small town like all others. It once had big-city dreams, but its growth had been equally nurtured and stunted by the Railroad. A Quick Mart was attached to the filling station. It advertised the sale of "package goods," the broad term given to alcoholic beverages.

Other than its five hundred residents, those who set foot in

Ideal were usually taking a restroom break at its sole filling station, grabbing a few snacks, and reboarding the Greyhound. For that reason, when anything more than exhaust and dust remained after the bus's departure, news spread quickly. It usually started with the chess club. The Ideal Chess Club wasn't an official club, meaning that none of its members actually played chess. They were a group of retired men who congregated outside the Quick Mart to watch the sparse daily activities of the town. There was, however, a chess board, as well as several mismatched chess pieces that had been placed next to their collection of rickety chairs and milk-crate seats against the building. But they were only props inspired by the town's long-standing joke of calling them the Ideal Chess Club. Occasionally, someone would drop off a chess piece they had found from some long-forgotten set, saying, "Hey, I found this here bishop piece. Y'all ain't got enough of them, do you?" The pieces were collected and dutifully added to the board more or less in their proper positions. The chess club wives, bearing the clichéd moniker of the Ideal Sewing Circle, actually did sew and were stitching club baseball caps.

Disembarking from the bus, Eve shrugged out of her corduroy jacket. It may have been autumn in Chicago, but Macon County was still very much in the heat of summer. Her white canvas sneakers were immediately covered in red clay dust as she began to move toward the bus's exterior cargo compartment. Eve had been ready to welcome the fresh Georgia air and sunshine after being cramped on the bus for so long with the lingering odor of things once pleasantly classified as aromas at the start of the journey. Fried chicken, perfume, and freshly washed clothing and bodies had all become stale with time and distance by their arrival in Macon County over twelve hours later.

Beyond looking up Ideal in her aunt's Rand McNally road atlas, Eve hadn't had much of a plan for her trip. But Ideal was incredibly small, smaller than her South Side neighborhood. So she had packed a week's worth of clothing in one of her aunt's green leather suitcases and jotted down the addresses of the two places that could help her the most—the public library and a motel. There was only one of each. Like all small southern towns, Ideal had one grocery, one package store, and a funeral home run by the same family for generations—with its requisite only son who had forsaken the family business. There was a diner and a service station with a mechanic who wore denim overalls every day and had perpetually grease-stained fingernails. Outsiders called the town quaint as they drove through to more appealing cities. In case of emergency stops, they cursed it as hell, unable to imagine being happily stuck there.

Eve imagined that it looked the same as it had over twenty years ago when her mother left. She made her way toward the Quick Mart. Her suitcase pulled her heavily to one side as a map fluttered from its folds in her other hand. Although several passengers were behind her, Eve was the only one toting luggage. The rest were simply making a pit stop on their way to other destinations. The line at the register was long, so Eve decided to wait until the other passengers reboarded the bus. She dropped her suitcase next to the ice cooler against the building and sagged down beside it to consult her map.

Deuce leaned over from his seat a few feet away. "Fresh off the bus and already lost? T'aint the best start, little missy."

Eve glanced up at the kind-looking old man. Wrinkles waved across his brown face in accordance with the humor in his eyes and smile. He wore both suspenders and a belt beneath his ever-present sport coat. The shine on his shoes defied the Georgian dust.

"Nobody needs a map in Ideal." He pronounced the city *I-dear*. "It's smaller than an ant's ass." He laughed, and the wrinkles smoothed, allowing Eve a glimpse of the handsome youth beneath the old man's years.

The town consisted of three main parallel roads and various smaller streets veining out into the few neighborhoods. Main Street ran through its center and connected it to the sister county towns of Oglethorpe and Montezuma. The main road, Front Street, weaved through the white residential area while Back Street sliced through the Black neighborhood.

Eve joined in the laughter. "I'm looking for some people. I don't even really know who they are, or if they're still alive or living here."

Deuce smiled. "Hell, gal, you don't need no *lie-berry*. I'm eighty years old and been living here all my life. I'm John Johnston, but most folk call me . . ."

"Let me guess," Eve interrupted. "J. J."

Deuce laughed. "Nawl, but you got the right *i-dear*. Deuce . . . on account of the double *J*s." The nickname, typical of southern logic, required an extra step. They hadn't gone for the ease of J. J. but had continued on to think of two *J*s as a deuce.

"Nice to meet you, Mr. Johnston. I'm Eve." She extended her hand. "Eve Mann."

Deuce's hand froze in the handshake, and his smile faltered. Her face had been familiar to him in the haziness of one who has seen too many faces over many years. Now Eve's face and name coalesced in Deuce's mind. "Mann, you say?"

Eve, slightly unnerved by his piercing gaze, nodded. "With two *n*'s."

"And who you say you lookin' for?" But even before she had dug out the picture, Deuce knew.

Eve handed it to him. "Any of these people or information about them."

Deuce stared at the picture, his eyes never leaving the face of Cornelius Gaines as Eve pointed, reintroducing faces he hadn't seen in years.

"This is my mother . . . Mercy. She died in childbirth having me . . ." Eve plowed through her descriptions with a speed that did not take into account the weight of the information.

Deuce had often wondered what had become of Mercy, yet he scarcely had time to register her death before Eve had moved on in her account.

"This is my aunt Ann. She raised me. This is my grandmother Gertrude. Never met her. And I think this man is my grandfather, but he's got a different last name, and my aunt never talked about him."

Deuce silently handed the photograph back to Eve. "I 'spect you staying at the inn down yonder?"

Eve nodded.

"I can give you a lift in my truck. Let you get settled in, and maybe you come round the house this evening for dinner? The missus loves company. Always going on about what she seen on the television or read in the magazines. I'ont half pay that stuff no mind, really, but she'd love to have a city gal to chat with."

Eve smiled, uncertain. "That's awfully nice of you, Mr. Johnston, but . . ."

"I can tell you 'bout your kin."

Eve paused. The lure of revelations quelled her protest. She'd spent most of her twenty-one years inquiring about her family, mostly from Mama Ann, her aunt and childhood guardian. She couldn't believe her good fortune at arriving in her family's hometown for the first time and immediately finding someone with the information she'd been craving her entire life. She hadn't known what to expect, but this was definitely a pleasant surprise.

"You know these people?"

Deuce sighed. "I knew 'em. When they was alive." He slowly rose and rubbed his leg. "Whew. This getting up shole is harder than it was when I was your age."

He insisted on carrying her suitcase as they walked toward his truck. He dropped Eve off half a mile down a barely paved road at Johnita's Inn. Before driving away, he said, "Lemme see that map of yourn." Deuce tapped the tip of a pencil to his tongue and circled an area on the map. "Now you know how to find me once you get settled in."

Johnita's Inn was a large two-story Georgian with an impressive wraparound porch on the first floor and a balcony on the second. Like Deuce, it was weathered but showed hints of youthful times beneath its exterior. The wooden sign bearing its name was repainted every five years or so, and its former name—Johnita's Place—was no longer visible beneath the colorful coats. The stairs creaked as Eve ascended toward the screen door but remained firm under her weight.

The interior revealed a parlor room with two faded wingback chairs and a sofa arranged around a small but capable-looking fireplace. A small stand-alone bar had been converted into a reception desk manned by a tall, slender woman in her sixties with smooth dark skin, save for a few long strands of curly gray chin hair. The comparatively black hair on her head had been straightened and brushed back into a severe bun atop her head.

As Eve made her way to the desk, she was greeted by the same intense stare she had gotten from Deuce.

"I'd like a room, please." Eve smiled despite the strange look she was receiving.

"Name?" the woman asked.

"Eve Mann," she said. "With two *n*'s."

The woman exhaled slowly and nodded as if resigned to some fate. "Eve Mann, then," she stated more than questioned. "Hmph."

Eve cocked her head in confusion. "Yeah. Um, yes ma'am. Do you know me?"

The woman plowed through her greeting, "I'm Ms. Johnita, sole proprietor of Johnita's Historic Inn. We've got you settled on the second floor in room three. Follow me."

Eve could barely keep up as Johnita whisked from behind the desk and strode through the parlor to the stairs. She paused at a row of framed photographs on the wall. "This is B.B. King!" she exclaimed and added, "And Lucille, his guitar!" pointing at a picture of the bluesman with his guitar slung at his side and one arm draped casually across the shoulders of a younger Johnita.

"Yes, she didn't have a name back then," Johnita allowed a chuckle to penetrate her stoic demeanor. "Neither of 'em did back in . . ." she hesitated to place the date and sighed, then said, "Shit, 1940?" It was more question than statement.

Then, casually waving her hand across the photo array, she rattled off names, "They all came through here, mostly to stay. We were listed in that Green Book directory for years. But once they stayed, they'd always end up playing a bit. Back then, this place was more juke than inn."

A photograph of a fair-skinned woman standing, mouth agape, in front of a microphone caught Eve's attention. A band consisting of a guitarist, drummer, and saxophone player flanked behind the woman but seemed diminutive in comparison.

"Is that . . ." Eve began before Johnita interrupted.

"No."

Eve's face slowly crinkled in confused disbelief. "But you didn't know who I was going to say."

"Everyone—well . . ."—Johnita smirked—"everyone who wasn't alive or was just nursing their mama's milk think that's Billie Holiday. But she ain't . . . She wasn't."

Eve nodded. "She's beautiful. She looks like she sang well."

Johnita stared at the photo, eyes unblinking. Her voice softened and sounded to Eve as that of an entirely different woman. "Claude definitely had a voice."

"Claude?"

"Claudette," Johnita supplied. "My best good friend."

Johnita abruptly turned on her heels and continued up the staircase, leaving Eve to quickly gather her suitcase and stumble to catch up. In her quick departure, her shoulder bumped a photograph. The black-and-white image of Hezekiah Mann seated between Johnita and a fair-skinned woman at a small table shifted slightly in Eve's wake. She hadn't noticed, but on Johnita's return to the front parlor, she automatically corrected the tilted photo with absentminded resolve. The frames always seemed to get jostled about, even when there were no guests. Frequent vacancies had been the norm since the closing of the train depot. And Ideal, along with Johnita's Place—as it was known in its juke joint heyday— withered like leaves on a dead vine.

Once checked into her small room, Eve was as exhausted as she was elated. As much as she wanted to follow the map directly to Deuce's home, she needed to wash away the Greyhound journey and sleep horizontally in a bed. Three complimentary "Welcome to Georgia, y'all" postcards caught her attention on the small desk. As she glanced deeper into the images, Eve realized that the building on the three identical postcards was a younger-looking Johnita's Inn. If she had to put her finger on a more acute description, she'd say that it looked more vibrant.

Eve scribbled identical "Made it to Macon County" messages on two of the postcards and carefully addressed them. One to Professor LeRoi and the other to her best friend, Nelle. She began to write the third to her aunt but got no further than the "Dear Mama Ann" salutation before her pen faltered, unsure of what more to add to the small blank space.

It was as if the white space perfectly illustrated the unknowingness she'd felt her entire life, and sending a blank card to the person responsible for it seemed appropriate to her. Eve pressed a hand to her temple, took a deep breath, and wrote the same message she had on the previous two and added "I love you" before pushing them all to the corner of the small desk.

Too tired to shower, she lay on the bed, closed her eyes, and fell into sleepful memories of her journey from Chicago.

PART I

ONE

mercy's ounce

We're the daughters of those old dusty things Nana carries
in her tin can. . . . We carry too many scars from the past.
Our past owns us.
—Eula Peazant, *Daughters of the Dust*, by Julie Dash

Before Every Mann and her aunt moved to the house in Avalon Park, they lived in Bronzeville, a thriving area for Blacks in mid-1950s Chicago. It was before the overcrowding due to large influxes of southern Blacks migrating for jobs. Before the lack of housing options precipitated a real estate decline that wouldn't begin to reverse itself until the new millennium's gentrification efforts. Before drastic property tax increases made it impossible for long-term residents to afford their already paid-for homes. Before the evictions of the very senior citizens who in 1955 had been the young and vibrant lifeblood of Bronzeville.

Every's earliest recollection from that time was of a crush she had on a boy when she was nearing five years old. Ann had often teased her whenever she came home full of stories about what the precocious little boy had done in school. Her aunt thought the crush funny until she saw him one afternoon as she was picking up Every from school. The boy was hanging upside down from the monkey bars, doing his best monkey imitation for his adoring five-year-old fans. His dark skin glistened with sweat, and his wooly hair stood more pronounced as he dangled. The display—already a stereotype—had traveled through centuries of propaganda by the time it greeted Every and her aunt on the playground. Bucked eyes, grotesquely large red lips, and a bulbous nose all planted on a simian-shaped caricature had graced advertisements for everything from nineteenth-century minstrel shows to twentieth-century Lux Soap, which featured the backs of two of such characters, hair drawn explosively outward with the guarantee that Lux Soap "won't shrink wool." By the 1950s the chicken and watermelon themes had been firmly entrenched for many decades, and a chain of restaurants used the same stock character with a red-and-black striped bellboy hat perched atop its head and the words "Coon Chicken Inn" inlaid on the teeth of its massive mouth. This was the visage that greeted Ann as she stared with open contempt at the boy. Her horror-stricken eyes darted from him to a couple of white teachers on the playlot. She snatched Every's hand and charged down the street as quickly as she could, her niece struggling to match her stride. Ann muttered about "colored folk acting like monkeys," her mind far from events beyond the bubble of Bronzeville, like the Vietnam War, which was just getting underway. She sought to distance Every from boys like this one, who would be shipped off to Vietnam thirteen years later.

Every stopped mentioning the boy to her aunt after the monkey-bars incident. She especially did not disclose their encounter two years later when he said that she could watch him urinate behind the school building. Every stared amazed as he lowered his pants and gently removed his "thing" with pride. Afterward, she watched as his wide eyes narrowed with disappointment when she squatted over a bush to show him that she could also pee outdoors. Her spray, seeming to come from nowhere in particular, lacked the showmanship of the "thing." Strangely prophetic, this two-year juvenile romance from kindergarten to second grade ended with the disappointment that often results after nudity is introduced into a relationship. Mystery gave way to indifference, and the boy's attention drifted toward a potato bug before she had even finished.

Every's childhood memories were packaged in the small Bronzeville apartment that she and her aunt had called home. She had used these times to ask her aunt for information about her deceased parents. When Ann came home exhausted from emptying bedpans days at Michael Reese Hospital and cleaning office buildings nights downtown, she would boil water for a hot toddy, carefully measuring a half shot of the Old Fitzgerald whiskey she kept in the farthest corner of the highest shelf, and sometimes she'd beckon Every to her. *Let's see 'bout that crow's nest on your head.* During those times, Every sat on the floor with her back between her aunt's legs as Ann carefully took down the plaits in her hair and the warm whiskey and honey coaxed small details of her childhood from her. Every sat, afraid to draw a breath for fear that it would disrupt the flow of information into her hungry ears.

Ann would share stories about growing up in the church and chores, even a tale or two about a boy she liked back home. *James was such a fine boy.* Sometimes she'd give Every advice that she claimed had come from her own mother, Gertrude. *Daddy used to call her Trudy,* Ann had said. *I can't believe I remember that.* Nostalgia etched her face like lines of lightning across a dark sky, and then it was gone, as thoughts of her father opened the gate to those she would rather shut out. During those times, she'd start to speak and then falter. *Uncle Cornelius taught me . . .* Returned to an unknown place, it was repackaged and put away like unwanted Christmas gifts rediscovered, remembered, and rejected. Though often truncated, Ann's memories extended to everyone but Every's mother. The only exception was the time she offered her niece solace when she found her gorging on ice cream late at night after viewing a weight-loss advertisement in one of the ladies' magazines Ann had brought home from work.

"If *not* eating it makes you lose weight, then maybe I should have it every night," Every muttered between spoonfuls.

Ann pulled a spoon from the drawer and joined her niece. "You know, your mama had attention from the finest of boys, and she wasn't but an ounce bigger than you."

"No," Every sighed. "I didn't know."

Every's teenage years brought more probing questions. As she grew, the hair-straightening sessions moved to the kitchen. She sat as her aunt parted a small section of hair and oiled it. Every closed her eyes and inhaled the acrid smoke from the steel-toothed comb being heated on the stove's eye. Then came the muffled thump of her aunt briefly placing the comb on a towel, an attempt to regulate its heat. Every's muscles clenched as the fire-heated comb moved millimeters away from her scalp and sizzled through her tight curls until they were crisp and straight. The latest sounds of Chess Records on WVON—"Voice of the Negro"—calmed Eve just enough to endure the next pull of the hot comb through her hair.

The weekly hair sessions placed Every's thoughts on unanswered questions. After each press, she opened her eyes and stared across the kitchen to a wall of framed black-and-white photographs. Every's glance fell on one photograph in particular. Her gaze often lingered on the black-and-white of the smiling woman in the picture who resembled her so much. Rooted to her chair, her movements limited and eyes only able to either stare ahead at the photographs or close and commit to a mental facsimile of the image, Every was in weekly communion with her unfamiliar heritage. The rare face or eye contact between Every and Ann made it easier for Every to ask those questions as if the thoughts belonged to her eyes, searching the photographs for hidden messages. It was a unique torture—the close physical proximity to the pictures and her aunt hovering above her head with a searing comb—as the conversation allowed her to shift attention from her hair yet threatened to ignite resistance from Ann if she pressed too hard. *Don't press too hard*, her frequent admonishments to Ann's slow draw of the hot comb through her hair also served to remind Eve to exercise care with her questioning.

But her aunt's tidbits of information dried up. "Leave the past where it is, Every."

"Mama Ann, please!" she begged. "I'm old enough to know something more."

"Age don't got nothin' to do with it, Every." Ann tightened her lips. "Some thangs young and old just need to let lie."

"What things?" Every tried to turn her head but felt the heat of the comb dangerously close.

"Hold still, Every," Ann hissed. "You know how you get when this grease burns you."

"Blame it on the grease."

"What?"

"Nothin'," Every sighed. "What things need to let lie?"

"Hold still!"

"I am holding still." Silence swirled upward with the smoke from Eve's half-pressed hair. "Mama Ann?"

"I cain't tell you what I don't know, Every."

Every paused before delivering her final attempt. "But you know more than what you say."

"Well," Ann exhaled slowly, "let that be my cross to bear, then." Taking note of her niece's perceptiveness, Ann felt the generations of secrets beginning to swell within her. It happened from time to time. Names, dates, and faces seemed to surge from the pit of her stomach and travel on nerve endings until they nested at her temples between her skull and skin. She would shut her eyes, press her fingertips to her hairline, and will them into submission. Ann opened her eyes, thumped the pressing comb on the folded towel until the smoke subsided and her headache cleared, leaving only the acrid odor of hot hair grease mingled with the stench of words left unsaid.

Dejectedly, Every slid down into the chair. She'd been here before over the years, asking about her mother, father, grandparents, uncles, aunts, if any even still lived or existed—everybody, somebody, anybody. Literacy introduced new worlds in books but also brought an understanding of the unusualness of her name. Every. Not "Avery," as it seemed to be pronounced on the southern tongues of her aunt and her peers—products of the Great Migration. For Every, there were always more questions than answers.

Ann had to exorcise her own demons of the past, leaving Every with nothing but a sense of weightlessness.

"Sit up, baby," her aunt spoke gently. "You should be happy you can make your own past. What you do from here on is up to you, Every."

This was no consolation. Every sighed and stared at the woman in the photograph and wondered how she managed to look slender and sophisticated. In it, her mother was laughing, and her pose—unlike the stoic, unsmiling ones of the other black-and-whites—was full of motion. Her hands rested protectively on her stomach, cradling its secret, and her head was slightly thrown back. She was seated in a wooden chair with one foot resting on the stretcher. Only her eyes, staring directly into the camera, revealed that the shot was not candid but posed. It was as though the antiquated camera, in a feat to match that of its successors, had caught Mercy in a fit of boisterous laughter. It was unblurred. Seven years later, it seemed that her mother's eyes and laugh belied her knowledge of many things. If Every stared hard enough, she could imagine Mercy's skirt moving slightly in the draft. Still gazing, her hands self-consciously tugged her knee socks over her narrow calves.

Every longed for the warmth of reminiscent feelings. Although she could think back on countless activities with her aunt, her main memories involved the probing questions of her classmates during the earlier years of childhood. "Ain't you got a daddy?" Not a daddy. Not an uncle. Ironically, the Mann family had a shortage of men. Thinking of her aunt's words emphasizing that she was in control of her own life, Every began to make a very conscious step to assert that control.

———

It is said that in the early 1960s, Nation of Islam leader Elijah Muhammad used a white ghost buyer to purchase twenty-six homes in the southeast neighborhood of Avalon Park. The brick ranch-style houses and impressive Georgians were sprinkled in a quaint area extending eastward from Stony Island Avenue to the lakefront and ended south at the boundary of the Pill Hill neighborhood, so named for the number of white doctors residing there.

The purchase placed a Muhammad on nearly every block. As the Nation of Islam grew, so did the financial prosperity of the Muhammads and, by extension, middle-class Blacks, who further integrated the neighborhood in the wake of their Black Muslim neighbors. The flight of white residents from Avalon Park, Pill Hill, and other Chicago neighborhoods, was a form of mobile segregation. Black folks moved in, and white folks moved out. Nineteen sixty-five brought the Chicago Freedom Movement, the collaborative effort of Martin Luther King Jr. and the Southern Christian Leadership Council to end slums in the city. While King moved his family into a North Lawndale slum in protest, Every and Ann were taking advantage of the South Side's Muhammad legacy.

In 1965 Ann purchased one of the recently constructed brick ranch homes. They'd always lived frugally, and although Ann no longer lived in the South, she adhered to Black southern financial planning learned from her upbringing: don't trust banks, and own your home. Every bragged about how "fly" it was to her best friend, Nelle. Ann testified in church to how "blessed" she was to be just "a stone's throw down yonder from Pill Hill." She hadn't forgotten the sight of that boy hanging like a monkey in the Bronzeville playlot and felt that her niece needed to grow up with a yard of her own. Some place away from the dangers of the city and, in Ann's mind, little nappy-headed boys who would grow up to be hoodlums.

Every flourished in the house, dancing with carefree abandon in front of the new black-and-white television to *Red Hot and Blues*, the early show that featured in-studio Black dancers and music, and a precursor to *Soul Train*, where Black dancers of every shape contorted in tune to the latest rhythm and blues. With the change of home and school and a figure that had inherited Mercy's ounce, fourteen-year-old Every began to develop.

One evening while her aunt worked the hospital night shift, Every and her best friend, Nelle, snuck out to a basement party where she had her first kiss from a shy brown-skinned boy named Jericho. His lips were soft, and she would have continued to press against them had she not been caught by the surprise of his tongue wiggling into her mouth. It was weird. It was wet. But later that night, it had been all she could think about as she hugged her pillow and willed sleep to stifle the shivers that pulsated downward from her abdomen. This new confidence—nurtured by her friendship with Nelle and a burgeoning young, gifted, and Black climate— was creating a desire for change.

She had endured the grade school teasing in her old neighborhood, where her schoolmates crafted urban mythology about *every po' man*, a character who, as punishment for unknown family transgressions, was destined to eat children but could gain little life-sustaining weight from them. It was an effective torture that linked her to the social outcasts of the neighborhood. To them, Every Mann was just a younger embodiment of the drunkards and homeless who held on to their vices in lieu of family. *Just as po' as no-man's-land*, they taunted. Someone had discarded Every, and her peers didn't need to know who or why.

Back then, Every had spent most of her recess time tucked into a book, but on occasion she'd be drawn to a crowd by the contagious excitement of children gathered around the inappropriate, mischievous, or unexplainable. Such was the case that drew her eyes from the adventures of *Heidi* and to a circle of classmates. Every walked around them until she found a space to squeeze between two larger seventh graders. At first, all she could see was a pool of water in the middle of the playground, and like her classmates, she was in awe of its size. It seemed a lake had grown on the gravel. Within it, an ecosystem developed where hundreds of worms writhed. Her thoughts joined the murmur of questions in the crowded hive. *How many were in there?* And slowly, someone's attention turned to whether it was enough to feed *every po' man*. Every felt two hands ram into her back and then she pitched forward into the playground lake of worms.

Her fierce shrieks and the rapid approach of teachers scattered the crowd except for Nelle, who reached down and pulled Every out of the mire and protectively wrapped her arms around her.

Once the tears stopped, the silence began. Every didn't speak to anyone for a week. She couldn't process how anyone could do something so vile, and it short-circuited her thoughts of everything else. At the end of a week, she let go to Nelle, who had been her constant companion during the time. "I can't help not having parents. I don't know what awful thing they did that they're not here."

Nelle nodded. "Maybe they didn't do anything awful. Maybe sending you here was something good . . . like heroic."

"What do you mean?"

"Well," Nelle thought carefully. "Didn't baby Moses' mother send him away? And then he ended up being raised by Pharaoh's daughter and saving a whole bunch of folk from slavery!"

Every smiled and then frowned.

"What?" Nelle asked concerned. "You can't see you as a leader of our people?"

"I can't see Mama Ann as a daughter of Pharaoh!" Every chortled.

Eve didn't know the origins of Every and detached from it quite successfully, manipulating clerks at her new high school to lose the "ry" in this record or that document, assuring them that it was one clerical error gone haywire. And who could doubt such a story? Who would ever name a child Every? Every Mann at that.

Her name adaptation was trivial compared to the changes of the time. Chemically straightened hair was slowly being abandoned. Skirt hemlines were creeping higher. Surnames were replaced with *X*s to break identification with ancestral slave names. Eve stepped further away from the skinny, thick-haired girl who cringed at her name whenever she sat in the straight-backed kitchen chair in front of the stove.

When Eve stopped questioning her aunt, Ann was grateful for the respite. All she wanted to do was raise her sister's child to be an upstanding, God-fearing woman who would not repeat the mistakes of her mother. Ann was afraid of her niece's curiosity. *When you shut the door to keep Satan out, you don't crack it open for a few questions.* The only thing her niece needed to know was that her mother, Ann's sister, had died in childbirth and that she was her legal guardian. But the truth was that Ann didn't know how to process the image of her sister bleeding out on a hospital table and blabbering seemingly incoherent phrases. Nor did she know that her sister, Mercy, looking up at those white faces in their surgical masks, died praying not for herself, or for her child, but whispering in her final utterance that every man is a child of God. Ann could not communicate these things, and so she took relief in the absence of her niece's inquiries.

Yet the questions hadn't disappeared from Eve's mind. They

remained never too far from the surface, sharing space with adolescent thoughts of who could dance the best Watusi and who would be the first to buy the new Temptations album. Eve's adolescence ended amid an increase in cultural tension throughout the city.

A few months after they moved into their home, Malcolm X was killed. It was widely speculated that the Nation of Islam, from which he had recently been excommunicated, had arranged his murder. As the community mourned, the Muhammads in the twenty-six homes gave way to Johnsons, Williamses, and Washingtons. By the time King was assassinated three years later, nonviolent movements went the way of shirtwaist dresses and straightened hair.

Eve felt even more lost in the melee, as her personal woes seemed part and parcel of a myriad of community sacrifices. Her mourning of those dead long ago was supplanted by that of recent martyrs, and her thoughts turned from finding herself in family to finding herself in the conflagration of society. When the news cycle rotated through the assassinations to the controversial renaming of one of the city colleges after Malcolm X, Eve's longing for connection and desire for knowledge coalesced into an idea.

TWO

in search of beginnings

The end is in the beginning and lies far ahead.
—**Ralph Ellison,** *Invisible Man*

It was 1972 in Chicago. Some remember it for bringing the worst commuter rail crash in the city's history when the Illinois Central Gulf train overshot the Twenty-Seventh Street Station and received the clearance to back up just as the heavier 720 Express was huffing and puffing its way at full speed on the same track. Forty people were killed and over three hundred injured.

That same year in the Windy City—as at least two thousand audience members can attest—Jesse Jackson, sporting a large afro, corduroy trousers, leather vest, and Martin Luther King medallion entreated them in call-and-response fashion with the mantra "I am . . . somebody." Even the dope fiends, the poor, and the uneducated were not exempt from this proclamation.

For Eve Mann, whose nascent political awareness began to blossom just as organizations like the Black Panther Party dwindled, 1972 Chicago placed her in a Black studies class at Malcolm X

Junior College, eager to learn the intellectual side of the social struggles that dominated her South Side existence from the outskirts of her community. If she could not answer the question of who she was, then perhaps she could decide who she would become. On the first day of class, she trained her eyes and focused on the professor.

He introduced himself as Brother LeRoi—not LEE-roy, as many in the class were accustomed to hearing the name, but luh-ROY. For some reason it sounded more intellectual that way, and this Brother LeRoi, by virtue of a shift in spelling and stress, was distanced from the Leroys that they knew.

"Who are you?" His voice rumbled and encompassed the class with the query. "Who am I?" he continued. "Who are we?" Standing just over six feet tall, with the light from the overhead fluorescent bulbs reflecting off his clean-shaven scalp, Brother LeRoi commanded attention, and the students at once ceased their knapsack fumbling, nail picking, and first-day chattering. The class was silent save for the occasional creak of chairs—unfortunate holdovers from years past.

The students were mostly young Black men and women—some too scared to leave the comforts of home and go away to a four-year college. A few had grown up with southern parents who had terrified them with stories of the South and continued to seek refuge in what was still thought of as a land of greater opportunity. Several, like Eve, had actually struck out on their own as prodigal children only to return to their homes, products of having too much of something or not enough of something else. These were the older ones in the class. Ranging from early to midtwenties, they had acquired just enough maturity to prompt skepticism of Brother LeRoi and silently question whether his dashiki was real, as in really from Africa, or one of the Taiwanese knockoffs sold out of the trunks of T-Birds on Forty-Seventh Street. Some were taken aback by the contrast of his light skin against clothing that had been long associated with Blackness. But they all were mesmerized by the voice that reached out to them, beckoning and promising, beseeching and bequeathing connection to a shared legacy. They were a generation that turned toward Pan-Africanism, while previous ones had shunned it. Brother LeRoi could deliver Africa, a vision that bestowed value on their West Side, South Side, Cabrini Green, Ida B. Wells housing project existence. They wanted to know the origins of their rhythms. They wanted to know whose children they were before they were the children of slaves.

Her seat in the last row, close to the exit, afforded her a view of the backs of several afros of varying heights, two bobs, a press-and-curl like her own, and one long blond—no straightening agents needed. Brown eyes of various shades periodically grazed over the drop of buttermilk spilled among flies. Pale legs flowed from a gold miniskirt and landed in matching platform shoes. A macramé bag with a "Chisholm for President" button rested against them.

Watching her, Eve absently raked fingers through her own pressed hair. Her hands came away slick with the remnants of Ultra Sheen, that aqua-blue-tinged grease that promised to lubricate Black hair into submission when slathered onto carefully parted scalps. Her one foray into the afro resulted in neighborhood boys calling her cotton swab. Eve rubbed her greasy fingers on the ends of her hair, which always seemed to dry out quicker than her roots, being so far from the Ultra Sheen's initial point of contact.

Brother LeRoi rumbled on about cultural identity as he dropped mimeographed papers onto their desks. They were hot off the press and immediately smudged black ink on fingertips. Eve's attention returned at the lure of the freshly deposited syllabus and reading list. She was reaching for the syllabus when Brother LeRoi cleared his throat and adjusted the black-rimmed glasses that rested on the bridge of his nose. "But let's not get too far into things. Back to my first question . . . Who are you? Not as a people. Not yet, anyway. Who are you as an individual person? Who are your people as you know them? Mother? Father . . . ?"

Afros nodded in agreement, blond hair swung, and a quiet but distinct "Right on" acknowledged that he had their attention. Brother LeRoi dabbed away a trickle of sweat that ran from under his kufi with a crisp handkerchief, a mannerism familiar to those who had attended the evangelical or Baptist or revivalist services from various churches—sans kufi, of course. It subconsciously signaled the impending crescendo in a sermon, song, or speech. And they responded in kind with "Right on" in lieu of "Amen." Like her classmates, Eve was entranced as Brother LeRoi rattled off bits and pieces about Black genealogy and uncovered (as noted on the syllabus) "the unknown neg(he)ros before discovering the African kings and queens to which we all claim relation."

Brother LeRoi slowly exhaled the decreasing cadence of his lecture, "Before we get into all this theory, let's start with a little genealogy project of our own." He explained that they would be tracing their own genealogies by gathering information from their relatives and collecting family pictures, legal documents, and obituaries.

"Careful though," Brother LeRoi warned. "Obits don't always contain accurate information. They share only the information that the relative providing it wants the public to know."

Eve's excitement quickly dissipated with the realization that she would be unable to complete the first assignment—or any, if they involved speaking with family members. In her case, it was family *member*—singular. Her attention waned, and she hung her head like a church parishioner when the collection plate circulates and lost herself in memories of the last time she was in a classroom and her failed matriculation at Tuskegee Institute.

She'd been so happy to get her acceptance letter from Tuskegee and had mistakenly thought her aunt would share in her enthusiasm. It was Mama Ann, after all, who had demanded that she be forward thinking. Eve could still recall their argument clearly after three years.

Eve and her best friend Nelle sat, shoulders touching, on her bed, staring at the envelope. Nelle had received her acceptance letter days earlier.

"I'm too nervous to open it." Eve shivered and handed the envelope to Nelle.

Nelle held her palm up in refusal, "Nawl, sista. College is finally being grown, and that's gotta start now. I'm here for you no matter what that letter say."

Eve inhaled deeply and slowly turned the letter over to unseal it.

"What y'all doing?" Ann bellowed from the doorway, startling them both.

"Shh, Mama Ann!" Eve clutched her dashiki-clad chest. "I'm trying to see if I got into Tuskegee."

"Well, what I got to shush for? How's my talkin' gonna change what's in that letter?"

Nelle gave a pleading look to Ann, who acquiesced but remained in the doorway. The brief silent respite was broken by Eve's shrieks. "I got in! I got in!" she leapt from the bed and embraced Nelle. Turning toward her aunt, she was met by Ann's swiftly departing backside.

Nelle slung an arm around her friend's slumped shoulders. "Take some time to enjoy the moment."

"It's already over." Eve's enthusiasm departed. "I may as well get this talk over with now."

Nelle turned Eve to face her and grabbed her hands. "We are going to Tuskegee, sis. It's all we've talked about through high school."

Eve nodded. "I know."

"Then I'll let you get to it." Nelle grabbed her jacket off Eve's bed and exited, leaving her friend to the inevitable argument.

Ann derided Eve for her dashiki and railed about "backward Black youth who don't know why their parents left in the first place."

Eve countered with "guardians not sharing information being the reason why so many young Black folk are returning to the South to retrieve it."

In the end, Eve reminded her aunt, "You left home, Mama Ann! Nobody stopped you.*"*

"Yes!" Ann shouted back.

"You came here!" Eve matched Ann's volume. Their shrill voices vibrated against the walls.

"I came here to take care of you, Every! It wasn't a choice!"

Eve sighed and held up the acceptance letter. "Well, this is, and I'm going."

Eve was whisked out of her memory by a blue jean bell-bottom whipping past her ankle. Class was dismissing, and she scrambled to gather her things so as not to be left behind.

Brother LeRoi spotted her and smiled, misinterpreting her lingering. "Did you want to speak to me about the project?"

Eve shifted uncomfortably in the chair-desk combo and for a fleeting moment felt herself relapse into her childhood as Every Mann—po', skinny, motherless urchin.

Brother LeRoi's eyes shone brightly behind his glasses. A smattering of freckles adorned his cheekbones. He waited as Eve silently debated with herself. She hadn't enrolled in the class just to give up on the first day. She had known it would place her face-to-face with the gaps in her family history. In fact, she had counted on it, although she hadn't realized it would occur so soon. Eve struggled to form the words that would open one of her deepest internal conflicts to this stranger. She wanted to share but not overshare. Not that she had enough information to constitute oversharing.

"Well, Mr. LeRoi . . ."

"Please, Brother LeRoi," he interjected.

"Ah, right. Brother LeRoi, I'm not sure how successful I'll be with this first assignment. My—" Eve stopped short as she caught sight of movement from the door, a flash of blond hair and the macramé bag she had admired earlier. Brother LeRoi followed her gaze and cleared his throat.

His eyes returned to Eve, but his tone was clipped, impatient. "Look, sista . . . um?"

"Eve." She stood, compelled by his sudden urgency yet not fully understanding its motivation.

He smiled. "Sister Eve—biblical first woman; I like that. See me during office hours tomorrow. It's on the syllabus. I'm sure we can work through whatever hesitations or problems you're having with the assignment." Brother LeRoi's eyes darted quickly toward the exit; still, he waited with raised eyebrow until Eve smiled and agreed. He then covered the distance from Eve's seat to the exit in a few long strides. As Eve packed her bag, she glimpsed the simultaneous departure of gold platform shoes and the macramé bag.

———

The Milwaukee Service transfer to Jackson Park train shuttled Eve through the city's racial landscape as passengers progressively darkened the farther south it traveled. Dark skin dominated the train cars after passing through Bridgeport, and chatter increased as tongues and bodies visibly relaxed into the commute. Eve rode nearly to the end of the line before catching the eastbound Eighty-Seventh Street bus to Stony Island Avenue and walking the final block and a half home. Eve let herself into the house that she shared with her aunt. She dropped her bag beside the couch and watched the contents, including Brother LeRoi's syllabus, spill out onto the floor.

"Every, is that you?" Ann called from her bedroom at the rear of the house.

"Yeah," Eve sighed. "It's me." Entering her bedroom, she switched on the radio, collapsed onto the bed, and let herself believe that the Staple Singers could fulfill their promise of "I'll Take You There." This was one of the times when she wished she had kept her own apartment. But Ann's strange illness, which first manifested when Eve went away for school and for which doctors could find no cause or cure, seemed to recur in Eve's absence. One nurse had slipped and mentioned the word *psychosomatic* within Eve's hearing. It had not been a shock to her. But she didn't know what to do.

Ann appeared in her doorway. "Well?"

Eve sat up. "Well what?"

"How was your first day?"

Eve sighed. "I've got a project, but I don't think I'll be able to do it."

"Of course you can do it. You're such a bright girl—"

Eve cleared her throat, and Ann corrected herself: "A bright young lady. You'll always be a girl to me, Every. Keeps me from becoming an old woman." But Ann had been an old woman for a long time, not in years, not even in experience. She had inflicted age upon herself in her inhibitions, hesitations, and the strange illness that left even her suspecting some unknown mental culprit.

"It's a family history project," Eve searched her aunt's face for emotion.

Ann sucked her teeth. "Hmph. I thought this was a African Studies class you was taking? What they need to know about your history for? I tole you, you got to be careful about giving personal information to those folk."

"What folk, Mama Ann?" Eve tucked her legs beneath her. "The Black professor? The university . . . ?"

"It's all the same thang. Government. It's a city college, ain't it?"

Eve pursed her lips. "Tell you what. I'll drop the class if you just tell me the information. That way, we can keep the government out of things."

Ann didn't know why Eve insisted on baiting her. She thought to tell Eve that perhaps the class wasn't such a good idea after all, but as she looked into her niece's eyes, she knew that it was not the time to argue her point.

Eve stared at her aunt. It was a practiced look—not a glare, which could be construed as disrespectful, but a wide-eyed, questioning expression, defiant only in its openness.

Ann pressed a hand to her forehead and left the room. The painfully familiar gesture no longer held the same power it had when Eve had packed for college a few years prior. It was around that time that her aunt's headaches began. Eve abandoned her suitcase in the same manner she would later abandon her studies after one semester and rush to her aunt's side. Her nervous excitement for the South, college, and freedom had quickly been replaced with concern for Ann's health.

Still, she liked to revisit the memories, as brief as they were, starting with the bus ride with Nelle to Tuskegee. She thought about Nelle's assertion that college was about adulthood and choices and how, as they cuddled together on the Greyhound bus, neither had a clue about the choices that would later test the seams of their friendship.

Jogged by the memory, Eve grabbed the receiver of the telephone and spun out her best friend's number on the rotary dial. It was Nelle who had urged her to take a Black studies class as they sat one evening having dinner at Gladys's Luncheonette in Bronzeville. Eve had been in the middle of trying to explain to Nelle the emptiness she had been feeling.

"Maybe I should've stayed in Alabama and finished school with you," she confided as Nelle pulled a compact from her brown suede knapsack whose fringes reminded Eve of moccasins. Nelle reapplied her lip gloss and frowned in the mirror as she patted her hair. It had been her attempt at an afro, but it had more curl than the regal fluff required for an impressive girth. She looked at Eve's hair, which had been pressed into submission by Ann's hot comb.

"You don't know how blessed you are, Every. Dig?" Nelle's inquiries were always punctuated by the latest slang. It would have been an annoying habit, especially as it was shared by so many of her contemporaries, but Nelle had a way of owning such indulgences of popular culture so that they seemed to have belonged to no one before her.

Eve sighed. "Take the damn hair, Nelle! I don't want it."

"Chill, sista," Nelle gushed. "C'mon, Every," Nelle and Ann were the only ones who continued to address Eve by her given name. "It's time. You got all this confusion inside, like so many other sisters out here. We're all trying to find out about ourselves as a people. You don't have to do it by yourself."

"Don't I?" Eve responded. "Every time I try to find out about my family, I get shut down. And every time I try to move around not knowing, I get kicked back to needing to know. And Mama Ann—" she faltered. Eve had only been at Tuskegee for one semester when Ann's illness worsened. She came home that winter break and never went back. But Nelle had stayed and graduated with an English degree and an eye toward journalism.

"I ain't talking 'bout Mama Ann." Nelle smiled.

Eve had been curious, and the more Nelle spoke about how Blacks were doing research to uncover their family histories, their ancestries, and even reaching back to Africa, the less restriction she began to feel in her chest. Eve sighed. Her next breath filled with the heavy aroma of collard greens, northern beans, and smothered chicken placed before her by an enviably Afroed waitress.

"Just sign up for one class, sis." Nelle extended her palm to Eve and smiled slyly. Her attention drifted and lingered on the waitress depositing their food.

Eve loudly cleared her throat drawing Nelle's focus back to her.

As the waitress departed, Nelle shrugged. "What? She's cute."

Eve pressed a finger to her temple. "Can you not do that around me?" They ate their meal in silence.

In her room, phone pressed to her ear, Eve continued to stare at the space her aunt had occupied moments before. When Nelle answered, all that Eve could muster was a half-hearted, "Hey."

Nelle read Eve's tone. "You could always bunk with me. We could get a righteous two-bedroom in the old neighborhood right now."

Eve was silent. It wasn't an option for her. Nelle was her best friend, and there wasn't anything she wouldn't do for her, but living with her was out of the question. She groped for what had become a familiar excuse. "Mama Ann's health . . ."

On the other end of the line, Nelle sighed and wondered why she continued to offer. Although Eve had left before completing her degree, the experience had disrupted their friendship. "Yeah. Sure. Mama Ann may not realize it, and you for damn sure don't realize it. That woman ain't old! Shit, my own mother is knocking on fifty. Mama Ann is gonna tap dance on all our graves."

In the background of Eve's room, Mavis Staples crooned from the radio, "I know a place . . . ain't nobody cryin' . . . I'll take you there . . ."

"Thanks for the offer. But I just . . . you know." Eve lowered her voice, cowering away from their unspoken issue. Discovering Nelle's sexuality, as much as anyone can discover another's fundamental qualities, had devastated Eve. Her own understanding of sexuality had been carefully curated by Ann and the Baptist Church that claimed their Sunday mornings. Both were clear on the matter: homosexuality was a sin. Although the church also claims that people are born into sin, it was clear that in the unofficial hierarchy of sinning, where unmarried sex is bad, same-gender sex is worse. Eve didn't know if there was a worst place in hell for the sinniest of sins, but she did know that she didn't want to be there bearing witness to what the minister regularly labeled "unnatural acts."

"Yeah, I know," Nelle conceded. She didn't fully understand Eve's withdrawal from their friendship. It reminded her of her early foray into literary theory, when she would read a sentence, know all the words it comprised, yet fail to comprehend the concept or thought it intended to communicate. Nelle had attended the same church as Eve and her aunt, heard the same dogma, but had no clue how they arrived at a conclusion so completely different from what she believed. She bore witness to the same brutality to women—Black women in particular—by every race and gender on the planet and did not understand how Black women did not make a covenant of loving each other in any manner—intimately, romantically, sisterly, maternally. Still, Nelle was intent on serving as an example of nonthreatening lesbianism to her friend.

"So, what's it gonna take to get you out your funk this time?" Nelle asked. "Food? Drink? Both?"

The smooth sounds of the Staple Singers gave way to the strong percussion rap and electric guitar of Funkadelic's "Cosmic Slop." Eve's lips cracked into her first smile of the day. "How about getting deeper into the funk?" She cranked the volume up, and she and Nelle sang along, temporarily drowning out her anxiety and, seconds later, Ann's timid knocks on her bedroom door.

THREE

motherless child

Guided by my heritage of a love of beauty and respect for strength—
in search of my mother's garden, I found my own.
—Alice Walker, *In Search of Our Mothers' Gardens*

When Martin Luther King Jr. came to Chicago in 1965, he targeted two white neighborhoods in which to stage protest marches against unfair real estate practices: Cicero, site of the prior decade's infamous race riot, and the southwestern neighborhood of Marquette Park. King's safety was entrusted to the Blackstone Rangers, both a street gang and political organization—a double consciousness nonexistent in successor gangs.

Lee Roy Duncan would find a home with the Blackstone Rangers that provided a stability that had been missing in his own home. Raised by his paternal grandmother, he felt the absence that the Rangers spoke of when recruiting men who were missing men in their lives. His grandmother was old, and they moved around each other in the ways of people who care but really have nothing in common outside of their mutual responsibility to one another. Lee

Roy's condition couldn't be reduced to a simple need for a father figure or peers or a mother; it was all of them, or maybe even none of them. He was what they called a "high-yella" boy, a redbone. It caused his face to redden when it ought not to have. Betrayed by his complexion, Lee Roy blushed when pigtailed girls sauntered past. He flushed when other boys bristled before him, extending their chests, their darker skin tones never betraying their fear or embarrassment. Some say the mark that Cain bore was what became known as a racialized darkness to set him apart from more fair and righteous men. Surely Lee Roy was the inverse of this myth: marked by paleness and punished for this difference.

As a youth, he was bullied. And because the source of his neighborhood combatants' disdain for him was the fairness of his skin, it was on this that they exercised their abuse. The world whispered to them that he was beautiful, or as close to beauty as a Black boy could get, and they were ugly. They could not reach the world, but they tried by pushing their fists through Lee Roy's buttermilk skin. He fought admirably. Sometimes he won; sometimes he lost; yet the easy bruising of his delicate skin would corroborate whatever narrative his assailants concocted. At which point they no longer wasted their energy on trying to best him but settled for scoring a "red mark," a blow whose evidence would remain.

Eventually the bullying fell to a standstill during Lee Roy's late teenage years as he became adept at blocking and dodging hits to his face. By the time the early1960s rolled out Muhammad Ali, the smooth-skinned world champion boxer who boasted about protecting his "pretty" face, Lee Roy had been in the practice for years. He was able to hold his own for a while—until the poling. This is when the Rangers found him. They saved him. They had watched Lee Roy with growing interest over the months, witnessed

41

his dexterity and strength in fending off the neighborhood darkies, as they called the other boys who shared their rich skin tones but fell short on the ideology of brotherhood, boys whose anger had turned inward like the hairs that abscessed in their chins, making them lash out at everything in their vicinity because they could not reach the true cause of their condition.

They meted out their frustrations in lighthearted jostling matches with each other that were always bound to turn serious, each destined for a moment when the playful shove of a comrade would catch them off guard and anger would flash across their faces before being quickly reeled in. But pulled punches build, and such was the case the final time the neighborhood boys laid hands on Lee Roy.

They had been hanging about in the alley, when Lee Roy ambled past. Tiny, the largest one, had beaten everyone in slap boxing and was looking for a new challenger. The rest, weary of their losses, encouraged Tiny's trash talk directed at Lee Roy. But Lee Roy didn't stop. He pushed past their sweaty bodies until dark, damp hands grabbed his shoulders.

Lee Roy swung furiously, taking them all by surprise. He jabbed and pounced until all they could do to end his barrage of punches was lift him, each struggling with one of his flailing limbs, uncertain of what to do with the fitful form. Then Lil Joe, the smallest of them, thought of a most sinister punishment. "Pole his yella ass," he directed.

They hesitated. "What the hell y'all waiting for?" Lil Joe screeched. "This boy think he white. Let's show 'em what it is to be nigga."

Tiny nervously drew his large palm across his forehead. "C'mon now, Lil Joe. Ain't no cause for that. We just—"

"You just gonna ram that nigga's nuts right into that pole, Tiny," Lil Joe interrupted. "Shit, better from us. We educating him."

A weary moan escaped Lee Roy, and they nearly dropped him as he became dead weight in their arms. They strengthened their hold and marched, two grasping him under the shoulders and two each grasping a leg—slowly parting from one another as they picked up speed. Lee Roy clenched his eyes and mouth, bracing for an impact that never came. He opened his eyes to what seemed to him a battalion of men in red berets. The Blackstone Rangers had watched him enough and decided to intervene.

Lee Roy felt a sense of wholeness when he wore the Rangers' trademark red beret and strolled through their Woodlawn neighborhood. He felt a strength unparalleled in any other aspect of his life as he joined in their refrain: "Look out, stranger. Here lurks danger, if you're not a Blackstone Ranger." He even had a mentor, the closest he'd ever known to a big brother. Rick had singlehandedly pulled Lee Roy from despair beginning that fateful day when he stopped the neighborhood poling.

To his credit, Lee Roy threw his entire being into his Ranger identity. He worked their community events, attended all the meetings, and was even employed in their businesses. He could have stayed in that place forever, locked in brotherhood, but the Rangers were about progression and movement, even if their progression did not result in a political movement. Eventually, they absorbed twenty-one local gangs and became the P. Stone Nation, symbolized by a twenty-one stone pyramid. What occurred afterward was somewhat typical of large organizations: opinions differed, the focus changed, and leaders split off to form their own factions, like the Islamic-based El Rukns. Street gangs dropped politics and picked up drug distribution. Criminal activity was no longer a means to an end; it was the means *and* the end.

Rick tried to explain, "Look, Lil Brotha, this game is rigged.

We follow the rules, we get slammed. We are lab rats in our communities."

"Then why sell poison in our own communities, Rick?" Lee Roy pleaded more than queried.

Rick's silence had been his answer. The drug game was not for Lee Roy. He needed something else.

By early 1965 adulthood and neighborhood politics made friends of Lee Roy and his boyhood tormentors. They helped him adjust to leaving the Rangers and were his support when his grandmother died. Much of Lee Roy's spare time prior to her death had been spent in the library, discovering books. Lee Roy looked to the past to find out how previous generations had handled the color issue. The pages of DuBois courted him, but Lee Roy found the most encouragement from Booker T. Washington's autobiography and his Atlanta Exposition speech declaring that he should cast down his bucket where he was. But Lee Roy was in limbo. He felt his own greatness stifled in Chicago. A nascent Chicago revolutionary, Lee Roy was a redundancy. He could not build what already existed. But the South could use him. Weren't all the Black folks flocking north?

The morning of his grandmother's funeral, he sat in her small apartment and cried until his shoulders ached from the convulsions. He cried harder than the time his grandmother told him that his father wasn't coming home, harder than when she told him his mother was a white woman—which was a fate like death to his seven-year-old sensibilities. He cleaned his tear-streaked face and took the Cottage Grove bus to Leak Funeral Home.

A. R. Leak Funeral Home had been laying out dead Black people since 1933. One week prior to Lee Roy's grandmother, Leak opened its doors to the thousands who attended services for legendary soul singer Sam Cooke. The crowd swelled until it crushed the parlor windows, and James Brown had to leave before paying his respects. There was no swollen throng of grievers at the funeral of Lee Roy's grandmother. No Ray Charles to sing "The Angels Keep Watching Over Me." Just Woodlawn neighbors, an organist, and soloist singing "Trouble of the World" in a voice that was nothing like Mahalia Jackson's. It was too high to convey the trouble of the world as so tiresome and burdensome that the decedent had found relief in death. This soloist sang as if the trouble were manageable.

Lee Roy sat in the front pew, feeling a loneliness that paled that which had compelled him in those earlier years to join the Blackstone Rangers. Neighbors spoke of his grandmother in two-minute praises. Community organizations gave resolutions in her name. She was eulogized by a minister that Lee Roy did not know at a church that he had not attended.

"Clara was a godly woman . . ."

"Always feeding those in need . . ."

The testimonials ran into each other, and faces blended into a single conglomerate of brown, wrinkled skin and woolen hair thickened with gray. His grandma Clara present in the words of her community.

"She was always taking in those who was put out."

Lee Roy raised eyes to the last remark and found apologetic hands that pressed envelopes into his loosely clasped palms. His grandmother hadn't taken him in from any out. She'd been with him from the very beginning. He never understood the fictions neighbors wove to patch the gaps in their knowledge. Lee Roy had not been taken in so much as his parents had been put out—long before his own memory ignited.

They filed in a line to his seat, squeezing his shoulder in passing. Elderly women embraced him in heavily powdered bosoms.

"Thank you," he murmured to no one in particular and everyone in general. It was a parade of sympathetic brown eyes and then . . . a pair of blue ones.

He looked into a face that was so similar to his own, but much paler, that he knew it instantly. "Your grandmother was an amazing woman. She was more of a mother than I could have been, you know."

He was paralyzed. It wasn't until her gaze shifted to a teenage girl beside her that he blinked. She told the girl, "Go ahead, Amy."

The girl had been clutching an envelope to her chest. Receiving the woman's permission, she thrust it into his hands. "Sorry for your loss," the girl added shyly.

He nodded and watched them descend the aisle to the exit. Not knowing what to do with the experience, he filed it away—as he did the unopened card when he returned to his grandmother's apartment. He loosened his tie and sat in the living room. In the kitchen and dining room, women he didn't recognize bustled about, dishing food onto Dixie plates and cramming aluminum-foil-covered dishes into the refrigerator.

The boys with whom he had once run the streets of Woodlawn were, like him, now adult men, but that is where their similarities ended. One kept refilling the red plastic cup in his hand. "This my nigga, right here!" he exclaimed, sloshing Crown Royal from the bottle to the cautioning cries of the others. "So, you say you gonna go down south now? College, huh? Ain't fuckin' with them Rukn Ranger niggas no more?" He continued without waiting for a response, "That's good. Slanging all that dope in the neighborhood." He pointed his glass toward the framed photo of Lee Roy's grandmother. "She probably turnin' in her grave. Rest in peace."

Lee Roy nodded. "Yeah," he replied, glancing at the photograph. He hadn't thought much about college after high school and had been content with the community service jobs that membership in the Rangers had afforded him. It allowed him to stay and care for his grandmother when she most needed it.

Tiny furiously shook his head. "Negroes leaving the South in droves and you carrying your simple ass against the motherfuckin' stampede."

Lee Roy tried to explain to them about Booker T. Washington building the school from nothing. Even making the bricks for the buildings. He snatched up Washington's autobiography and pointed emphatically to the cover. "I mean, he was like the man, y'all."

Tiny stared at the book. "I ain't never seen no Negro on no book. Not like that."

Someone quickly chimed in, "And how many books have you even seen, Tiny?" which caused an eruption of laughter from everyone. "Seriously," the prankster continued. "You say this Booker T. man started this school with his wife and then had a woman on the side too that he married?"

Lee Roy frowned. "Not at the same time. Why you gotta focus on that?"

Tiny laughed. "You know we got folks like that up here too." He paused for effect. "We call 'em pimps." He clasped Lee Roy on the shoulder nearly upsetting his drink. "Nigga all highfalutin' nah! Gonna have hisself a shitload of degrees." He beamed at Lee Roy, who stared blankly back. "Man, we gon' hafta call you Luh-Roy. You too sharp to be a Lee Roy." The others murmured their agreement.

"Hey, Tiny, how long you gon' hang on to that Crown, man? We thirsty over here."

As the bottle made its way across the room, Lee Roy felt his body relax and his mind numb. He found himself smiling and

47

laughing with Tiny and the others. When they slipped into calling him Luh-Roy, he didn't correct them.

————

Brother LeRoi sat in his office. It was the anniversary of his grandmother's death. Later in the evening, he would meet his old neighborhood friends to toast her memory. He'd pick up a bottle of Crown Royal, knowing they would feign surprise and promise to grab the next one.

He thought of his students. There were those who diligently took notes and would return with the requisite amount of information and would uncover enough "new" family history to judge the course a success. Then there were a few who wouldn't want to do the work. He'd find the class enrollment decreased by this number in the upcoming weeks. What he searched for were the ones who had more questions than answers. They came to his class searching because they had not found answers in the comforts of their own lives. Under his tutelage, they emerged from the cocoons of their own darkness into the knowledge of daylight. This is what he perceived as he waited for Eve Mann to arrive at his office.

There was a knock on the door, and when he said "Come in," he was only partially surprised to see pale skin and blond hair instead of the darker woman he had been expecting. Other than her appearance in class, he hadn't seen her since his grandmother's funeral. She was taller, and the teenage roundness of her face had slimmed into young adulthood.

"Brother—" she began.

"I have an appointment," he interrupted.

Unperturbed, she plopped into the chair across from his desk

48

and dropped her macramé bag onto the floor. "Well, it's not like you've allowed me to make an appointment. So I thought the element of surprise would be best."

"Oh? And you felt you didn't achieve that when you showed up for my class?"

"Brother—" she began.

"Stop calling me that."

"Why? Everyone else gets to. But I guess it's just weird from me, huh?"

Brother LeRoi leaned back into his chair and exhaled. Perhaps he was going about things the wrong way. "Look, Amy, I guess I can understand things from your end. But this is not the way to forge a relationship with me."

"So, what would you suggest, Bro— I mean, Professor?" She smirked.

Brother LeRoi removed his glasses and slowly cleaned the frames with one of the many lens-cleaning cloths he kept. "Drop the class, Amy. You don't need to be here."

Amy stood quickly, nearly upsetting the chair. She snatched her bag from the floor. "This isn't fair. How can you be so hypocritical?"

"This whole thing has been unexpected. Just give me some time. We'll talk." He gave a reassuring smile.

"You promise?" Amy wavered.

He did not want to give her promises. He wanted to reject her, like their mother had rejected him. But she was not his mother, and he couldn't take out the ambivalence that he felt toward his mother on her. "I promise." He searched her face. "But I need you to drop this class."

"Fine, but I'm not going anywhere."

"Duly noted."

Outside of the office, Eve listened and quickly jumped back upon hearing noise moving toward the door. When Brother LeRoi opened the door and ushered Amy out, his eyes rested on Eve's. He wondered what, if anything, she had overheard.

She entered and took a seat opposite his side of the desk and they proceeded to play a game of manners, knowing but denying with their silence that they both had engaged some taboo. Eve, guilty of eavesdropping, felt justified given her discovery of Brother LeRoi's covert meetings with the enemy. She imagined him spouting Black patriarchal rhetoric while lusting after white hippie girls. Eve had known brothers like him during her brief time at Tuskegee—the ones who'd bring giggling white girls from neighboring Auburn University to the Soul Inn on the outskirts of town.

Brother LeRoi was the first to speak. "So, you have concerns about the assignment?"

"Yes." And now she had concerns about other things—his ethics, his personality, his taste in women, his professionalism, his commitment to the community. Eve glanced skeptically at Brother LeRoi, thinking that he would not be the first to attempt to fashion himself in the *Shaft* mold. Black America was in the early titillating thrall of *Shaft*. Written by a white man, the originally white title role went to Richard Roundtree, instantly making race a major factor in the script. *Shaft*, the movie, targeted Black audiences with the lure of a Black male protagonist restoring the racial balance of New York one corrupt police department, racist white man, lusty white woman, and insubordinate Black woman at a time.

He interrupted her thoughts. "What seems to be the problem?" The tension was palpable. He knew what she was thinking, or at least some version of it. They were employing a game of double-talk, inquiring on two levels of conversation.

"Well, it's kind of personal . . ."

"I see."

They were at a verbal impasse: Eve unconvinced she could trust Brother LeRoi with personal information, Brother LeRoi called to convince her that he was deserving of such trust. He tried a different tactic. "You know, whatever you discuss here with me is confidential. I can't share what you tell me with anyone."

She smiled. This was a chess game, and he had her in checkmate. He couldn't share her personal information, neither would he be able to share that of another student, a white one in particular. Eve relented. "I don't have a family history to gather information from."

"Well, that can't be right. We all have family histories. Some—many in fact—just aren't known to us. Is that your concern?"

"Sort of." Eve inhaled and exhaled several times. She'd never discussed her feelings about her lack of family history with anyone other than Nelle.

"Please, go on."

When Eve finally spoke, it all came out in a rush of words lubricated by slow, fat tears that took her by surprise. She told him about her aunt and the little that she knew of her family, which only amounted to her mother's death and her grandmother's a while later from cancer. She searched his face for a hint of the teasing she had experienced as a child, for a sign of the pity that she sometimes got from Nelle, for the irritability her aunt often displayed. She found none of those things reflected back at her, but still, she had to make certain. "I may be sobbing, but this isn't a sob story. I'm not looking for pity."

The information surged over Brother LeRoi. "Mother's sister?"

Eve nodded.

"I assume—" he began but stopped himself. He did not want to make assumptions. History is buried for many reasons. When one digs, one must be ready for what may be uncovered. "Why are you here, Eve?"

"Because you told me to see you during office hours."

Brother LeRoi raised an eyebrow.

"Sorry," she said and took a moment to compose thoughts that had coalesced into the most intense desire of her life. "I'm here because I'm tired of not knowing. I don't know what it is. I don't know what it means. I sometimes feel as if I don't know a very large part of myself."

Brother LeRoi handed her a tissue and busied himself inspecting a preserved bird's egg that he kept on a stand on his desk. "Well, I can help you."

"How?" Eve dabbed at her eyes.

"In class we'll be looking at many resources for gathering information outside of the family. I'm sure once your classmates start sharing their stories . . ."

Fear flooded Eve and she stood. "No. I can't do this in class. It's hard enough talking to you about it here. I can't . . ."

Brother LeRoi turned the egg quicker in his hand. "Okay, okay. Calm down. Have a seat. Let me think. Just, please . . . sit." He handed her another tissue for the new batch of tears that threatened at the corners of her eyes. He pulled out a pack of chewing gum and held it toward her. "Juicy Fruit?"

Eve looked at Brother LeRoi's eyes, wide and full of unexplained loss, and laughed. She took the gum and relaxed in spite of herself. She felt some strange kinship with him in this moment and wondered about his own story. "I went there too." A hint of jealously tinged her words. She nodded in the direction of his wall, toward a row of framed diplomas and degrees. Her eyes narrowed on the framed degrees from Tuskegee University.

"Yeah?"

"Just briefly though." They hadn't known each other then, of course, but they had surely passed one another occasionally on campus. "My best friend Nelle stayed the whole time."

"Nelle?" The name was familiar to Brother LeRoi. He remembered Tuskegee. Professor Woodridge. He remembered Sammy and his fraternity days. Then the name appeared. In 1968 he had officially become Big Brother LeRoi to a group of anxious young pledges. There was one that nearly hadn't crossed, being so heartbroken by a woman called Nelle. *To hell with Nelle*, he had encouraged his pledge with the mantra. LeRoi had assured his pledge that once he crossed over into full membership, there would be a girl like Nelle for every day of the week and two on Sunday. Looking back on the advice, it troubled him. The sexual politics of manhood always seemed work to the detriment of women.

Brother LeRoi was no John Shaft. He remembered how it felt to be bullied into nearly accepting a lesser version of himself and was reminded of it whenever he noticed the same tactics applied by men against women. Brother LeRoi did not attend the mix of feminist meetings and organizations. It wasn't his place; nor would he have been particularly welcome in the mostly white female space. He recognized that some of his friends did have a thing *for* white women, but Brother LeRoi had a thing *about* white women—which was a considerably different experience.

Unlike Eve, Brother LeRoi had no questions about family. He knew his mother's identity, had even met her briefly at his grandmother's funeral. But there was nothing more that he cared to know about her. It was fully understood why a white woman would give away a Black child even at this moment in 1972, and it was understood even more when he had been born, some thirty years earlier. He felt that he had nothing to search for. But Eve's plight ignited his historian's thirst for a vicarious treasure hunt.

"Don't come to class," he said.

"What?" Her thoughts flashed back to the eavesdropped conversation, and she feared that he might be telling her to drop the class.

"Don't come to class. This can be an independent study. You can meet with me here once or twice a week." The idea came so suddenly that it took even him by surprise.

"We can do that?" Eve wondered how many times he had offered this arrangement to other students and if his previous visitor had a similar agreement.

"Yeah. Yes, we can." His voice deepened in an effort to appear more confident than he felt. There was doubt in his tone, but it was the hopefulness, previously foreign to her, to which she responded.

"Give me a few days to gather some helpful information for you," he added.

"What should I do in the meantime?"

"You live with your aunt?"

She nodded and he hesitated before continuing, aware of the implications of what he was about to recommend. "There's information in that house. Somewhere. You see, we hide things from others and ourselves. We don't want to see them, but we don't want to destroy them either. It's there, Eve, you just have to look." His own secrets were still buried in an unopened envelope in a box in the back of a closet. Had it contained perishables, it would be foul-smelling and leaking. He regarded it as if it were such, from the scripted name he no longer claimed written in block letters

54

across its front to the weighty thickness of its unknown contents. He thought of the hidden envelope even as he suggested to Eve that she violate her aunt's dark corners and closets. His hypocrisy was not lost on him, and he recalled that he had just been accused of such.

Eve wondered whether she would find treasure or curse on her information hunt. She thought back to her last demand for information from Mama Ann before leaving for Tuskegee.

"You know, if you're really my mother, you should just say so," she said softly as she packed.

"That's just nonsense, Every," Ann responded, clearly flustered as she fumbled together a care package for Eve's dormitory life.

"Is it?" Eve paused. "I mean, if you and that boy James got into a little . . ."

"Every!" Ann shook. "Things moved different back then."

"If that was the case, then I wouldn't have been born to an unwed teenager," Eve shot back.

Ann moved directly in front of Eve, grabbed her face, and slowly turned it toward her. "Your mother was Mercy Mann. She was my baby sister, and she's dead." Releasing Eve's face, Ann left the room and the haunting thoughts of sending her dead sister's child into the very South that Mercy escaped during the steady hemorrhaging of Blacks that migrated north.

Eve shook off the memory as Brother LeRoi continued to maneuver the egg around his long fingers in accordance with the speed of his thoughts.

"What is that?" Eve nodded toward the egg.

LeRoi smiled. "Someone once told me it's a beginning."

Because Brother LeRoi and Eve didn't know what else to do, having shared what felt like too strong of an intimacy for their relationship, they shook hands. Determined to escape the sentiment foretold in the popular refrain of a Negro spiritual: "sometimes I feel like a motherless child," they were two people living alternate versions of themselves, from their conscious revisions of their names to their decisions to rewrite the migration stories they had been given to perform. Stories that migrated with people and snaked across the country as veins pumping blood to new transplants.

FOUR

the hillbilly highway

They're American-born white-skinned natives, with
no racial, religious, or language characteristics [except
southern accents] to set them apart as an ethnic group.
Yet as a group [steadily increasing] with specific,
recognizable culture patterns that are completely alien
to urban life, they pose one of the most serious problems
in Chicago's projected plans for industrial expansion.
—Norma Lee Browning, "New 'Breed' of Migrants
City Problem," *Chicago Daily Tribune*, March 4, 1957

It would have been an easy task for Brother LeRoi to burn his mother's letter. He could have thrown it out on trash-collection day and most assuredly never have come in contact with it again. He could have used it as kindling and set it ablaze during one of the community cookouts or shredded it and flushed the fragments down someone else's commode—heaven forbid a paper floater claim determined resilience in his own toilet. But people have a habit of hiding things that they wish never existed. When faced with possessing what could arguably be the very key to their physical, emotional, and mental undoing, something prevents them from destroying it.

So LeRoi didn't discard it, nor did he open it. Not that either mattered when the information contained in its pages—the family narrative of which he'd decided to remain in blissful ignorance—sauntered into his classroom, pressured him to meet, and presently sat across from him in a small South Side coffeehouse.

Amy generously poured cream into her tea until it mirrored the milky dusk complexion of LeRoi. She rambled on about school and witnessing North Side racism as if her first-meeting jitters had compelled her into a false sense of familiarity. LeRoi waved away the proffered cream and silently sipped his coffee. His thoughts drifted to the price of coffee, which had steadily increased over the past decade. His attention pushed away toward the South American farmers who produced the beans and snapped back as Amy continued.

"And Mama's been a little under the weather . . ."

LeRoi frowned but said nothing.

Amy's brow creased. "Don't you even care to hear about your mother?"

LeRoi slowly set his mug on the table. "The woman who mothered me died several years ago."

"Your grandmother, but—"

LeRoi interrupted, "There is no but."

Amy sighed. "I'm sorry. I—"

LeRoi held up his hand. "What is it exactly that you think I can do for you, Amy?"

She smiled widely. "Actually, it's what I can do for you."

"What does that mean?" LeRoi sneered. His thoughts were on

unwanted trust funds and family relics. Perhaps his mother was dying and needed an organ donation. He did not want to give to them or receive from them. Not that he had a choice in the matter.

"Have you ever heard of the Melungeons?" Amy asked, and then it did not matter at all how long their mother's letter had been wedged into the recesses of LeRoi's closet. The letter was an errant thread that threatened to unravel the entirety of a garment. In a most callous well-intentioned act, Amy had opened her mouth and freed its contents. She had released his parents, LeAnna and Roy.

Theirs was no love story. It was not the strangulation of young love by feuding families. Nor was it the controversial tale of taboo miscegenation between a president and his enslaved mistress. They were not even an Othello and Desdemona. LeAnna and Roy hadn't had much of a chance to be anything more than two equally poor teenagers working the same land neither of their families owned. Whites had simply been too poor to segregate themselves from their Black counterparts. Poverty may have made better neighbors than good fences. Between white and Black lived the Melungeons, isolated on a ridge just beyond the small town of Sneedville, Tennessee. Their features varied, as did the curl patterns of their hair. They were any combination of pale, olive, bronze, or brown complexion and kinky, curly, wavy, or straight hair.

Nowhere were these variations more present than in Roy's own family. His widowed mother, Clara, was buttermilk in tone with a broad nose and full lips. Both brothers possessed the olive skin associated with those from the Mediterranean and straight hair. Roy was as brown as the Tennessee soil on which they lived with hair that curled against his scalp when short and became fuzzy if left untended. His father had been a dark man. So dark that he had been thought to be Black. Unable to prove his Melungeon heritage, the family had been excommunicated and forced to relocate to the bottom of the ridge. Clara had violated a fundamental rule of Melungeon freedom: the distinction between them and Negroes. Melungeons best resembled those with whom they were in close proximity. It was no wonder that they tended to marry their white neighbors and lighter variations of their own ethnicity.

LeAnna and Roy did not fall in love, nor did they fall in lust. Their fall was in fear. They were not colorblind, for such a thing does not exist. LeAnna did not just notice the expanse of Roy's muscles, she reveled in the contrast—the coloring within his body lines, Roy as her polar opposite: male and dark—while Roy could not see her absent her paleness. Color had been such a part of their lives that it certainly must have infiltrated their attraction. Yet they shared the same heritage. Their most recent ancestors had successfully argued in early court cases that they were not of the Negro race. It allowed them to remain free as many of the same complexion were enslaved and subsequently legally discriminated against during LeAnna and Roy's time. Their freedom came with a shadow that Roy knew all too well—a constant threat of it being upended should there be one dark smudge on their Melungeon lineage. They were Melungeon, but Roy, with his dark skin and coiled hair, was a dead branch on the tree.

LeAnna and Roy didn't make eyes at each other as they passed in town. They didn't carve hearts with their initials in trees. They ended up at the same place in a sense broader than merely arriving at Mullens Field at a specific time one evening. Namely, both were running from their lives on the ridge—the inescapable expectations that came with being Melungeon and the realities of propagating an ethnicity that seemed to exist only in Appalachia. They were trapped.

LeAnna often snuck out of the house to sleep under the stars. It wasn't a romantic engagement with nature; she fled because she had exhausted her ability to keep her drunken uncle from entering her room in the night. She found a haven in the field they sharecropped. Shrouding her thoughts of leaving the ridge in the darkness of night, LeAnna wondered if her history could exist outside of the ridge. What would she be? She wasn't white or Black. Would she only be as she appeared to be to those who looked upon her? Would they take in the straightness of her hair and grayness of her eyes and peg her as white?

Mullens Field similarly harbored Roy and his feelings of stagnation. The ridge simultaneously labeled his dark skin problematic and protected him from the harsh realities of American Blackness circa 1940. He could be relatively safe if he remained in the bowels of the ridge. Yet the knowledge that his station there would be tied to the complexion of his mate and their children, since his own already counted against him, kept him up nights, visiting the field. Since work at the mines had been greatly reduced, many were packing up and leaving the ridge. He worried about what could happen if he left. On the ridge, he *might* be Black. Away from it, he'd be nothing other than it. He'd be nothing other. He'd be nothing. Some nights as Roy sat silently gazing at the stars, LeAnna slept soundlessly across the field—each unaware of the other's presence. Until that night when the sky opened.

Lightning, accompanied by a deluge of rain, illuminated the field in bursts of near daytime intensity. LeAnna's fear of lightning harbored memories of her uncle creeping into her room and blinding her with a flashlight beam, a smile hidden behind the darkness. *Just a joke, baby girl.* His eyes lingered on her. *But you ain't a baby no more, is you?*

Roy's fear was of shotgun blasts of thunder that cracked the sky's flesh open like a whip. He shuddered and thought of the loud noises in the night that often accompany the deaths of colored men in the South, even within the purview of the ridge. Although they were escorted by flashes of light, Roy remained unconvinced that the sounds were those of some dark body being brutalized. He stood, eyes scanning the horizon for lynch mob shadows. They landed on LeAnna standing paralyzed by fear, and his first thought was that his imagined vigilante posse served as a premonition since it didn't get much more dire than being a dark man in a field with a soaking-wet white-enough woman. He resigned himself to the fate of a dead man already tried and punished for whatever did, could, or was about to happen.

Hail fell or hell fell—it was all the same to LeAnna and Roy as they moved toward each other, hurried along by a fear of everything outside of themselves. Their progress was revealed in flashes of lightning, their mud-caked footfalls silenced by thunder. They clung to each other until all that remained was night and a steady rain.

She kissed him. She didn't know why, but she did. He responded. They, who moments earlier lamented the constraints of their lives, cast them off in the first way that presented itself.

Without speaking, they disrobed slowly. They reached for each other because there was no one else there to reach for—and no one else to see them reach. They were young birds exercising their wings before attempting flight. Their same time and place was one night's moment of freedom. When light returned, so did they— to what they were.

LeAnna's family did not care about the origins of her stomach bump. Some figured the uncle had finally won. Others chalked it up to the inevitable result and purpose of menstruation. What mattered most to them was where this latest addition would sleep in the already overcrowded three-room shack. Marriage suggestions brought inquiries about the father, and her silence, first regarded as the shame of a spurned lover, soon began to cause greater concern among her relatives. The question became not *whose* baby was in her stomach but what *kind* of baby.

She was eight months swollen and constricted by her nightgown the next time her uncle visited her bedroom. On her right side facing away from the door, LeAnna didn't see him enter. The flashlight flickered three times before it released a consistent beam. She turned into the depression of the bed with his weight and eyed her uncle wearily as he placed a hand on her stomach.

"What's in here?" he hissed in her ear.

"My baby," LeAnna whispered.

"What's it gon' look like? Ain't gon' look like me, is it?"

Moisture spread from her. Her uncle dabbed it with his fingers. He knew before she did. Her water had broken. He ran a hand through his sweaty black hair. "Imma go wake your momma."

LeAnna faced the door and wiped away tears. Pulling herself up, she slid her bare feet into work boots and shuffled out of the house as quickly as her contractions would allow.

When she knocked on the door, she was in full labor and could only manage to gasp in front of the older Black woman who opened it. Brown faces peered at her—the youngest with curiosity, and the oldest with fear. LeAnna's eyes found Roy's, and he reached for her and guided her into the room he shared with his two brothers. His mother Clara followed, soon ushering him and everyone else from the small bedroom, barking orders for towels and hot water, then staring at her eldest son with despair before closing the door in his face, isolating her and LeAnna from the rest of the house.

It was five hours before the door opened again, bringing the shrill sound of a crying newborn. The baby entered the world swathed in fresh sheets laundered for middle-class white women by his paternal grandmother, the woman who would raise him. He lay nestled against LeAnna, while Roy sat beside them. The fear in the house was palpable. They noted his pale hue, aware that an infant's color darkens with age, before counting his tiny fingers and toes.

Baby Lee Roy, later known as Brother LeRoi, darkened, binding their fate to his complexion. When he reached the color of cinnamon, they knew that they would not ascend the ridge. Roy and his family wouldn't return to the Melungeon community, and LeAnna would be similarly expelled from it. They would leave, as so many others had, on the Hillbilly Highway.

———————

With great flourish, Amy sat across from her half-brother, LeRoi, and announced, "You're not Black. You're Melungeon. We both are. We're the same, LeRoi. The exact same."

Brother LeRoi belted out a deep guttural chortle that shook the table and caused a questioning glare from Amy. LeRoi didn't need to hear the details of his mother and father's migration from Appalachia. He had no knowledge of their multiple stops along the way or how many places refused them service and entry. LeRoi didn't need to know about the final time his father, Roy, claimed not to be Negro—to two white men at a filling station not far outside their Tennessee home.

"Nigger says he ain't a nigger."

"What kind of nigger is he?"

"Whatever kind of nigger he is, it comes with a nigger-lover," one said, nodding his head toward LeAnna seated in the pickup truck.

"That right?" the other answered.

They beat the Melungeon out of him. When Roy arrived with his family in Chicago, he was Negro and LeAnna was white. The only way for them to live was apart, as pegs pressed into the holes they closest fit.

Amy began to repeat, "You're not Black. You're descendant of—"

LeRoi grabbed her hand inciting an audible gasp from several of the mostly white patrons around them in the coffee shop. A white man seated across from them half-rose until LeRoi removed his hand and stood.

"Right." LeRoi winked at her. He tossed enough money to cover his coffee and her tea on the table and left Amy to fantasies of racial loopholes and sibling harmony. All that Amy's instigation had accomplished was to stir up the sediment of his repressed feelings about his matriculation at Tuskegee.

FIVE

beneath the veil

He lifted the veil of ignorance
from his people and pointed the way to progress
through education and industry.
—Inscription, Booker T. Washington statue,
Tuskegee Institute

I am standing puzzled, unable to decide
whether the veil is really being lifted,
or lowered more firmly in place;
whether I am witnessing revelation or
a more efficient blinding.
—Ralph Ellison, *Invisible Man*

The second rising of the South did not occur in the way expected by the old Confederacy. It arrived with the South's racial underclass clawing their way out of oppression. Booker T. Washington's aptly titled autobiography *Up from Slavery* recounts the process for Tuskegee Institute's first president in 1881. It was a slow and arduous climb.

When Washington arrived in Tuskegee, Alabama, to serve as the first president and sole instructor at its new school for colored folk, there were no buildings in which to teach, no materials, no staff, and no land. It isn't technically correct to state that he founded the Tuskegee Normal School, as he was brought into service by George C. Campbell and Lewis Adams, an ex-slaveholder and ex-slave, respectively. Yet it would be an extreme disservice to history not to claim Washington as the founding father of the Tuskegee Normal and Industrial Institute (the school's fourth name), the man who first learned and then instructed its growing faculty and student body in agriculture (the primary economy of the South) as well as brickmaking and masonry, much in the way he had taught himself to read and later became the head of an educational institution.

Two decades after its founding, the school would boast a total of forty buildings—all constructed by the students. The turn of the century's contagion of progress was evident all over the country. Yet parts of the old Confederacy rallied against this particular aspect of southern uprising by memorializing the lost war in monuments like the Daughters of the Confederacy's stone statue in Tuskegee's town square.

The lone stone soldier of the Confederacy stands with an unwavering gaze directed beyond the desolate square. His concrete eyes pierce space and time as the town center crumbles around him and the institute rises seemingly from the alabaster rubble. This statue glares from the growing shadows toward another—that of Booker T. Washington, immortalized in metal as in deed.

The bronze sculpture depicts Washington lifting the veil of ignorance from a kneeling slave at his side. Washington did not live to see the statue erected in his honor or the post-Reconstruction Jim Crow era, which sparked millions of Blacks to flee the South beginning the year of his death. Like an omen, perhaps Washington could see the futility of his life's work, encouraging southern Blacks to "cast down their buckets" where they were. Exhausted by violence, lynchings, and stolen legacies, southern Blacks packed their buckets with their meager belongings and migrated north while the Confederate soldier stared on.

Yet Lee Roy Duncan had found answers in Washington's autobiography as he grappled with the changing landscape of Chicago gang life. Lee Roy saw himself surrounded by people surviving poorly, and Washington's words spoke directly to him. At first, he just wanted to see the campus that had been built by the hands of students and teachers and Washington. He tried to relay the stories of Washington's triumphs to his fellow Blackstone Rangers, yet his awe failed to inspire.

"We got plenty dead niggas for you to dig on right here, right now," they chided him. It was true. His friends were pouring liquor onto cement steps in Malcolm X's honor—three weeks dead after delivering a fiery speech on "The Spectrum of Political Ideologies" at Tuskegee Institute. They would continue the practice for each murdered activist, and it wouldn't be a stretch of the imagination to see how, later, King's assassination would serve as the final nail in the political coffin of the Blackstone Rangers. There seemed little profit, social or otherwise, in peaceful protests. They could not protect their king, so they acquiesced to building empires constructed of powder—heroin for broken heroes.

When Lee Roy exited the Greyhound bus with his single suitcase, he didn't even know the way to campus. The town square was desolate, bereft of the major businesses usually located in such central districts. Lee Roy looked anxiously around the square, hoping that its emptiness was not an indication of what he could expect from campus life. Wandering the square, Lee Roy found himself before the stone soldier—a most unusual welcome committee. Yet the Confederate statue was not the only soldier in the square.

"You look lost."

Lee Roy turned toward the voice to find a slender young man near his own light complexion approaching. "Yeah, a bit." Lee Roy grimaced. "I guess I didn't think things down to the small details."

"Looking for campus then?"

Lee Roy nodded and took the proffered hand.

"Sammy." Sammy tipped his cap toward the statue and smirked at Lee Roy. "Well, come then. It's only 'bout a mile."

Lee Roy grabbed his suitcase and followed Sammy as the soldier gazed on. Behind them, the Greyhound bus pulled away from the station, leaving a dust cloud that wouldn't settle until the two new friends had arrived at their destination.

Sammy had enrolled at Tuskegee about a month earlier. "But I've been around here most of my life," he told Lee Roy. "Graduated from high school right around there. Then went into the navy, but . . ." He patted his side. "Kidney failed me. They took it and sent me packing. You serve?"

Lee Roy shook his head and tapped his glasses. "Eyes good enough for everything but that. Detached retina." He waved his hand beside his right ear. "Try not to stand over here."

Sammy smiled. "Well, can't fight with guns . . . Guess we just have to make our minds into weapons. Plenty to fight for down here."

"Right on." Lee Roy felt the beginnings of a belonging he hadn't known since his days with the Rangers. "I should've been down here sooner." He faltered. "Brother Malcolm . . ."

Sammy stopped walking and slowly bobbed his head. "He was something. He was really, really something. And it needed to be heard. Here."

"What do you mean?"

Sammy snorted. "Brother, if you think you found some sort of Negro paradise, you mistaken. There is lots of work to be done in Tuskegee. Don't worry. You haven't missed the rapture. I'm sure there's plenty more death and struggle to go round."

And there would be. It was 1965 in a segregated Alabama town where statues of a white Confederate soldier and a former slave turned educator were planted on parcels like opposing chess pieces. They made pawns of the inhabitants of towns like Tuskegee, and the first college student casualty of the battle for civil rights was Sammy Younge Jr. It was nearly a year before his untimely fate that he befriended Lee Roy, leaving a legacy etched in the hearts of many, although void of the commemorative concrete and bronze avatars afforded to the soldier and Washington.

———

Lee Roy's commitment to the cause had been reignited. It made sense that his quest to aid the civil rights struggle would take him to the South. Although his childhood friends did not understand. Tiny had been the only one to brave the late February winter hawk and take him to the bus station.

"Your backward ass belongs down there," Tiny's breath visibly puffed toward him in the car. Lee Roy reached for the door handle, and Tiny roughly planted his hand on Lee Roy's chest. "Don't get yourself killed down there."

It was a heavy remark in the wake of his grandmother's funeral and Malcolm X's assassination. People were dying. The movement that claimed the reformed Nation of Islam leader was not responsible for the death of Lee Roy's grandmother. Yet her demise served as a reminder that passings brought about by injustice in no way lessen those from natural causes.

"I'll be a lot safer down there than in this piece-of-shit car of yours," Lee Roy shot back. They shared a laugh about the four-year-old Corvair that decades later would be deemed one of *Time* magazine's fifty worst cars of all time.

With Sammy as a guide, Tuskegee offered Lee Roy innumerable opportunities to participate in the civil rights battles. Nineteen sixty-five was a hotbed year of local and regional activity that brought not only Malcolm X in February but also Martin Luther King Jr. in May to deliver the commencement speech. Although Lee Roy missed the activism fostered by the Blackstone Rangers in their earlier years, he had also latched onto them for more personal reasons—the brotherhood they offered. Attending Tuskegee brought fraternal bonding by way of four Panhellenic organizations thirsty for new pledges.

The behavioral changes in Lee Roy—ones that seemed to accompany all fraternity pledges—were not lost on his new friend. "You know you're starting to look like an undertaker," Sammy remarked as they sat outside of the dining hall in early March. Lee Roy looked up from the sign he was painting.

"What? You don't like the suit?"

"Well," Sammy chortled, "I did the first couple of days, but now it's just too much."

Lee Roy carefully placed the end of his tie over his right shoulder. "They say—"

"They?" Sammy raised an eyebrow.

Catching his near error, Lee Roy cleared his throat. "It's good for colored men to be seen in business attire."

"So *they* say," Sammy sneered.

"Look, man," Lee Roy slid back from the sign. "We are more than capable of being involved in all manner of business. If only folk just—"

"White folk," Sammy interjected.

"Yeah. Yes. White folks. If they just got used to seeing us this way . . ."

"Then what? They gonna bring us their business?"

"Yes!"

"Bullshit." Sammy tossed his paintbrush into a bucket of water at his feet. "You know, most students are tired of unimportant 'business as usual.' Here you got your fancy fraternity telling y'all to just wear a suit and tie but ignoring the threat of nooses that are far more likely to be put around your neck. It's a joke."

"I get you." Lee Roy resumed painting. "But what's wrong with working both ends of this thing? Why can't I march and also pledge?"

Sammy sighed. "Because colored folk never get a choice on which end of anything. You even thinking that you have one is just a distraction. If you aren't full-time, then you part-time pledging to the movement. You can't be part-time for life and death." He stood and pointed to Lee Roy's sign. "And this? Where you gonna be on Sunday?"

"I'm there." Lee Roy's voice was strong with conviction. "Imma march." Sammy snatched up his own sign and bucket and trudged away leaving Lee Roy to paint the final red *a* in Selma. But the institute had different plans, delivering notices reminding students about the mandatory Sunday chapel services and doubling down on the mandate with the threat of expulsion for absentees.

The original Chapel, completed in 1898, required 1.2 million student-made bricks and years of trial and error learning the brickmaking trade, including three failed brick-burning kilns and thousands of useless bricks. By the time of its completion, the Chapel was the Pyramid of Djoser of its day. Perhaps Lee Roy and the other students compelled to attend Chapel every Sunday would have felt some deep reverence for its history had it not been destroyed by lightning in 1957. The replacement chapel, a wonder for its astonishing acoustics and lack of right angles, would not be constructed until 1969. Meaning that Lee Roy spent his weekly services in Logan Hall, the gymnasium.

Lee Roy sat in the well-worn wooden seat with the indescribable sense of being out of place or placed out of being. The chaplain—unaware of the irony of his lecture "Pray Not Play"—droned on about student responsibility and morality from a makeshift pulpit in a building designed for play. Most faculty members sat toward the front of the room, and every time the chaplain spoke of play, a small but distinct cough sounded from one of the front seats. Straining to see past the rowed seats in front of him, Lee Roy could only make out the back of the culprit, identified by the occasional raising of the arm to cover his mouth in a perfectly synchronized dance with the throat-clearing noise. Lee Roy's focus on the arm revealed a dark suit jacket, the one-inch bright tab of white shirt peeking from the jacket sleeve as the arm bent upward, and the exotic flash of a gold watch fastened around the wrist.

With his eye on the culprit, the chaplain switched his focus to moral standards, eliciting a double cough from the offender. Lee Roy watched in rapt fascination, wondering if anyone else noticed the hidden war being waged. None knew of the very public war happening about eighty miles to the west on the Edmund Pettus Bridge. The chaplain spoke. The coughs repeated. Lee Roy watched, hypnotized by the rhythm of it all and transfixed by the gleaming timepiece.

It came to be known as Bloody Sunday—the first leg of the Selma to Montgomery March. Fifty years later, the first Black president of the United States would participate in a re-creation of that final leg of the march in commemoration of both the struggle and progress, of which he was the most prominent legacy. In its entirety, the distance between the two cities was slightly more miles than years to this future event. It was far less commodified in its original incarnation. No one wanted to have to do it, and yet they marched by the thousands. Spectators gathered to lend support or hurl their opposition in racial epithets. On this leg of the march, six hundred souls linked arms and attempted to cross the Edmund Pettus Bridge—named for the Confederate general and Ku Klux Klan grand dragon who died in the summer of 1907, a year after Tuskegee's stone soldier emerged.

The bridge—opposite of the sun's ascension and decline—rises on its western end, the direction from which the protesters traveled. It reaches its peak at the center, one hundred feet above the Alabama River. The bridge's uphill march revealed nothing beyond pavement until the activists reached the pinnacle and looked down toward policemen. Dogs. Batons. Violence. The future of their battered bodies to be immortalized by the unimaginably horrifying amounts of bloodshed on that Sunday.

Bloody Sunday had awakened a hesitancy in Lee Roy that was matched only by the conflagration it ignited in his friend Sammy. They both attended the student protest against the violence of the event three days after its occurrence; however, where Lee Roy withdrew from the movement, Sammy was consumed by it. Lee Roy leaned hard toward the academic activism of the civil rights movement, while Sammy was entrenched in its physicality. There were no more debates between them—just silent acceptance of the other and the permeation of loss.

That July, Sammy was brutally attacked while working to desegregate a church in Tuskegee. Lee Roy visited as he convalesced.

"Can't you see how dangerous this is becoming?" He argued to no effect. It seemed to Lee Roy, reflecting on his Blackstone Ranger years, that the most effective strategy against institutional racism was to work your way into those institutions and fight from within.

Sammy's voice was weak, but the conviction was as strong as ever. "No. Not becoming. Always been dangerous."

"Then why do this to yourself?" Lee Roy implored.

Sammy attempted a chuckle but winced in pain. "You think I did this to myself?" He pointed emphatically at his bruised and swollen face.

"Of course not."

Sammy sighed. "So, what would you have me do, brother?"

Lee Roy touched the Greek letters on his sweater. True to his natural inclinations, he had retreated into the safety of a fraternal order. Alpha Phi Alpha, stitched in raised Greek letters, glared outward. "Live." He gently placed a hand on his friend's shoulder. "I'd have you live, brother."

"To what end?" Sammy whispered.

"A natural one!"

A smile managed its way across Sammy's face. "What kind of natural order says that my life should be without the vote? inferior? separated from anything good in this world? What life is that to lead?"

"There are other ways to, to, to fight." Lee Roy stammered. "In writing and petitioning and . . ."

Sammy blinked languorously. "Fighting . . . eventually involves . . . fighting."

Two months later, Sammy was arrested in the neighboring town of Opelika. Lee Roy heard the news from one of his fraternity brothers. There was often unvoiced reverence for the foot soldiers of the movement. Not everyone was built for marching, but they found ways to support it. The fraternity brother pressed a collection of crumpled bills into Lee Roy's hand. "You know . . . for the brother's defense or whatever." Lee Roy nodded wordlessly. He was seeing less and less of Sammy but would make sure to get the money to him and to also relay the names of its donors.

Autumn rolled into winter, and the New Year saw the birth of 1966 and the death of Sammy Younge Jr. one year after his enrollment at Tuskegee Institute. Lee Roy mourned heavily. He thought of his first meeting with Sammy at the Greyhound bus stop—the same place where Sammy met his unfortunate end.

It was at a voter registration drive near the Standard Oil gas station where most everyone with a vehicle refilled their tanks at some point. After using the whites-only bathroom, an argument ensued between Sammy and the station attendant. The attendant—sixty-seven years old and well reared in the ways of the Old South—pulled a gun, and Sammy, still with fight in his footfalls, fled. The first shot rang out and missed him.

Sammy made it to the Greyhound bus station just as an Atlanta-bound bus was boarding. He ran onto the bus, but safety was short-lived. The driver forced him off and back into running. It was the second shot that hit his temple, and Sammy fell bleeding against the back of the station.

Lee Roy's anger bubbled within him, and it could not be quelled by the constant coddling of his fraternity or quieted by the consolation of his classmates. The buildings, with their student-made bricks that he so admired, appeared weak and inadequate. They were an illusion of stability. They could not protect against what the movement moved against. Lee Roy no longer saw the lush greenery of the campus. He saw complacency, and as he maneuvered on the night of Sammy's death, inebriated and carrying a pint of whiskey in one hand and a tire iron in the other, he found a scapegoat for his blame.

In the pitch dark of the night, he raised his eyes to the bronze statue of Booker T. Washington and yelled, "Were you there?" Then followed it with a whispered, "Were you there?" He stood poised with the tire iron raised for the blow.

The response came as a soprano melody from the night. It sang back to him, "Were you there when they crucified my Lord?" It gained intensity and asked again. "Were you there . . . when they . . . crucified . . . my Lord?"

Lee Roy leaned with his back against the statue and slid to the ground as it moaned, "Oh, ooh, ooh-ooh . . . sometimes it causes me to tremble . . . tremble . . . tremble. Were you there when they crucified my Lord?" Lee Roy, shaking in response, sat on the cold ground.

"Were you there when they nailed him to the tree?" Tears streamed down Lee Roy's face during each crescendo of the refrain, "Were you there when they pierced him in his side?"

A loud sob escaped him before he could quiet it with his hand. "Oh, God," he cried. He saw Sammy running for his life and thought of their last conversation, where he'd pleaded with his friend to live safely. Mercifully, the voice stopped, and Lee Roy opened his eyes to investigate its source, the ending punctuated by the distinctive sound of flint to steel and a flame, at first small, then puffed large, reflected against a gold watch on the wrist that held it.

Woodridge emerged into the moonlight reflected by the statue. He puffed a mahogany pipe and exhaled. "You'd do more harm with that tire iron to yourself than the founding father." He took another long drag from his pipe. "The founder and I have always had differences of opinion on some things, but he's always been one of impeccable taste."

Woodridge smiled. His suit played tricks in the moonlight by appearing royal blue at some angles and purple at others. It was tailored beyond its time, fitting a little more snugly than fashion then dictated. Middle-aged, a slight graying glazed his temples and sprinkled what seemed at first a low haircut but in more light was revealed to be a fiercely brushed Caesar cut. His mustache and goatee were equally manicured.

Lee Roy stood attentive. He had heard of Professor Woodridge and the advice to avoid him and his apartment, for what the chaplain would call "morality issues." He cleared his throat. "I wasn't going to do . . . What I mean to say, sir, is that I'm cool."

Woodridge frowned into his inhale and exhaled. "Cool? I don't know what that means. I think language and semantics are wasted on the young. I take it you mean that you are not hot? Not hot, not now. But you look very hot indeed. Hotheaded. That is to say, not cool at all."

"I'm fine, sir."

"Don't call me sir." Woodridge stepped closer. "I only wish to convey that the statue is of bronze. You don't want to go clanging metal onto metal."

"Oh." Lee Roy exhaled.

Woodridge retreated into the darkness. "It's not like cement or concrete." His voice trailed off. "Now, I imagine a tire iron could do some damage to a statue like that."

Lee Roy stood fixed in place, catching the dwindling refrains of what had become a deep tenor humming, "Were you there . . ."

The campus was awash with news that the Confederate soldier in town had been vandalized. Not all of the damage was caused by a tire iron. Graffiti and trash lingered. When students individually and in groups encountered the statue after its initial violation, their impulse was to add to the cause. It became a community vandalization project until Tuskegee's white residents took note and began standing guard around the stone sentinel. Lee Roy, in particular, had lost what had become his nocturnal exercise in directed aggression.

One night not long after his encounter with Woodridge, he stood frozen at the door to the professor's apartment, fist raised, poised to rap on the forbidden slab of wood that was the subject of much discussion in student circles. Students were just as indoctrinated in the whereabouts of contraband and vice by older scholars as they were directed to systems of moral reinforcement by the administration. They knew that a juke joint could be found at the very end of Church Street. Ladies in trouble might find a solution at a small brick house right on the edge of town. There was a still ten miles into the woods toward Shorter that sold the worst moonshine since Prohibition. And if you felt a sense of unbelonging, you could knock on Professor Woodridge's door around ten o'clock at night during his evening libations.

Woodridge, quite undeniably, was homosexual, and during the course of his tenure, some students struggling with their sexuality did visit. He did not have any sexual interest in his pupils, however, and for their part, they were merely seeking answers to questions they were unable to ask in their heteronormed home lives. Yet most of the knocks on Woodridge's door were not from students suffering from a displacement of heterosexual desire; rather, they came from those suffering an intellectual displacement that did not successfully integrate with the institute's policies. Lee Roy had lost a friend, and there were protests by students, yet the institute kept its pace. Classes remained in session. The chaplain lectured on Black student morality, and Sammy stayed dead. His fist grazed the wooden surface and he waited.

Woodridge was not surprised when he opened the door. He had pegged this one. "Well, if it isn't the little tire-iron man." He frowned. "I'm still working with that one. It lacks a certain *je* ne sais *quoi.*" He gave names to all his special visitors, his outliers. The institute's most prolific young thinkers and writers, yet their true character lay hidden beneath the mask they insisted on wearing even in a racially homogenized space. These were his invisible men, frightened of their own selves. They mistakenly came to him seeking cosmetic fixes for their intellectual marginalization. They came to him wanting to learn how to hide more effectively. And one by one, he crushed their spirits while simultaneously setting them free.

They sat across from one another, Lee Roy in an upright winged-back chair and Woodridge on the chaise longue, eying him curiously. "I can offer you coffee, tea, or water."

Lee Roy wordlessly pulled a mason jar from his jacket pocket— bad moonshine—to which Woodridge commented, "And the advice that a gentleman carries a flask, not a jar." He wrinkled his nose. "And not of that Shorter swill, but you didn't visit for alcohol connoisseurship."

Lee Roy took a large gulp from the mason jar. "No, sir—I mean, Professor—I did not."

"Well . . . enlighten me. Why are you here?"

Lee Roy took a smaller sip. "I don't know where else to be."

"I see." Woodridge rose and poured a scotch from a glass decanter. "You know, you remind me of someone. He came to me late at night—as they all do—so full of despair. As much nightly despair as the daytime disdain that they have for me. I know you all pass by my door, snickering and pointing. I'm too . . . what is it you call it now? Fruity?"

"I imagine that's between you and your God, Professor."

Woodridge exploded in laughter. It was hearty and throaty and unexpected from the same body that could produce a soprano version of "Were You There When They Crucified My Lord?" He drank his scotch in one long progressive swallow. "Well, that is something. Because, between you and me,"—he winked conspiratorially—"you don't believe in God."

Lee Roy's hand was large and awkward on the mason jar. He looked at the decanter of scotch. "Can I have . . ."

"No. You cannot."

Lee Roy swished the moonshine around the jar. "A glass then?" Woodridge rose and disappeared behind a shimmer of satin curtains separating the kitchen area. Lee Roy sat in a haze. He hadn't processed it. God was something you took for granted and accepted as a condition. God was like Blackness. You might not agree with the ideal, but everyone else did, so you struggled along with it and its complications even though God seemed to be discriminatory in his blessings. You believed in God because of the miracles he had given others. You believe in their God, for them.

Woodridge returned with a hefty crystal glass and set it on the end table next to Lee Roy. He relieved Lee Roy of the jar so effortlessly that Lee Roy hadn't registered it until his drink was made.

Returning to his chair, Woodridge carefully plucked an egg from his bookcase shelf, cupped it gently, and snorted. "Let me tell you about God. You come here in your darkest moments, and you reach for someone else you imagine is in darkness—me, because of who I am. In the dark, it never occurs to any of you that what you crave most is light. Enlightenment. I appear as such with just a flick of the switch. You speak of God and miracles but would never regard me as such. And yet, who do you reach for in your darkest hours? Whose name do you invoke? For your God . . . you knock on *my* door." His eyes remained trained on the egg, which he delicately turned in his hand.

"What is that?" Lee Roy's eyes were also fixed on the egg.

"Exactly!"

"No," Lee Roy specified. "I mean, that in your hand."

Woodridge held the egg toward Lee Roy in his open palm. "It's you."

Lee Roy gently retrieved it. "It's an egg?"

"It's a beginning," Woodridge emphasized. "At least symbolically. In reality, that," he pointed to the egg, "is a barbaric travesty. Do you know ornithology?"

Lee Roy shook his head slowly and felt the moonshine's countercurrent movement.

"Ornithology is the study of birds." Woodridge had been fascinated with them since his youth. Their majesty and freedom and gaiety proved to him that if those qualities were possible in birds, under the dominion of humans, then surely he could manage a modicum of the same traits.

"You know, you can't profess to love birds," Woodridge continued, "and murder them for your own collection. And puncture their eggs and drain out the embryos because you love them so much.

That egg is a reminder of a dark time in my life when I was willing to kill the qualities that I most admire."

Lee Roy rotated the egg and spied the tiny puncture wound in its fragile shell. "What kind of bird was it?"

Woodridge dragged on his pipe. "A mockingbird."

Lee Roy reached out to return the egg, but Woodridge held up his hand. "I want you to keep it. I don't need it any longer. I have much to remind me of the past."

The mockingbird egg saw Lee Roy matriculate in title and name. He buried the Lee and Roy parts of himself alongside the helplessness that he felt about Sammy. He became good at burying things over which he felt little control. The push and pull of integration, the gap between his studies and the real-world application of them, and the realization that there was absolutely no difference between the inner workings of his fraternity and those of the Blackstone Rangers. LeRoi greeted the new decade and its integration of Blackness into a system ready to acknowledge its legal equality if not quite a social one. The framed depictions of Booker T. Washington, Frederick Douglas, and John Shaft that adorned his dormitory wall loomed imposingly over a small shelf on which the tiny egg rested.

the new black

**If I didn't define myself for myself, I would be crunched
into other people's fantasies for me and eaten alive.
—Audre Lorde, "Learning from the 60s"**

Eve and Nelle sat with eyes glued to the screen, focused on the breakout star of *The Big Doll House*. Busty and brown, Pam Grier portrayed a prostitute in the women-in-prison flick. When she ordered her heroin-addicted lover to trade bunks with the new girl, stating, "I like to be on top," Eve's eyes shifted toward Nelle. The flickering light of the film highlighted her friend in a mix of colors. Eve wondered who played the dominant role of man in Nelle's relationships. She would never bring herself to ask and chided herself for the thought, which felt disturbingly impure.

Nelle refused to acknowledge Eve's stare. She frowned as Grier's character offered to exchange sex for drugs with a male food-delivery worker. When he tells her, "Forget it, Helen. I know you dig girls," Nelle snorted loudly as Grier replied, "I'm not this way because I want to be. It's this place. Pretty soon a girl gets strong desires. And it creeps up on you like a disease. But it's curable."

everyman

Nelle rolled her eyes and sighed. "I can guess the cure . . ."

"Shhh," Eve hissed.

On-screen, Grier disclosed the cure. "A real man. Like you." She reached through the bars of her cell and grabbed the worker's hand directing it downward, off-camera, toward her genitals.

"This is ridiculous," Nelle whispered only to get hushed again by Eve, who was finding it quite informative. It wasn't prison but college that brought out Nelle's same-sex appreciation. Eve may have been obsessed with the physical aspects of homosexuality, but Nelle hardly gave thought to the sexual acts—at least not at first. She hadn't spotted a beautiful fellow undergrad across Tuskegee's campus. She hadn't been seduced by an older female professor. She hadn't been abused by male suitors. Nelle had simply grown bored with male companionship and found herself preferring the company of women. Her desire did not emerge from the parted legs of a female lover, rather it unraveled itself between the pages penned by Black feminist writers. It stirred her in ways she couldn't quite communicate to Eve, although she tried. She gave her friend Nella Larsen's *Passing*, but void of overt same-sex desire, Eve—still focused on the sexual nature of her friend—failed to read anything more than the surface narrative.

What Eve did understand was what *The Big Doll House* would later illustrate: homosexuality as a direct result of white influence or isolation from men. Watching the shower scene, by this time a requisite feature of the women-in-prison genre, reminded Eve of Tuskegee. Eve thought back to the large dorm showers and her earlier aversion to sharing the space with Nelle. She felt as uneasy in the crowded movie theater as she did years earlier in the shared dorm room.

Eve couldn't reconcile Nelle's sexuality within the context of Blackness, the only conclusion that could be drawn was that Nelle was inauthentic. Eve saw her best friend become compromised in the ways of white folks. Somehow her best friend had become a bulldagger right under Eve's watchful eye as her dormitory roommate. At a historically Black college. In a predominantly Black city. Afro and all.

Yet it was not white power, nor the man, nor the government that overthrew that bastion of Black beauty and power. Afros were halos of Black pride. The manifestation of Black Is Beautiful. They were a declaration and refused to be demure. The bigger, the better. Still, afros were hot. Hot as in cool, as in good. But also hot as in sweat trickling down the sides of faces and backs of necks. Hot. The afro would meet its final demise in the eighties.

But Nelle and Eve were a decade away from the drippy coolness of the curl. And Nelle's impressively large afro was especially hot in their shared dorm room at Tuskegee. Eve may have ceased to be physically comfortable in the space since Nelle's disclosure, but Nelle remained true to herself, which included continuing to lounge in their room in her underwear when the temperature was particularly high. Eve used to join her, similarly clad, they would throw ice on each other from across the room. They had comfortably dressed and undressed in each other's presence since they were young. But the disclosure brought a close to such intimacies. Eve often dressed immediately after showering in the shared dormitory bathroom on their floor, ironically in full view of anyone who happened to be in the bathroom at the same time.

Eve had told her friend, "What you do disgusts me," without any actual knowledge of what Nelle did. In fact, at the time, Nelle had not done anything outside of reading a few books. She was still sleeping with the Alpha fraternity pledge. Her lesbianism, in its preliminary, theoretical stage, did not preclude sex with men. This did not go unnoticed by Eve, who silently turned her nose up at her friend when Nelle left on her dates with him. To Eve, the only thing worse than a lesbian was a confused one who continued to sleep with men.

"What about Paul?" Eve asked one afternoon as they walked from White Hall to the student cafeteria.

Nelle looked perplexed. "Who the hell is Paul?"

Eve nodded in the direction of a collection of men in black suits and sunglasses. "The 'almost Alpha.' Your boyfriend that keeps lurking around. Don't you see him always just happening to be where you are?"

Nelle shrugged.

"That's all you got is a shrug?" Eve frowned. "First of all," she glared at the fraternity, "anybody willing to join a damn cult—"

"Fraternities aren't cults," Nelle interjected.

"They dress alike and do whatever their leaders tell them," Eve countered.

"Fair enough," Nelle responded. "Your point?"

"My point," Eve stressed, "is that looks like some real fragile-ego shit and you'd better watch out for that."

Nelle shrugged again and opened the door to the cafeteria. "His name's Richard, by the way. So you know who to report when I get kidnapped."

Their debate continued sometimes for days on end, other times pausing for the occasional truce. Through it all, Nelle took heed of Eve's advice and distanced herself from Richard, whose recently increasing presence Nelle had felt so steadily that she became startled by its absence. She shared the observation with Eve as they sat on their respective beds.

"You gonna have to choose a side of the fence. And I don't know if I'll be able to be your friend if you choose the wrong one."

Nelle glanced across their dorm room at Eve. "This fence. Who exactly built it?"

"What?" Eve frowned.

Nelle shook her head. "Never mind." Then added, "So, you'd throw away a lifetime friendship because of who I may or may not date."

"I'd say the same to you. You'd prioritize this, this—" Eve stammered for a definition. "—this urge of yours over our friendship. Hell, over your salvation?"

"Salvation!" Nelle chortled. "You all of a sudden saved when it comes to my sex life? What about your own, Eve?"

Eve balked as Nelle continued. "We came down here to find ourselves. You to connect with your history, and I came down here to find myself too, Eve. Or did you just think that my own studies and focus would be about your shit as well?"

"I thought we'd still be—"

"Friends?" Nelle crossed the room to Eve. "Of course we'll—"

"Normal," Eve spat, stopping Nelle in her tracks. "I thought we'd still be normal down here."

Ironically, it was Eve's condemnation of Nelle that became the catalyst for Nelle's first sexual experience with a woman. As Nelle listened to Eve's disdain and disbelief that she could want to touch a woman, she actually became interested in doing so.

"You don't even know what you're talking about!" Nelle shot back. "Just because it's something different . . ."

"I mean, what do two women even do?" Eve sneered.

"I assume that's rhetorical." Nelle fanned her afro with a paper fan advertising services at a local church. She had no idea how it had come into their possession. Sometimes things just appeared as a result of communal dormitory living.

Eve recoiled, "I don't wanna know what you do." But she did want to know. It was a conundrum: wanting to know but realizing that those merely curious of such knowledge were just as damned as those who lived it. Eve didn't understand her anger but felt it nonetheless. She felt betrayed, as if Nelle had purposefully kept a part of herself from her. In Eve's mind it was this imagined betrayal, and not some antigay hostility, that allowed her to coddle a bitterness unperturbed by Nelle's exit punctuated by the slamming of the dorm room door.

Nelle, having no experiential knowledge, began to wonder herself what took place between two intimate female partners. She wasn't naive. Neither was Eve, for the matter. They both had assumptions based on their individual sexual experiences. Yet Eve's stomach turned as she tried to purge the thoughts from her mind, while Nelle's fluttered as her mind opened to embrace them. She couldn't talk to her best friend about what best girlfriends usually discussed, heartthrobs and heartaches. Nelle's heart palpitated between desire and a longing for an unknown home.

It was night when she knocked on Woodridge's door some three years after Lee Roy's visit. His hair contained more gray, and the goatee had been grown into a full, closely trimmed beard. He wore a satin smoking jacket and silk scarf tucked into the shirt beneath it. The visit both surprised and amused Woodridge. He stood with his hand still on the doorknob and appraised Nelle. "Well, this is most unusual."

Never had one of his student conversations been so straightforward. Nelle sat in the proffered chair. "I like women." The declaration was as far as she had managed to go into any exploration.

Men had been easier to a certain extent. They sniffed around women so early that girls learned to fend them off before processing their own desires. Now as she sat in Woodridge's living area, she felt she needed a guide, and Woodridge presented a most apt Charon into this underworld.

"My word. You are direct, aren't you?" Woodridge smiled. "Times appear to change slowly regarding the Negro, but I dare say, some things might be too rapid for their own good."

"You mean Black homosexuality?"

"We've had the desire to live as racial equals. We have marched. We have petitioned. We have died. But no one is going to gather for your rights as a sexual equal to love whomever you choose. They will tell you that it is the opposite of fighting for racial equality. They will label you a turncoat, a traitor to the struggle. They will tell you that there is no Black homosexuality, only deviance." Woodridge sighed. "Why are you here? Did some man touch you where he oughtn't?"

Nelle thought of June Bug and salt tombs, her mother and truthful lies. She slowly shook her head. "I'm having difficulty talking about this with my best friend. She . . ."

"You want her to be more?" Woodridge raised an eyebrow. "I'm no root doctor."

"I want her to keep being my best friend as I find myself."

Woodridge chuckled. "Do you have a map, dear?"

Nelle's face soured, and Woodridge rose. He opened a drawer in his secretary and stared at the contents. "Everyone wants to fly, but no one wants to be ungrounded." He removed a preserved egg, the last in a set distributed throughout the years. "I've given these to students over the years. The ones, like you, that visit me for . . . personal reasons. It makes them feel special—perhaps drives them to do what they were always going to do anyway. This is the last one." He handed the egg to Nelle.

Nelle turned it in her hand and tilted her head toward Woodridge. "Is this meant to make me feel special?"

"No," Woodridge responded drily. "But what I'm going to tell you will." He returned to his seat. "You cannot live your life for another, and you cannot hold yourself to the limitations of others. Think of that egg as the rebirth of yourself as one who knows herself capable of flight."

Nelle exited, leaving Woodridge to stare around his small quarters. The flourishes of color had been removed. No more soft silks danced with stoic wood sculptures or Greek statues. Everything except a few essentials—clothing, toiletries, scotch—had been neatly packed into boxes as Woodridge prepared to take flight in his own life.

Nelle began to date, or rather hang in the company of, those who appeared as if they could potentially be intimate partners. There was the well-intentioned white girl who was enamored with Black culture. She was the only white woman who regularly attended the Black feminist events on campus. There was only a shade difference between the two, yet vast lacunae existed between their thoughts and ideals. When Nelle asked how she'd come to attend Black feminist rallies, the woman confessed to often feeling uncomfortably tokenized in those situations.

"The issues of Black women are ignored in predominantly white feminist organizations." Her blue eyes sparkled. "I . . . I mean to be an ally to women's causes, for all women."

Nelle nodded, adding cream to her coffee.

"Sometimes it's hard though."

Nelle paused and raised an eyebrow, continuing to listen in silence.

"I mean, don't get me wrong, and it probably sounds so very wrong." Her eyes gazed, appropriately troubled. "But sometimes, I just kind of feel unwelcome. You understand? Out of place being the only . . ." Her voice lowered. ". . . white woman there."

Nelle gazed around the coffeehouse where she had agreed to meet, in a predominantly white neighborhood near a feminist bookstore. She glanced at the prevalence of white faces, noting that she was indeed the only Black person there.

Catching her meaning, her coffee date smiled. "I know, right. But that's different. I mean, it's not cool to say. I'm not saying it's cool at all, but Black people have had to get used to that. Being the only one in places, especially colleges and political activist events."

That was their final coffee date. As much as she tried to be open to the idea of breaking down barriers of racial interaction, Nelle could not imagine being with someone on the most intimate of levels who, willingly or not, contributed to her own marginalization. As she gazed around spaces in which she was increasingly the only Black person, she needed to be able to share a look, smile, or touch with someone who truly shared that experience. Otherwise, she would be a token not only in public space but in her private space as well—her home, her bed. She was just beginning to imagine what sexual intimacy looked like between women. She could not fathom what it looked like between Black and white women.

Then there was the butch, in her suit and tie and highly polished wingtips. Only a slight pitch in speech betrayed the female beneath the broad shoulders and wide stride. She told Nelle that she liked her femininity. Her heels and skirts. But when Nelle met her for coffee wearing jeans, there was an issue.

"What are you wearing?"

"Gloria Vanderbilt. You like?"

"Ahem . . . Yeah, but . . . they're not very ladylike."

"How can that be? I'm a lady."

"Yeah, but . . . I like my ladies a certain way."

Nelle's face bunched in confusion. Her date leaned across the table toward her. "Look, sista. I'm gonna give you a head's up. Save you lots of trouble. Women who look like you . . ." she pantomimed an hourglass figure, "typically date women who look like me." She straightened her tie.

"Why?" Nelle leaned in conspiratorially. "Why is that?"

"Because there's masculine energy and feminine energy . . ."

"But we're both women," Nelle interjected.

"Doesn't matter."

But it did to Nelle. That was their final coffee date. Nelle had unknowingly stumbled into the lesbian binary of gender identification. She enjoyed wearing skirts and platform heels just as much as she liked to wear her bell-bottom jeans and corduroys, unaware that each change of her wardrobe signaled some dress code violation within her nascent sexual identity. Nelle did not understand the gender language of this sexual politics. She had been searching for a home, yet once arrived, found herself ignorant of its cultural properties. She feared that she might just be a tourist after all, vacationing from a life less satisfying.

Nelle was tired of coffee dates. She'd started at the beginning of the fall semester and had continued until final exams. The Alabama temperature had dropped, and Nelle's enthusiasm was quickly following. She began spending more time in the campus library, refocusing her energy on the gothic elements present in Chopin's *The Awakening* and thinking what utter despair it must take for a white woman to drown herself in the ocean.

It was during one of these solo study sessions that Nelle caught notice of a young lady staring at her from the next table. She smiled, and the woman took it as an invitation to join her. They were in a local feminist-theories reading group. Her name was Audrey.

They talked of class. Cixious and Beauvoir. *The Feminine Mystique* and *The Federation of South African Women*. They talked of white women who found themselves trapped in wallpapered rooms. And Black women who wished for rooms of their own. If white women were the second sex, they wondered, then what were they—as Black women—the unsexed? They got hungry and went for lunch.

They thought of the women of the world. Colonized everywhere, even among the colonized. If the disenfranchised created methods of subversion in chitlin circuits, from the Blacks to the gays, could the same be said of women? Were there female versions of the chitlin circuit? Female enclaves resisting patriarchy. Nelle certainly didn't think so.

"Race will always matter," she assured Audrey as they sipped water in the cafeteria. "Between women, race will always matter."

"Men too," Audrey added. "But who gives a fuck about them?" She smiled. Their eyes sparkled, and suddenly men didn't matter to Nelle at all. Not all men. Not any men. And certainly not Richard the pledge, entitling himself to her periphery.

Nelle and Audrey talked until dinnertime, pooling their pocket money to splurge on two dinners at the Chicken Coop. Between bites of chicken, collard greens, and macaroni and cheese, they wondered aloud where they fit in the Black nationalist rhetoric.

Audrey asked, "Where are women outside of traditional relationships with men?"

Nelle's eyes widened.

Audrey held up her hand, "I didn't mean to offend . . ."

"No," Nelle interjected. "I'm not offended."

"Oh, what are you?" Audrey asked. She stuck a hot-sauce-covered finger into her mouth and sighed. "My God, this is heaven."

Nelle watched, intrigued. Her food had sat untouched on her plate for quite some time. She averted her eyes and drank heavily from her sweet tea. When they shifted onto Audrey, she met an unflinching gaze.

"Aren't you hungry?"

Something behind Nelle's eyes recognized its own reflection in Audrey's. "Yes," she replied. "I think I am."

They left the restaurant and continued talking as they walked, but it was not an aimless stroll. It was not in the direction of Nelle's dorm, where Eve sat turning the pages of Ellison's *Invisible Man*. Their meandering placed them at the steps of Audrey's dormitory. Unsure of anything, they sat on the steps and stole questioning glances at one another as what was being said became noticeably secondary to the unsaid.

Nelle was in the midst of an explication of Black women's roles in the Black Power movement, when Audrey interjected, "My roommate's gone for the evening." Embarrassed by her own outburst, she clapped her hand over her mouth in a gesture that was so girlish that Nelle felt comforted.

"I don't mean that . . ." Audrey began.

Nelle laughed and grabbed her hand. "Show me your room, Audrey." As they rose together, a figure emerged from the shadows.

"Nelle, can we talk?"

The whispered voice was almost difficult to distinguish from the night air, but Nelle recognized it as belonging to Richard. Nelle released Audrey's hand. As she descended the stairs toward him, she felt her energy lowering. By the time she stood in front of him, an exhaustion had overtaken her. Nelle was tired of explaining and reexplaining to him that she no longer wanted to date.

"Richard, we don't have anything more to talk about."

"We do!" he shouted, then lowered his voice. "You have to explain why . . ."

"I have explained it, Richard. I shouldn't have to defend my right to date and not date whomever I want. I no longer want this."

"But why not? We were good together. I am good!" Richard took her hand and placed it on his chest.

"Please don't do that," Nelle sighed.

Mistaking her exhaustion for a moment of emotional weakness, he stepped forward into an embrace, muffling her response. "What's that?" He pulled back slowly.

"You are quickly becoming not good." She exhaled.

Appalled and then angry, he released her. His lips curled, "Well, you . . ."

"Number Four!" A voice boomed toward them, startling Richard into attention.

"Yes, Big Brother!" Richard's eyes stared past Nelle into nothingness while she scanned behind him toward the approaching figure of LeRoi.

LeRoi smiled at Nelle. His eyes never left her as he directed his question to Richard. "What time is it, Number Four?"

Richard's wrist shot up to his face. "A quarter to, Big Brother LeRoi!"

"A quarter to what, Number Four?"

"Ten, Big Brother LeRoi!"

"And what happens at ten, Number Four?"

Richard's face betrayed his rigid attentiveness. "Curfew," he whispered.

"I. Can't. Hear. You, pledge!" LeRoi's voice thundered, and Nelle jumped slightly. She wanted to leave but felt compelled to witness Richard's humility as a safeguard from future stalking. She was vaguely aware of Audrey waiting on the dormitory steps.

"Curfew, Big Brother LeRoi!" Richard shouted, chancing a glance at Nelle.

"Looks like you better be on double time then," LeRoi responded and turned toward Nelle as Richard sprinted through the valley separating the campus into male and female dorms.

"He won't be a problem anymore," LeRoi said.

"He wouldn't have been one in the first place if y'all didn't fill his head with all that alpha male bullshit," Nelle replied. "And you're standing in my face just as smug, like I should thank you for cleaning up your own mess. Well, Big Brother LeRoi," she sneered, "you can double-time it the fuck out of my face right behind his stalker ass."

LeRoi inhaled his shock and simply nodded and strolled back into the darkness. Nelle's attention had already returned to Audrey on the steps. She had no idea how to recapture a moment that was new in the first place.

But Audrey smiled and walked toward her. "Men make everything about men," she said. "We've spent this whole glorious evening questioning how to create something between women and the last vestiges of patriarchy sends us a fraternal order of epic mannishness. I think that means we're very close to something." She closed the space between them.

Audrey stood in the same close proximity that Richard had moments earlier, yet the experience was the exact opposite. Nelle felt recharged. She tried to dissect the excited tingle that started in the pit of her stomach and radiated outward to her fingertips.

Unable to contain it in her mind, she decided to let it guide her, and it propelled them both up the stairs, into the dormitory, and toward Audrey's room, where they embraced without bothering to light the darkness with either lamp provided.

Afterward, lying in her own dorm room bed across from Eve, Nelle thought of the sweetness of her evening. "You're the one who's going to have to make a choice." Her words sliced through the darkness toward Eve.

———————

Years later, in the movie theater watching Pam Grier's on-screen pantomime of thrusting the delivery man's hand into her as the cure for her same-sex relations, Eve saw an act of redemption: Grier begging to get back to the normalcy of a heterosexual home. Dirty work, but a hero's journey.

Nelle saw a woman used to prostituting her body for survival using her only asset to score heroin for her addicted lover. Grier was a lesbian navigating the gendered, heterosexist landscape to save her woman. It's never pretty, but Nelle saw the beauty in it. Grier was going through hell to get back to heaven. Had she the luxury of confiding to Eve, Nelle would have giddily answered her inquiry about what women do. She would have said that it was not so different from being with a man—and that it also was extremely different from being with a man. She would have explained the familiarity and comfortable awkwardness of softness and warmth. Described it as sweet and scary. Erotic and tender. And to her, not as salty.

SEVEN

marie laveau

Witch hunters is white women's worry.
—Marie Laveau,
American Horror Story: Coven

The past is not so much hidden as it is buried by people's shame. They tuck it away like unopened envelopes in the far recesses of dark closets. They cram it into crawl spaces, faded chifforobes, and dusty basement storage areas. People bury the past like Edgar Allan Poe narrators—beneath floorboards and behind bricked walls, often still alive. Still relevant. To them, still shameful. In its conspicuous absence they weave stories—first omissions that absolve them of their deceit, then tall tales that glorify their presence. This faux past weaves its way into historical narrative like a wolf straining the downy-white seams of a sheep's clothing.

It is rumored that New Orleans Vodou priestess Marie Laveau lived an unnaturally long life and bore fifteen children. Her life has been heavily sensationalized and fictionalized in works that purport to present the past. But how many Marie Laveaus are being pressed into a single narrative? Marie Laveau I—born around 1800—had two sisters also named Marie Laveau. She had five children, but only two survived infancy. They, too, were named Marie Laveau—Marie Eucharist Heloise Laveau, known as Marie the Second and Marie Philomene Laveau. Each of these second-wave Marie Laveaus had five children.

Written records are privileged over oral tradition, and in the burying of the past, it is the written word that must be plunged into hiding. It opens itself up to the reader, formed and solid. Nothing changes it. While the spoken history is in constant manipulation by the speaker. New tone. New emphasis. New words. New omissions. New additions. Marie Laveau II, the eldest daughter, continued her mother's work and perpetuated the rumors and folklore surrounding her mother in an effort to continue the legacy and blur the distinction between the real Marie Laveau and the not always accurate legacy.

Several generations later, and far from New Orleans, the only magic that Janette Marie Laveau Baptiste possessed was in her ability to bewitch male suitors—a skill she sought to instill in her daughter Nelle, hoping that Nelle's own Laveau magic would supply the missing element required to maintain it. For Janette Marie Laveau could charm men into her life, but nothing that she had could entreat them to remain there. Her husband, Nelle's father, had disappeared shortly after Nelle's birth. But it was no Laveau magic that vanquished him. In their neighborhood, single-parent households were not rare. Some men had left pregnant wives and girlfriends while they looked westward for better work. Births occurred in their absence. A few men made it through their offsprings' early childhood years only to disappear after a quick run to the store for cigarettes . . . or in the dead of the night . . . or with another woman . . . or after being threatened by the local dope man, loan shark, gangster. Frederick Baptiste, Nelle's father, had a penchant for all three—heroin, borrowing money that he could never repay, and gambling with borrowed money. He'd have been lucky to have made it west for work or to have found love in the arms of another, because chances were good that Frederick Baptiste spent Nelle's formative years at the bottom of a shallow grave.

About the time Nelle befriended Eve, her mother had taken up with a man called June Bug—*Uncle* June Bug to Nelle, who had acquired many temporary uncles over the course of her young life. She had had Uncle Paul, Uncle Harry, and Uncle Harold, and Nelle was growing tired of sharing her mother. She was tired in the way of young girls who feel more than they are yet able to comprehend.

Her mother managed to hold on to June Bug for three years—although to those who observed them, it wasn't a feat of difficulty or merit. June Bug rarely worked. He was a man of small stature who compensated for it with a loud voice and a lot of talk. He was always tapping a foot or fidgeting with his hands. And when his eyes, which often darted fervently around the room, fixed themselves on ten-year-old Nelle, Janette Marie Laveau immediately took notice of his notice.

June Bug liked women who were so light skinned that they could be called white, so enamored with love that they could be manipulated, and so young that they could be called girls. With Nelle's mother, he had found two out of the three. June Bug considered himself to be a pioneer of sorts. Yet he lacked the actual motivation and follow-through to make strides in any movements of racial or political importance. Seated at the dinner table of Janette and Nelle's small apartment, he dismissed his lack of involvement when the conversation turned to civil rights.

"I leave all that marchin' shit to Martin Kang an'em." He chuckled and took a swig of Night Train.

"You know they're always looking for men to help out." Janette scooped a spoon of mashed potatoes from the bowl to refill her plate.

June Bug shoved his plate above Janette's, and she plopped the last of them onto his plate instead of her own. "Well, it ain't gonna be me. You see that nigga got hit with a brick? Shiiiiiiit, that wouldn't be my ass!"

"Who got hit with a brick?" Nelle asked. They looked at her, temporarily having forgotten that she was at the table.

"Martin Luther the Kang," June Bug answered and laughed. "That nigga got smooth busted upside his head."

"June . . ." Janette admonished him.

June Bug swallowed a mouthful of potatoes and glared at Janette. Her eyes lowered slightly. "Baby, I just don't think she needs to be hearing about all that violence."

"You right," June Bug responded. "You just don't think."

Tension crept in like the chill draft that coagulated the remaining green peas on Nelle's plate. "May I be excused?" she asked.

"Hell nawl," June Bug answered before Janette could respond. "You asked a question, and I got answers for you. Now, your mama wanna keep you shielded from all the shit in the world. But I'm a man, and I know what you need to prepare you for the shit that's out there."

Male companionship was important to Janette. She took great pains to maintain her physical appearance and stressed the importance of proper care to her daughter. That said, having a daughter—a biological legacy to receive and continue the life's lessons, which by the time of Janette's generation of Marie Laveaus, had withered down to physical vanity—was of the utmost importance. And although Janette was missing the conscious cultural, spiritual, and political substance of Marie Laveau, she did feel compelled to protect and propagate the essence of her ancestor contained in dreams she did not fully understand and intuitions she blindly followed. June Bug's beady eyes had penetrated her daughter, and Janette intended to make sure that nothing else of his would do the same.

One day as she braided Nelle's hair, she asked, "Nelle, has June Bug put his hands on you?"

"Has he hit me?"

"Nooo . . ." Janette drew out the query.

"Um, he touched my hair one day. Said it looked nice?" Nelle raised the pitch of her voice toward the end, still reaching for a suitable answer.

"That all?"

"Yeah, Mama," Nelle answered slowly, her mind raced. Their mother-daughter bonding time had gradually been reduced to weekly hair-braiding sessions. Her ten-year-old brain reached for something that would prolong the rare moments in which her mother showed some interest. She thought of the way June Bug's beady eyes lingered over the softening places of her body. How he stuck out his tongue at her when her mother wasn't looking and made it wiggle, suggestive of things she wouldn't be aware of until years later. Without touch, he had made her feel soiled and aggrieved in a way that she could barely comprehend much less communicate to her mother. So she did what some girls have done when negotiating a space beyond their years. Nelle improvised. The words slipped from her mouth without the benefit of foresight as she described a scene that was a masala of her mother's eavesdropped phone conversations and the pulp romance novels she secretly read with Eve in her basement.

Had Janette not been so incensed, she would have been able to discern the obvious fantastical elements and the omission of the less than romantic ones that every girl remembers from her first sexual experience. But Janette did not hear the words as much as invent them to accompany the visual image that etched itself inside her head. An image of June Bug and her little girl. An electric current of tension shot from Janette's fingers into her daughter's hair follicles.

Nelle reached up and tenderly touched her scalp. "Ow, Mama. Not so tight."

Janette relaxed her hands, leaned down, and kissed the back of Nelle's head. "Sorry, baby." She rubbed oil onto the parts she'd made in Nelle's hair, placing particular care on those that were reddening. "You gonna go stay with your friend Eve and her aunt for a little while, okay?"

"Why?" Nelle asked. Her heart raced with panic, and she grew anxious that the lie would bring Janette closer to June Bug instead of closer to her.

Janette thumped the back of Nelle's scalp where moments earlier she'd planted a kiss. "Don't you why me! You just do as I say. You hear me, JaNelle Marie?"

Nelle placed a hand on her sore head. "Yes, Mama."

They sat in silence as Janette continued to braid Nelle's hair, yet her mind refused to be silent. Her hands worked through her daughter's long tresses on muscle memory and her thoughts turned to that unknown ancestor of whom she knew so little. Even the stories and speculation about her lineage had been so distant that they seemed more rumor than truth. She wished for it to be true. She longed to be able to take care of things, as Marie Laveau had.

No one knows what happened to the first man Marie Laveau married. He disappeared into the creole-thickened New Orleans air and was never heard from again. A death certificate was issued years later, although no body was found. There was no inquiry. It had been a thing that was taken care of in the way women have been known to take care of things. Almost magical in its mystery and craft. Yet, something of it remains. It must, because nothing ever truly disappears into nothingness. There are bones to be buried. Trinkets to be stashed. Souls to be exorcised. Laveau's first husband was never found, not that anyone dared to look for him, yet in its stead looms the disappearance itself.

While Janette silently plotted June Bug's exit from their lives, Nelle couldn't wait to share the recent developments in her household with Eve. They would escape to the basement of Eve's house, where all secrets were shared, and exchange ideas about the adult world within its cold concrete walls.

———————

A decade later, the basement walls had been insulated for warmth and covered in wood paneling. Although they were better equipped for keeping secrets, none had been told between Eve and Nelle since their time at Tuskegee. Still friends, the dismissively classified "separate paths" had redefined closeness. It was apparent in the stiff one-armed hug that Eve gave Nelle when she entered the house. Nelle briefly pressed her cheek against Eve's, and they both pulled apart, relieved to be done with a ritual that had become archaic.

The living room had changed little since they were girls. Ceramic elephants littered the surface of the faux fireplace's mantel. They threatened to burst from the glass curio cabinet. Elephants loomed majestically from several paintings on the walls. They had doubled in number since the time of Nelle's two-week stay while her mother rid the world of June Bug. Elephants have long memories, and if the ones that lined Ann's house could talk, they could have spoken volumes on the silent strains of Eve and Nelle's friendship.

Nelle eased past Eve into the living room's interior just as Ann arrived there from her own room down the hall. Ann welcomed her in a warm embrace. "Nelle! I been asking Every where you been."

"Hey, Miss Ann. It's good to see you. How you feeling these days?"

"Oh, I'm fair de middlin'," Ann slipped into the familiar drawl of the South reserved for home. The tension Nelle felt moments earlier eased. Ann reminded Nelle of the South, where the weather, food, and people were all warm and soothing. "How's your mama?"

Nelle smiled. "Oh, you know Mama, Miss Ann. Looking for a new husband."

Ann and Nelle's chuckles drifted conspiratorially into a simultaneous "hmph." Eve brushed past them and walked down the hall and through the kitchen to the basement stairs. She paused and turned her head back slightly. "You coming?"

"What y'all gotta be runnin' down to the basement for at this age?" Ann asked, nervously clutching Nelle's arm. "I know y'all don't have little girl secrets still."

Eve sighed. "We already talked about this, Mama Ann."

"But, Every . . ." Ann began to protest but thought better of it.

Nelle reassuringly patted Ann's hand before detaching and excusing herself to quickly follow Eve down the stairs. Ann reluctantly returned to her bedroom and the Harlequin romance book that awaited her.

In the basement, boxes of varying sizes had been pulled from the storage room at the rear and now sat in rows blocking the sofa and loveseat. They sat atop the wooden card table. They leaned against the secretary and perched haphazardly on the mahogany floor-model television.

Nelle pressed Eve for more information on their goal. "So, you're just gonna go through her personal things then?" Although it was apparent that Eve had already begun her search. Some boxes were open, their contents spilled out in front of them like eviscerated organs.

"What other choice do I have?" Eve defended as she tossed two pillows with stitched images of elephants.

"You could try talking to her again."

"I've been trying to talk to her about this ever since I could talk!" Eve lowered her voice. "Funny you giving advice on talking to parents."

"What's that supposed to mean?" Nelle frowned. "What are we even looking for?"

Eve searched her brain to remember information from her meetings with Brother LeRoi. "Letters. Photographs. Obituaries." Then added, "And you know exactly what it means."

Nelle sat on one box and began rummaging through its neighbor. More elephants. Little bags with elephant earrings and brooches, gifts that were too ornate for Ann's prudish tastes. A dark purple Crown Royal bag stuffed with other balled-up velvety Crown Royal bags. Nelle held up a small glass elephant figurine and peered at Eve through its translucence. "So, we're finally going to talk about the elephant in the room?"

Eve suppressed a chuckle that would have threatened the seriousness of the mood. "So, you want me to talk to Mama Ann, which I've done practically all my life, but you haven't given so much as a whimper to Miss Janette about yourself."

Nelle's face twisted. "It ain't her business."

"No? She seems to think it's her business to get you married off to some Billy Dee Williams. It'd save her a whole lot of trouble if you just told her." Eve smirked. The onus of the conversation had switched, and she gladly shared the guilt of conversational omission. Their conversation overtook their initial task, and neither noticed as they ransacked the boxes that they had entered the age of the owl, the elephant's predecessor. They had ceased to unwrap the newspaper-bundled trinkets, assuming them all to be elephants. They were too engrossed in personal conflict to read the newspapers that had been repurposed as wrapping paper. Nelle missed reading about the "accidental death" of one Jesse "June Bug" Birch in the *Chicago Defender* dated twelve years earlier. The words "June Bug" nestled in the palm of her hand as she replaced the wrapped owl with moveable bead eyes into the box. A small sound escaped as the eyes shook in their plastic sockets, but neither Nelle nor Eve heard.

"Told her what?" Nelle feigned innocence.

Eve was taken aback. She looked around but had no reply.

Nelle smirked. "Yeah, that's what I thought. You wanna talk about it? 'Cause I'd love to talk about my life with my best friend who completely lost interest in it once I told her I was a lesbian."

Eve's eyes widened and Nelle's confidence was bolstered. "Yeah, I can say it. I can say it all day long, and you'd be used to hearing it by now if you quit acting like that part of me didn't exist. Don't you even care?"

"I care about you, Nelle. But . . ." But Eve had been indoctrinated in the 1960s Black Power politics of Black babies for the revolution, and gays and lesbians could not naturally produce them. She still struggled with the idea of tying reproduction to Black liberation, especially since she, herself, did not want to have children. At least, she didn't think that she did.

"But?" Nelle pressed, knowing that they were skating close to previous arguments. She wanted to push hard against the weak spot in Eve's beliefs on the "natural."

Eve snorted. "It's not just me. I mean, even Maya Angelou wrote that—"

"Oh, that's bullshit," Nelle argued. "The world of the pervert, right? Angelou got the brunt of being painted as unwomanly, which is the case for all Black women, mind you. Especially tall, dark ones like she is."

"But—"

"But nothing! She takes that same definition of unwomanly hurled against her and turns it on lesbians. Jive bullshit, and so disappointing."

"But—"

"But what?" Nelle shouted in exasperation.

"But I just don't care to hear about *that*." Eve's words swirled around them, commanding time to slow itself just enough so that they could float weightlessly between an intake of breath and its inevitable exhale. They spread themselves amid the boxes of the storage room, climbed the shelves of the storage racks, and stole away into the cedar closet snuggling with quilts and spare pillows. The words filled the small storage room so that there seemed little room for Eve and Nelle. Little room for conversation, so they continued to rummage through boxes in silence. Eventually it seemed not enough space for the words themselves, and they drifted upward to a vent and slid through its evenly cut slits into the aluminum shaft that circulated cold air in the summer and heat in the winter to various parts of the house.

Unknown to Eve and Nelle, the vents distributed more than air. Sound, too, traveled through the shafts, and it was in this way that their words reached Ann as she sat reading her romance novel in her room. It was no secret to Ann that the vents served as the house's informal intercom system. Actually, it was more a listening device than an intercom, as sound seemed to be interested only in traveling upward from the basement and not the reverse. Ann had made sure of this years ago, after discovering that she could hear her niece's basement activities. It had always served as a secret resource, like so many others that only parents and guardians are privy to and which reinforce their seeming omniscience in their children's eyes.

Through the years, Ann had learned more about her niece by eavesdropping than by actual conversation with her. She had listened as Eve described her first kiss to Nelle. It had been with a boy named Jericho. Later, Eve had been surprised by an uncannily pertinent talk Ann had randomly initiated about the sexual motivations of teenage boys. Ann had shakily listened to details of Eve's first sexual experience, and the following day Eve found a pack of Trojan condoms on her bed with the note "Better safe than sorry."

Eve had been more disturbed by the note than the condoms, which she had immediately discarded. Her aunt was an unwanted presence in her sexual acts. But she had kept the note, rereading it nearly every day for months and wondering whether her birth had been a sorry consequence of sex. Eve hadn't asked her aunt for clarification. Their cycle of indirect communication continued, with Ann listening through the bedroom vent to Eve's life and commenting on it in ways which she felt were appropriate and Eve, in turn, adding those comments to the growing list of questions she had about herself, her aunt, and what intersections, if any, existed between their lives.

As Eve and Nelle sat in the basement, Ann received their

conversation as disembodied voices floating into her room. There were no elephants or owls in Ann's room. There were no trinkets or figurines. No photographs. No knickknacks. The bed was a modestly full size. She had a white nightstand, white dresser, and white chest of drawers. Everything else—from the curtains to the bedspread, from the throw pillows to the carpet—was some shade of green. Celery-colored doilies adorned the furniture. Forest green pillows were carefully arranged on top of a mint-green duvet. Pastel blue-green, olive, and asparagus hues leapt at the eye from different items.

Ann placed the laminated bookmark she had received from church during Lent between the pages of her romance novel—which she had previously learned through the vent was called "Mama Ann's soft porn" by her niece. The quote on her bookmark was taken from the book of Mark, chapter 1, verse 13: "And he was there in the wilderness forty days, tempted of Satan; and was with the wild beasts; and the angels ministered unto him." The biblical quote found itself pressed between pages that included, "She could feel the palpitations of his throbbing manhood against her and could no longer resist unbridling her own passion." And so, temptation and Christ were placed in strange collocation with two others in a dance of resistance and surrender. Ann placed the book facedown on the bed and gave her attention to the vent. She thought it was no wonder that Nelle had turned into a lesbian after the June Bug fiasco. Ann was just relieved that Eve hadn't "turned funny." There was bad blood in every family. She had tried to share some information with Eve the last time she asked. She had hoped it would satisfy Eve's curiosity. But her version of events was truncated.

Eve's voice rose through the vent. The cadence was so much like that of the mother Eve had never known. At times, Ann would close her eyes when Eve spoke and could see her sister, Mercy, as clear as day in her mind's eye. It seemed to her that Eve was becoming more like Mercy, and Ann couldn't understand how it was possible. Ann always thought of Mercy, particularly during the times Eve and Nelle were huddled together in the basement. She had told Eve that Mercy had come to Chicago pregnant and disgraced. *We had some people up this way, and your mama came for a fresh start, I suppose.* But now Ann allowed her thoughts to travel backward, past Mercy's death, past Eve's birth, past Chicago to Macon County, Georgia, in 1950.

———————

Sixteen-year-old Ann crept silently through the woods, keeping a careful eye on her target: the two giggling girls weaving their way around the trees. She was tired of having to always look out for Mercy, who still seemed too young for her years in so many ways. There were chores to finish. Yet when Ann looked out of the kitchen window to see how Mercy was coming along, she found the back stoop empty. Instead of cleaning the catfish Uncle Cornelius had dropped off for them, Mercy was traipsing through the woods with her friend Geneva Thompson.

It didn't matter how many times Ann caught her sneaking off from her chores. Their mother's punishment—all mundane church-house-related chores—didn't even seem to set Mercy in her place. Mercy acted as if whatever she was getting herself into was worth all the trouble. She didn't even get mad at Ann for telling on her. In fact, she was nice toward her older sister, always acquiring an extra candy, magazine, or trinket for Ann when she received one. It annoyed Ann that Mercy's first request upon receiving gifts was that she have an extra for her. Ann could not help but think that maybe Mercy felt sorry for her and acted on her behalf. She did not want Mercy's pity. She was the older sister after all and therefore should be entitled to first experiences and generous gifts that she would then dole out to Mercy, and not the other way around. But Mercy was simply more outgoing, which netted her more friends, more experiences, and more gifts than her sister.

Ann continued following at a safe distance. She didn't have to worry about being quiet. Mercy and Geneva were in their own world, singing and swinging around the trees. Ann wondered where they were going. An abandoned shack loomed ahead, and the girls raced toward it. Geneva reached it first and jumped up and down shouting, "I won! I won!"

Mercy panted beside her. "'Bout time. I guess I got tired of winnin'."

"Oh no you don't, Mercy Mann!" Geneva argued. "Don't even think 'bout tryin' to say you let me win."

Mercy grinned. "Naw, you won alright. Let's go in and you can git yo' prize." They hurried into the shack.

Ann wasn't sure what to do next. There were things that she needed to finish before their mother returned from her work at the church. But the chores were not the biggest thought in her mind at the moment. She wondered what prizes Ann and Geneva exchanged. Maybe she could stay a little longer and peek through one of the windows.

Ann made her way to the back of the shack and peered into the darkness. As her eyes adjusted to the dark, she gazed around the space. She recognized a quilt from their house spread across the floor. There was an oil lamp and stacked wood was being used as a table. Ann and Geneva sat in the middle of the quilt.

"C'mon, Mercy." Geneva scooted closer to Mercy, and Ann frowned as her view was blocked. She heard them giggle but could only see their backs.

Ann racked her brain to figure out what the prize could be. She wondered if it was the cookies she had baked. She became incensed with the thought of it. Her fists tightened against the wall of the shack. Finally, Geneva moved slightly, creating a gap between her and Mercy and a break for Ann's line of vision. Ann breathed a sigh of relief. There were no cookies present, but moments later she wished that there had been. Her breath caught in her throat. Eyes and mouth agape, she stared unbelievingly at her sister and Geneva with their arms wrapped around each other and their lips pressed together like she imagined hers with her unrequited love, James—who in a few short years would remind her of the smooth-skinned folk balladeer Harry Belafonte and inspire Ann's first celebrity crush, ironically because of Belafonte's likeness to James, as opposed to the other way around.

Her mind ran through the usual intimacy exemptions: women sometimes kiss each other to say hello. Sometimes it's to say good-bye. But none made the uneasiness building in the pit of her stomach subside. She could not look away and began to count in her head. *One, two, three . . .* And the realization that women don't kiss each other that long—*seven, eight, nine*—brought the thought that only husbands and wives kiss like that. Quick flashes of past images of Mercy and Geneva played through her mind like a picture show: their lingering gazes at one another; long, boring conversations; the way their hands always seemed to find each other. Ann realized that she and everyone else had witnessed the courtship of the two.

Ann's mind latched onto one of the foremost principles in the

Bible Belt South: that intimacy was between men and wives and, even then, belonged only in private thoughts and holy matrimony. It did not belong in a shack in the woods of their property, where Mercy and Geneva sat with their lips pressed together. *Oh, God, thirteen, fourteen, fifteen . . .* Ann hated her sister with more power than she had known existed. Hatred incubated in their sibling rivalry and fed on Ann's resentment about being older and more mature; for having to complete Mercy's chores when she left them unfinished; and for being invisible to James, while he pined for Mercy. Hatred coursed through her body and pulsated violently. She bit down on her lip in an effort to regain control. She tasted blood and tears.

"Eighteen! Nineteen! Twenty!" Ann's rage found voice, and Mercy and Geneva were startled out of their kiss. It was a disturbing image, Ann immobile and enraged with a trail of blood on her chin and eyes glossy.

Inside the shack, Geneva's mouth froze in a cartoonish circle as she expelled an "Oh, God!"

The words released Ann and she fled through the trees. She was panting, running without thought, but moving instinctively toward home. Branches scratched at every bit of skin exposed by her sleeveless sundress. Her ears attuned to the sound of twigs snapping behind her, revealing Mercy's pursuit. Ann pressed harder, allowing her anger to fuel her pumping arms and burning thighs. Her toe struck something hard. Before she could process the pain, she felt herself falling.

The memory was a haunting dream for Ann, and it took several moments to calm her breathing and return to the present moment. If it is true that the brain doesn't distinguish between the memory of an event and its actual occurrence, then to remember is to relive, reexperience, reinflict. Ann sat amid her tousled green covers and willed away Mercy's voice from her head as she slowly left Georgia behind. It all had nearly disappeared when that same voice, more ghostly than ever, seeped through the vent and returned her attention to Eve and Nelle in the basement—both digging for some sort of connection.

Eve searched for history, while Nelle hoped that by supporting the process, their friendship would return to its former intensity. When Eve's allergies succumbed to the dust particles encapsulated in boxed memories, Nelle wordlessly supplied tissue paper to quell her friend's sneezes. They fell into a familiar pattern of near-silent communication, allowing their history to lull them into comfort and propel their task. In silence their bodies could move about like sisters accustomed to sharing space. Boxes were opened, contents rifled, and abandoned in their tiny assembly line until, returning to the closet for the next box, Eve's hand faltered on a rough-edged photograph, and her gasp brought Nelle rushing to her side.

The photo that they found—not in any of the boxes, but crammed in the recesses of the storage closet—was a notable step for each of their goals. Eve's hands trembled as she swiped across the dusty, black-and-white image. Her fingers traced the face of Mercy, whom she recognized from the only other photograph she had seen of her mother. The tension between Eve and Nelle was forgotten as they retreated from the closet into better lighting. Eve scooted next to Nelle and shared view of the picture. On its backside was scrawled "Cornelius, Gertrude, Mercy, Ann. (Ideal) Macon Co., Ga. 1950."

EIGHT

the uses of salt

a lie

is

simply a lie.

it draws its strength from belief.

stop believing

in

what hurts you.

—Nayyirah Waheed,

"Power," *Salt.*

There are more than fourteen thousand household uses for salt. In addition to accenting the flavor of meats and vegetables, salt solutions have valuable uses outside of food preparation. Yellowing in enamel bathtubs and toilets can be reversed with a salt and turpentine solution. Salt drives moths and ants away. It has antiseptic properties that make it an effective mouth rinse. It can also improve skin complexion when used as a massage mixture.

It was salt that killed June Bug. Not as in hypertension. Although in the end, he had become both hyper and tense.

Nelle didn't eat salt. Not after the salt incident with June Bug. She lived a salt-free life before the advent of low-sodium canned goods and sea salt versus iodized salt standoffs. She couldn't bear the taste of it. Even looking at the tiny crystalline specs filled her instantly with disgust. Nelle even hated the smell of salt. Its acrid bitterness was an assault on all her senses. Tears are salty, so she didn't cry. Sweat is salty, so she tried not to exert herself.

In college she found herself as most do, discarding the old skin of childhood and discovering new things. Still, the salt incident loomed large, refusing to be discarded as childhood folly. She moved from dating men to dating women, oblivious to the debates on whether her sexuality was determined at birth or through choice, if her sexual orientation was a lifestyle or a life lived. Nelle was no advocate. The truth of the matter is that men and women taste differently, and to Nelle—with a newly discovered aversion to the briny fluids of lovemaking—women were simply less salty.

The salt incident occurred in 1961, when Nelle was ten years old. Everyone involved could at least agree on that. Yet it was actually a series of events that played out differently for everyone. If they had bothered to speak of it—if they could have spoken of it—the events would have spun into very diverse stories. Nelle would have said that it started with the lie she told her mother about June Bug.

Janette would have said that it started with June Bug's interest in her daughter. His inappropriate glances when he thought she wasn't looking.

Eve would have said that it began with a late-night knock on the door, which once opened, revealed her best friend Nelle, Janette, and an empty can of green peas.

Ann, upon hearing Janette recount the details of June Bug's alleged transgression against Nelle, would have surely recognized the language of Harlequin Romance novel number 528, *Wife by Arrangement*, and perhaps the salt incident would have ended there.

But they did not speak of these things. They held firmly to their silence, guarding their individual knowledge against self-incrimination, and the salt incident began as most incidents do—as the consequence of an infinite number of choices made by people with a very limited understanding of their present moment.

The only time Janette, June Bug, and Nelle were together was when they sat in mismatched chairs at the small dining table. June Bug, seated in the brown vinyl chair, talked nonstop while shoveling food into his mouth. Janette, in the white chair with yellow printed flowers, chewed silently, periodically returning to the stove to refill June Bug's plate, so her own meal became cold by the time she was able to eat it. Nelle, from her small green plastic chair, watched them both and greedily soaked up information on male-female relations that she could later share with Eve.

It was already an interesting sort of relationship. When June Bug entered their lives three years earlier, Janette was taken by the more chivalry-cloaked chauvinisms of having doors opened for her, bags carried for her, and garbage emptied for her. They both subscribed to the separation of duties for men and women. Janette did not expect June Bug to cook—although at times he had. Standing over the charcoal grill, with a cigarette dangling from the corner of his lips, June Bug would claim that he wasn't cooking but 'cueing on a man stove.

Those days had been good for Janette. At forty years old, she was his senior by ten years. *Cougarism* had not yet been coined in 1961. It was two years before the publication of *The Graduate* sensationalized the exploits of a younger man and a much older woman. Janette counted herself lucky to have June Bug, even when the good days began to sour. When his hustle dried up. When his chivalry turned to plain chauvinism. When his attention went elsewhere. To whispered phone calls. To late nights. To the second-floor apartment. To Nelle's budding preteen form.

"Why you so quiet?" June Bug asked Janette through a mouthful of meatloaf. A small particle escaped his mouth and landed on the floral plastic tablecloth.

"I was just thinking . . ."

"Oh lord," June Bug exclaimed.

"Never mind."

Nelle's eyes volleyed between them. "What you thinkin', Mama?"

Janette smiled at her daughter and slid her eyes toward June Bug, who sighed and said, "Well, if Lil Bit wanna know, I guess we gotta hear it then." He winked at Nelle, missing the sneer that spread across her mother's face. Not that it would have mattered had he caught it. June Bug considered himself to be the head of the household. His own upbringing informed him of what that meant. Do the heavy lifting. Protect the women. And as his own father had dictated, prepare the daughters for marriage.

Janette's eyes burned into the side of June Bug's face. "I was thinking about going to the beach tomorrow." She was not. She had been thinking of what she always had been thinking about since Nelle told her about June Bug. Since watching him watch her daughter. Since the thought of his hands on Nelle had penetrated her waking moments such that she nearly burned dinner and plagued her nights such that she barely slept.

"What beach?" June Bug sucked at meat fiber lodged between his molars.

Janette slowly chewed her food before delivering a very

calculated response. The idea was to incite an argument that would result in June Bug eventually storming off into the night. "Rainbow Beach."

June Bug's fist slammed onto the table, causing Nelle and the plates of food to jump. Janette paused, a forkload of green peas at her lips. June Bug grabbed her wrist, shaking the peas from the fork. "I said no to that months ago, 'Nette! Them other fools can go out there and sit-in or wade-in or whatever the hell they wanna call it. But you ain't going."

Nelle slid from her chair and slowly began to pick up the scattered peas. June Bug said, "Leave it. Your mama will clean up her own mess." He looked at Janette. "Fix me some more peas."

Janette rose and moved toward the stove. "J. B., don't you get mad at anybody 'sides me? Don't you get mad at those white folk who say we don't have the right to sit on nature's beach and swim in the earth's water?"

Hugging Chicago's South Shore neighborhood, Rainbow Beach had been legally desegregated for a year. But that did not prevent the neighborhood's white residents from forcibly keeping Blacks off the city-owned property. When the NAACP led a protest, one of its young members was hit in the head with a rock by an opposing mob. She'd still have a pronounced limp fifty years after the incident, when Rainbow Beach and its surrounding neighborhoods had long since become predominantly Black areas. Maybe if June Bug had known in 1961 that they were just a few harsh years away from equal housing legislation, he would have insisted that Janette become a part of its history.

His eyes momentarily softened, but Janette's back was to him and she didn't see. "Woman, you gonna get yo'self kilt just to get on that rocky patch of beach? And then who gon' take care of Lil

Bit?" He grinned and winked at Nelle again. This Janette saw. Her eyes burned with hatred and bore into June Bug. He turned his head toward her and grinned.

It was a stare-off that seemed to last an eternity. Neither looked away. Nelle sat immobile, unsure whether to speak or be silent. Finally, Janette brought her attention back to the pot of peas boiling on the stove. She opened the cabinet to the right and rummaged around until she found a small glass jar of salt that she had borrowed earlier from Ann. She sprinkled it onto the peas.

June Bug watched. "What's that?"

"Salt," Janette answered without turning around.

"Bring it here."

Janette marched the jar to June Bug and set it on the table. "It's just salt, J. B."

"Just salt, huh?" June Bug's skepticism was unconsciously perceptive. Salt had never been "just salt." It always has been a form of currency, and a channel of power. It presented itself as no different in Janette's kitchen.

Amused by June Bug's sudden paranoia, a slight smile tugged at the corner of Janette's mouth. "Taste it if you don't believe it." It was a tiny grain of empowerment, not much bigger than the salt crystals in the jar. She held onto it in the place where she nurtured ideas of Laveau magic and women's intuition. From this same place, Janette made a choice—perhaps even a lie of omission—to not disclose that the salt was in a jar because it was borrowed.

It is considered bad luck to borrow or lend salt. In ritual practice, salt is a finicky tool. It protects those who use it in their own homes but opens vulnerabilities to those who deploy it in the homes of others. Salt, like toilet tissue and sanitary napkins, should be in constant supply and replenished by the person who will use it.

Janette had been vaguely aware of this when she decided two days prior to borrow it. But she also had known that Ann's apartment was closer than the grocer and she could leave the black-eyed peas she was cooking that night simmering on the stove while she was out.

Black-eyed peas are thought to have their own lucky properties, dating back to the Civil War. They were planted as a food staple for slaves. When Sherman's troops stole and decimated other crops, they ignored the vast fields of black-eyed peas. But the magic of black-eyed peas reveals itself only when they are consumed on the first day of the new year, and it was not New Year's Day when Janette stirred green peas—as opposed to black-eyed peas—with borrowed salt at the stove while she poked at June Bug's discomfort as one does a sore, feeling the sting of weakened skin. Her voice said that it was just salt in the jar, but her tone hinted otherwise.

"I ain't tasting shit." June Bug placed the jar on the table.

"Fine." Janette retrieved the peas from the stove and spooned them into the bowl on the table. "Here's your peas." The moment was passing, and Janette had enjoyed the balance that the small battle had afforded her. A confidence was blooming in her gait, and June Bug felt it.

"C'mere, Lil Bit." He held out his arm to Nelle, who continued to sit silently across from him.

Janette turned back toward the table alarmed. "J. B., leave her be."

"Nawl, Lil Bit gonna taste it."

Nelle hesitated and looked at her mother. June Bug reached across the table and grabbed her arm. "When I say come here, you come here."

Nelle's lip quivered. "I don't want no peas, Uncle June Bug."

"Aw, now ain't nothin' to cry over, Lil Bit. I ain't gonna make you eat no peas." He smiled and rested her on his lap. His hand held her firmly in place by the arm. He reached for the jar with his other hand.

"J. B., stop it now; you proved your point. Let her go!" Janette tried to grab the salt jar from him. June Bug shoved her away.

"Mama!" Nelle cried. June Bug held tightly to her as he brought the salt jar to her mouth. Nelle's head whipped back and forth as she tried to move away from it. June Bug stood with her still on his lap, pinning her against the table and forcing her mouth open. Janette scrambled from the floor. Her eyes were wild and a sound, more war cry than scream, escaped her lips as she charged toward June Bug. She reached him two seconds too late. His hand was around Nelle's small throat. Her gaping mouth, struggling for air, received salt instead.

They arrived at Ann's door late in the evening. Ann, early to bed and early to rise, had already started to drift to sleep when the doorbell rang. Eve—just ten, but already the night owl—was the first to the door.

"What you doin' opening the door this time of night?" Ann whispered suddenly at Eve's side. "Get over here." She pulled Eve behind her and peered through the peephole. The distorted image coupled with Janette's tear- and makeup-streamed face, made her nearly unrecognizable. Ann slowly opened the door. "What in God's name, Janette?"

Nelle was huddled against her mother. Her skin was paler than usual. A purple bruise encircled her neck, a large blotch on one side that had been June Bug's palm jutted out into four elongated spindles on the other—his fingers. Her curly brown hair was tousled. A few ponytail holders and barrettes remained as vigilant reminders of the hairstyle that had existed before salt. She clutched an empty can to her small chest. On it, a red banner with white lettered words spelling out the Hanover brand was just barely visible through her fingers. Ann opened the screen door and yanked them both inside. She peered up and down the block before slamming and locking the door. They sent the girls to Eve's room.

For Eve, the salt incident started with watching her best friend shake and spit into an empty can every few minutes. Nelle spat her salty saliva into the empty can that had contained the green peas June Bug had refused to eat. Nelle's hacking, the can, and its contents were the salt incident for Eve. She was unsure of what to say to Nelle, so she said nothing. The salt incident struck some sort of balance for Eve. Many times Nelle had been Eve's protector on the school playlot, shielding her friend from schoolyard taunting about her thick hair, dark skin, and sinewy limbs. But now that it was Nelle who needed protecting, Eve was at a loss for how to proceed, while every time Nelle tried to form the words to share with Eve what she had told her mother about June Bug, all the moisture left her mouth—absorbed by the excess salt, she was sure. Their silence was punctuated only by Nelle's sporadic hackings into the can.

Nelle felt that this was punishment for the story she had told her mother. Ashamed, she couldn't bring herself to share the lie with Eve. In a few short hours, Nelle had matured beyond her ten years and the lie revealed itself as the juvenile ploy of an insecure girl. No longer that girl, Nelle couldn't bear to admit to Eve that she had once been her—the girl who spun dangerous tall tales for her mother to hear. She had lied about June Bug, which isn't to say that he was completely innocent.

June Bug had poured salt down her throat, but he was no child molester. He didn't lure young girls into dark places, whisper lewd lines into their small ears, or become their first-time sexual experiences. June Bug looked at girls in the way many men do: with comments in their eyes and knowing smiles creeping beneath their mustached lips. He was one of those who whistled at them from stoops, told them that they "shole was pretty," assured them that if they didn't have boys sniffing around them, "the knuckleheads wouldn't be long coming." He gave them candy, asking for some of their sweet sugar on his scruffy cheek. Yet his behavior was no different than that of most of the men in a young girl's life—uncles, fathers, Santa Claus. It stepped into the inappropriate without crossing into pedophilia. But it only took a slight shift in perception for this same behavior to be considered predatory.

Fifty eyes peered at Janette. Most were from the owl figurines and paintings in Ann's small living room. The only live set of eyes belonged to Ann, but they stared at Janette with no less inquisitiveness. "You a fool to go back to that apartment tonight." She sipped a small amount of brandy from a chipped coffee mug.

A much larger amount was in Janette's cup, which remained pressed to her lips until she replied, "I'd be a fool to let him think he can lay up in my bed after laying hands on my baby girl."

Ann began to slowly rock herself in the straight-backed armchair. "What you gon' do?"

"What you think I'm gonna do?" Janette shot back. "I'm gonna get that poor excuse of a man out of our lives. I'm gonna kill him." She drained her cup and reached for the bottle of brandy on the coffee table between them.

"Janette, let's be serious . . ."

Janette glared at Ann. "I am being serious. Maybe something like this is hard for you to understand, not being a mother and all."

Ann's fingers clutched at her housecoat and she swallowed,

suppressing the sting of the comment and the flare of an angry retort. Janette was instantly remorseful. "I'm sorry. I know Eve is more than a niece to you."

Ann reached across the coffee table, nearly upsetting the brandy, and squeezed Janette's hand. "Let's call somebody. Let's get some of the men in the neighborhood . . ."

Janette gave a weary smile. "Girl, half of them run with June Bug and the other . . ." She trailed off on what didn't need to be said. The other half, married or otherwise, had all been at one time or another her lovers, prior uncles to Nelle.

"At least don't go back tonight," Ann pleaded. Janette rolled her eyes toward Ann but said nothing.

Ann continued, "We can plan something . . . together." Ann thought of the ways of womenfolk back in Macon County. Women's troubles or maladies always seemed to involve men, and the remedies required certain sacrifices. It had been women who had taken care of Big C after Mercy left with Eve still growing in her belly. "Even a small ax can fell a big tree," she quietly whispered, her eyes on Janette and mind in Georgia.

Janette tilted her cup down her throat and stood.

"Janette . . ."

"What?" Janette stared at Ann defiantly.

"Nelle needs you."

"I know," Janette replied. "Which is exactly why I'm going to do what needs to be done."

When Janette left Ann's apartment, she had no idea how to do what needed to be done. She returned to her own apartment. To the low moan of Bobby "Blue" Bland on the radio crooning "I Pity the Fool." To the sounds of June Bug snoring from the bedroom. To green peas and salt strewn across the kitchen floor.

She washed the dishes, gathered the errant peas, and was beginning to sweep up the salt, when she paused. Janette stared at the grainy scatterings on her floor. Instead of sweeping them into the dustpan, she brushed them into the corners, where wall met wall met floor. It created an anthill-like mound in one corner. The other corners of the room stood empty. Bare. Janette needed more salt. The urge was so strong that it could not be ignored.

Perhaps her Laveau magic—spurred by recent events—had awakened and risen within her like the kundalini snake uncoiling itself from the base of the spine. Like the loa taking possession of its supplicant and rejoicing in dance. Like crossing over into the place of no space and no time, she began to recall things. The placing of salt across doorways kept away evil spirits. Accompanied by an incantation, casting salt after the departure of an evil person prevented their return. Consumption of communion wine and wafers only proves that religions are just sanctioned magical beliefs and rituals. Any ritual, infused with enough belief, can be a spell. To believe is to think something into existence that wasn't previously there. It is conjure. Any object can protect or harm, and too much of anything can be a poison. Janette Marie Laveau Baptiste needed more salt.

Over the days that followed, June Bug never noticed that first mound of salt, and he had enough sense not to mention Nelle's absence. But when the mounds began appearing all over the apartment, he could no longer hold his tongue. He stood in the middle of the dining room watching Janette cook dinner. "What the hell is all this, 'Nette?"

"All what?" Janette cut a chunk of butter and dropped it into the pot of collard greens on the stove.

"This shit in the corners." He gestured frantically around. But it was more than in the corners. It lined the baseboards of every room. It snaked around furniture like chalk outlines of bodies at crime scenes. It traced thresholds and lined windowsills.

Janette, with a Morton Salt container in hand, sprinkled a careful amount into the greens. "Keeps the ants out."

"I ain't seen no damn ants."

"Must be working then." Janette checked the chicken baking in the oven.

They ate in silence. June Bug watched Janette, wondering if her food tasted as salty as his. But their food was flavored to the same degree, and whatever saltiness June Bug tasted had traveled to his senses through the moistened air of the seasoned apartment. He struggled to swallow but could not manufacture enough saliva. Water did not help but seemed to intensify the problem. His only relief was in the bottle of Old Granddad. The bourbon cut through the salt mines in his mouth, leaving a smooth alcohol finish in its wake.

Old Granddad was June Bug's lifeboat as he skipped around the apartment, avoiding salt trails like a game of hopscotch. After brushing his teeth, he rinsed his mouth with bourbon instead of the salt and water mix Janette had substituted in place of their usual Listerine. He stayed out of the apartment for as long as he could, sometimes sleeping on a friend's couch to sober up from the excess of Old Granddad. But they eventually sent him back to Janette's. No one wanted an out-of-work drunkard in their home for too long. So June Bug would meander back to the apartment to find more salt in unexpected places.

One night, about a week after Nelle had been sent to stay with Ann and Eve, Janette reached for June Bug in bed. His body stiffened at her touch. "'Nette . . ."

"Shhh." Janette could feel his fear. His heart beat rapidly against her palm. "You're so tense, J. B."

June Bug's breath heaved, filling the space between them with the smell of bourbon and the weight of remorse. "'Nette, I'm sorry for . . ." And in that moment he was sorry for everything. He was prepared to curse the salty oceans for freshwater bodies and purify the world of its saline dependency.

Janette shushed him again, pressing her lips against his and her body on top of him. "I know, baby. Just relax."

June Bug sighed as her hand kneaded into his neck. His body sank into the mattress. Janette reached for a jar on the nightstand, and June Bug's eyes flew open. "What's . . ."

"It's just massage oil," Janette cooed, and June Bug slowly allowed his body to relax again. Janette rubbed the oil into her palm and massaged it onto his chest. The texture, warm and grainy, eased his tension and exfoliated his skin as she raked her fingernails down his chest. It felt invigorating. Janette's hands moved downward, and June Bug felt his arousal.

More oil. More massage. More nails. His face twisted. The grainy scrub, against his sensitive member, felt more aggressive as Janette worked her hands to every part. June Bug felt a tingle that grew into a sting. He screamed. He shoved Janette off him, and clutching himself, ran to the bathroom.

June Bug straddled the sink. The cold porcelain pressed against his backside as he flushed his genitals with cold water. He returned to the bedroom shriveled, scratched, and wet, and asked the question to which he already knew the answer. "What was in that oil?"

"It's good for the skin." Janette switched off the lamp and rolled over toward the wall.

His friends began to notice the weight loss. They bought him food. Perch sandwiches from the seafood place on Forty-Seventh. Chicken dinners from Gladys's. Invited him over for oxtails, black-eyed peas, and Friday fish fries, but June Bug ate very little. The absence of salt at these gatherings loomed as large as its presence in Janette's apartment. He didn't taste salt in these dishes, and strangely enough, he missed it.

He was too quiet. When he did speak, he put his friends off with strange questions. Staring at the untouched plate of pork chops beside him on the stoop of George Wright's house, June Bug asked, "You think it's something out there that affects men and women different?"

George exhaled his Marlboro. "You mean like Mother Nature? Menstr'ation?"

June Bug slowly rolled his eyes upward to look at George. Large bags puffed beneath them, and eye crust stuck in the folds of skin at their corners. He licked his dry lips and took a swig from a pint of Old Granddad nestled in a brown paper bag. "Nawl. Like . . . salt."

"Salt?"

"Yeah, you think salt can act different in men than it do in women?"

George scratched at the bald spot spreading at the crown of his head. "I'ont know, J. B." A concerned look crossed his face, and he thought briefly about offering the couch to his friend that night. But his wife did not take too well the last time June Bug had stayed over. He'd broken one of her good glasses that he had insisted pouring his bourbon in, and she swore that he'd used the large house plant as a toilet, complaining to George that it reeked of urine. So George closed his mouth on the offer and watched June Bug stagger home for the very last time.

It would have shortened the distance had he taken the alley, but June Bug was in no hurry to get home. He half walked, half stumbled in the direction of the apartment. His shoulders scraped brick walls and chain link fences. He bumped into garbage cans and felt his chest tighten the closer he got to his destination. His thoughts did not go beyond placing one uncertain foot in front of the other. He was a lemming drawn to the cliff overhang of a raging ocean. He was a bit of cosmic debris in the inexorable gravitational pull of a black hole. He did not want to push forward, but he could not turn back. As it was with Lot's wife in the Bible, there was nothing to go back to.

June Bug reached the bottom of the back stairwell. He trudged up the first flight. The shuffle-clump of his footfalls reverberated through the empty night. The first-floor neighbors, accustomed to the late-night arrivals, remained fast asleep. Their five-year-old son—finally convinced that the rhythmic *shhh-cloomp* was not a monster dragging a body, but the drunken homecoming of their third-floor neighbor—slept soundlessly as urine trickled into his pajamas and spread across his bedsheets.

June Bug made it to the landing of his second-floor neighbor, a single mother of two. She thought Janette was a "high-yella heifa," and had slept with June Bug out of jealousy, regretting it immediately. He'd been too drunk to perform, passing out on top of her and dripping bourbon-scented spittle on her sheets.

June Bug sat on the landing and lit a Kool. He rubbed at the scruff of hair on his chin, feeling its contrast with his smooth cheeks, where hair refused to grow. His eyes peered upward to the apartment where Janette murmured strains of a blues song in her sleep. The next flight of stairs leading to the apartment was a minefield of salt. It saturated the crevices of the stairs so that June Bug was forced to perch on his toes. He could not square the irrationality of his fear. He knew that salt wasn't acid, yet he was afraid to make contact with it. He had tiptoed on the balls of his feet, hopscotching over the sagging fifth and sixth steps, so many times that he could do it drunk in the dark. Muscle memory guided him every night to land on the seventh step and take the final leap onto the concrete step at the back door.

Janette often thought that in a perfect world, he'd stumble and miss. It wasn't just the abundance of the salt that put June Bug off but its pristine appearance. He suspected that Janette frequently replaced the salt, and his suspicions were correct. She couldn't stand for grains of dirt and debris to dull its luminosity like snow that had been on the ground too long. If magic is belief plus intention and action, then clear intent must be represented in ritual. So she swept and redistributed the salt trails in his absence. Earlier that night, Janette had moved the salt line at the back door two inches closer to the stairs, and the imperfect world shifted into one moment of perfection.

June Bug stubbed out his cigarette and began the obstacle course by taking the first step on toe tips. He moved with the sobering dexterity of a tightrope walker. He hopped over the two sagging steps onto the seventh. His legs, accustomed to the movements and timing, sprang just as his brain registered the new salt line. He tried to correct but overcorrected. He tried to turn but didn't arc. He flinched. He landed wrong, teetering on the edge of the seventh step at a forty-five-degree angle, tilted with his back toward the stairs. He was frozen in time long enough to grasp at the wooden banister and miss. Long enough to grasp at a prayer but not to await its answer.

June Bug tumbled backward into the night. His nose was broken on the second-floor neighbor's landing. His neck was broken on the first.

The five-year-old on the first floor would find blood outside his back door the next day and once again believe in monsters.

The second-floor neighbor would add the incident to her list of why she was no longer jealous of Janette.

And Janette would awaken refreshed, "Two Steps from the Blues" lodged deep within her subconscious mind.

NINE

revolutionary remains

the Revolution ain't dead
its tired,
and jest resting.
—Carolyn M. Rodgers, "The Revolution Is Resting"

Chicago burned the 1960s down while civil rights leaders, social justice advocates, and agitators absconded in its rapture. The remnants were scattered attempts among survivors of political parties—not so much ushering in the seventies as clinging to the shipwrecked remains of the revolution.

The remains of the revolution lay next to Eve in bed. Ash was tall, dark, and not very handsome. He would've been at the Monroe headquarters when Fred Hampton was assassinated by the "pigs" if only he had completed the six-week political education classes. He was habitually absent, but good-natured. To Ash, there was the revolution but there was also the world. He could not reconcile his racial obligations and worldly aspirations. "Must we all be revolutionaries? Can't some of us be explorers?"

The party kept him around because of his idealism—a symbol

that although the answer to his query was no, they believed in a future where it could be yes. Eve kept him around because his inspiration was contagious. He was always off somewhere. The spiritual mounts of Machu Picchu. The Egyptian pyramids. Table Mountain. If not in person, then in mind.

He was a nomad driving a Chicago cab and sleeping in his parents' basement until he had enough money for his latest adventure. She enjoyed the freedom of not being pressured into marriage and making babies for the revolution. Ash looked at Eve like she was one of the few souvenirs brought back from an excursion. Not so much as a prize, but a memory that he enjoyed revisiting. Eve looked at Ash as she did when rereading a favorite novel: with familiarity and appreciation.

Currently he was unwittingly inspiring her to travel to Macon County, Georgia, without so much as a word goodbye. She would take a page from his book. Eve's naked body was wrapped snugly in the floral sheets from his parent's linen closet, leaving his own nudity on full display to her. Eve's thoughts meandered to when she met him after returning to Chicago from Tuskegee. Womanly curves teach girls to keep walking through the barrage of daily catcalls and calloused hands that reach for them from neighborhood corners. Yet Ash had a way of looking at Eve that made her linger. His look held more interest than lust. He had a quiet manner about him, and when he said his name, she found herself leaning closer to catch it.

"Nobody names their kid Ash." Eve smirked.

"Oh, you wanna know my *gubment* name?" he responded. "It's Ashford."

"Like Ashford and Simpson? You're joking!" Eve clapped her hands over her mouth and tried unsuccessfully to stifle the laughter.

"Go ahead. You aren't the first. Although I gotta say that I had

136

the name before anyone knew who Nick Ashford was. I mean, yeah, he's older, but think about it. When I was born, nobody knew him."

"Alright. You're right."

"And everybody can't have such a beautiful name like Eve."

Eve's smile quickly faded. Ash's abbreviated nomenclature mirrored her own name journey. Eve mostly liked when her name rolled off his lips in a whisper or was belted out in a postcoital shout. Eve felt truly to be her own woman, self-named and self-made. No mother. No father. Just the moment of now next to a man whom she had lain with for two years and could leave in a moment's notice. She caressed the thought in her mind.

That spring, she had listened to an interview of Fred Hampton's fiancée recounting his murder by Chicago police officers as they, too, had lain in bed. Eve wondered if their sheets had been as tangled as the ones in which she currently snuggled. She imagined police storming into the basement, disturbing her partner's sleep. Would he jump out of bed, action-ready? Or was that part of the training he had missed?

Eve believed in fighting for a cause and dying for a cause, but she could not fathom that a cause could be contained in one person. But so often that was the case. The lifting up of one leader at a time in the easiest manner only for them to be knocked down. Eve blamed religion. Jesus, Muhammad—the faith didn't matter if the practice remained the same.

Ash's eyes were upon her, crusted sleep still present in their corners. "What are you thinking?" It was his most repeated question. He always wanted to know what was on her mind.

"Our first conversation." Eve smiled.

A slow grin spread across his face. "The religion one or the sex one?"

Eve playfully slapped his thigh. The clap echoed through the basement. "The religion one."

"Ah, yes. The exaltation and subsequent destruction of men. That's what you called it. But why now?" He traced her thigh with his index finger. "Did you have a come-to-Jesus moment?" He gasped and dramatically clutched his chest. "Or was it Muhammad?"

She slapped his thigh again. "Neither. Did you ever meet Hampton?"

The playfulness left his face, and he slowly nodded. "Just briefly. He wasn't no Jesus or Muhammad. The chairman was just an intense brother with a message, dig?"

"I just don't know how his fiancée could risk her own life and that of her unborn child to try to shield him from bullets." Eve was certain that she would not have rolled on top of Fred Hampton as a shield. Of all the horrors of that event and the news program interviews with Hampton's fiancée, what Eve could not get out of her mind was the haunted look and deadpan stare, the words "I jumped on top of the chairman . . ." She believed in maternal instinct. Her spirit told her that she lived because her mother, Mercy, had sacrificed her own life. Eve rolled her eyes toward her companion and thought one simple word: *no*.

As if reading her mind, he chuckled. "Not a lot of brothers out there with intense messages."

"That beat maternal instinct?" Eve asked incredulously.

"But, Eve," he slowly dragged out her name. "That *was* maternal instinct."

"Bullshit."

"Who are the mothers of the movement? Its nurturers," he intoned.

"Don't go there," Eve warned. "You mean its nursemaids. Its domestic laborers. Its prostitutes . . ."

"Now *you* don't go there," he fired back.

"Its shields," Eve challenged.

He nodded. "Fair enough." The grin returned, and his hand shifted up her thigh. "Why don't you show me how it feels to be used for your gender?" He laid back on the bed and clasped his hands behind his head.

"Be serious." She frowned.

"I am serious. I'm not trying to make light. I'm trying to make love, but I dig it. On your terms, Ms. Eve. I'll wait."

In that moment, as she slid her body onto his, Eve knew two things: she could love him, but she would not. She saw it so clearly—the path to marriage that seemed to elude the ones who wanted it most. Eve veered decidedly away from it, and Macon County seemed a most appropriate detour.

Eve would miss his bed, but she realized that part of its appeal was that it was not her own bed in her aunt's house. She enjoyed freedom from the familiar creaks of Ann's floorboards as her aunt paced, busied with housework, or adjusted in bed. His basement had granted sanctuary from Ann's late-night coughing, bathroom breaks, and muttered commentary on her romance novels.

Her only other respite had been with Nelle, who returned to Janette's apartment after graduation. Nelle had repeatedly tried to convince Eve to share an apartment with her. Eve had been tempted, but every time she considered it, she thought of the things that occurred between her and Ash in this basement apartment. The sounds. The smells. The acts. She vehemently shook her head to Nelle. "I just can't do it."

Nelle sighed. "I'm not asking to share a bed, Eve."

Eve clinched her eyes as she thought of the countless times when they had shared a bed. It was standard sleepover practice during their youth. They'd sleep, pinkies entwined. *Sister from another mother.* Only Eve had secretly wished to discover an actual blood connection with her friend. Somewhere in her unknown lineage, she hoped that their lines linked together like their pinky fingers looped in slumber. She knew that it should not matter who Nelle slept with, but it did change things for her, especially when Nelle tied her sexuality to her feminism.

"Women loving each other, Black women especially, is the most radically revolutionary act we can do," Nelle had tried to explain.

"So, sleeping with women is feminist action?" Eve rolled her eyes. "I gotta sleep with a woman to be feminist?"

Nelle sighed. "This would be a lot easier if you'd just get over yourself, Every."

"What's that supposed to mean?"

"It means ain't nobody trying to get into them granny drawls of yours. It means that there are many ways to love a woman, and you just focusing on the sexual is some real mannish shit." Nelle stared at Eve and braced for a response.

Eve had not responded, and the conversation remained at an impasse, with Nelle insisting that their friendship remain unchanged and Eve demanding that they excise talks of relationships and romance from it. They were the best of friends within continually narrowing parameters. Sometimes Nelle would forget this in her excitement and mention a positive dating experience, eliciting a silent glare from Eve. Similarly, when Eve mentioned Ash, Nelle's "I don't wanna hear that straight shit" response cut quick and to the core.

Now that Eve had made the decision to go to Macon County without telling Ash, the person she most wanted to share it with was Nelle. She lay next to Ash and imagined the conversation where Nelle would ask, *What's the big deal? Why won't you tell him?* To which Eve would shrug her shoulders at first until Nelle gave a probing look, prompting a truthful reply. This familiar practice became the substitute for actual conversation, and it left Eve with the important information she needed: the realization that she was afraid that telling Ash she was leaving would prompt a change in their dynamic. That one or both of them would cling to the comfort of the other in the face of a new unfamiliarity. Eve was mostly afraid that it would be her clinging to him as she waded through the unknown terrain of family lineage.

Later, as Eve scurried toward the bar where she was to meet Nelle, she resolved to break the code of silence that plagued their friendship. She would talk to Nelle, and yes, she would listen too. Eve shuddered at the thought but trudged even more determinedly. Her loafers slapped the pavement as if high-fiving in support, and Eve sighed her first sigh of relief since uncovering the photograph of her family.

As she counted down the addresses toward her destination, Eve did not notice the shift in atmosphere. The Pub carved a smooth oasis within the concrete hustle and bustle of storefront shops and busy boulevard traffic. Entering the establishment, Eve was drenched in darkness and the light from outside quickly faded with the closing door. It took a few seconds to make out Nelle seated at the bar. Eve plopped onto the stool next to Nelle, who wordlessly held up two fingers to the bartender signaling their order.

"Look," Eve began. "I just wanna say that I've got something to discuss with you, and it involves a man . . ."

Nelle's mouth opened to speak, but Eve held up a hand to ward off any impending protest.

"I know. I know. We have boundaries, but—"

141

"Eve—" Nelle tried to interject. But was once again rebuffed by her friend's hand.

"Yes, I know that I was the one who established those boundaries." Eve lowered her hand and wrapped it around the cold beer placed before her. Nodding her gratitude toward the bartender, she continued, "But I just want to say that perhaps we should revisit things." She sipped her beer and gazed around. Eve's eyes captured images she had missed when she first entered the bar oblivious to its décor of rainbow flags and its ambiguously gendered clientele.

Three men laughed together at a table. Their rough jawlines rouged into softness. Toothy grins displayed none of the reservation they'd exercise once they left the temporary shelter of the Pub. A beautiful woman in a business skirt suit sat against the wall glancing nervously from her watch to the door. She reapplied already flawless lipstick before returning to the universal activity of waiting for another.

Nelle was speaking, but Eve hadn't heard a word. Her mouth did not leave the glass as her eyes scanned her surroundings, trying to make sense of what she was experiencing.

"I can't be here." Eve quickly rose and rushed outside, nearly bumping into what she first registered as a man but then realized was a masculine woman in a suit and tie. Eve stammered an apology, but the woman was already halfway across the floor toward her companion, the waiting woman.

Nelle signaled for the bartender, indicating that she'd return, and slowly followed Eve's path. She found her leaning against the wall, watching the cars pass on the boulevard. "You know this is not how it works, Every."

Eve's focus remained on the cars as she spoke. "Can't we just talk out here?"

"Not if you really meant what you said in there." Nelle's unwavering stare warmed the side of Eve's face as she continued to avoid eye contact. "Anyway," Nelle sighed as she opened the door. "I got a beer to finish." She left Eve leaning against the wall in perplexity.

Eve pressed a hand to her forehead in a motion reminiscent of her aunt. She couldn't shout the expletive banging through her head, so she mouthed it to the heavens.

A passing drag queen caught her silent protest and chimed, "Well, you're certainly in the right place, hot stuff."

Eve watched them enter and moments later followed. The unassuming door closed behind her, sealing out the light and traffic of the boulevard.

Nelle and Eve were two peas who had outgrown their shared pod and no amount of reconfiguration would see them returned to it. Nelle wasn't necessarily proud when Eve reluctantly followed her back into the Pub for drinks. No one should be applauded for finally doing what they should have been doing in the first place. But she was sympathetic to Eve's journey, so different from her own. Nelle didn't have a journey of self-discovery.

It seemed comical that Eve was just saying, ". . . to really find myself in this world."

Nelle nodded but muttered, "Such a straight luxury."

"What?" Eve paused.

"That you get to find yourself like some board game or TV show."

Eve scanned the bar; her outspread hands demonstrated her gaze. "Your bar. My topic. Isn't that the deal?"

Nelle nodded and dutifully lent her ears to Eve's talk about the man she'd been sleeping with and her decision to travel to Georgia.

"I just feel like I've spent my whole life in this back-and-forth of questioning and trying to move past what I don't know." Eve paused and sipped her beer. "Asking Mama Ann about our family, not getting any answers, and then trying to live without those answers."

"I understand," Nelle murmured absently while her attention drifted to a figure in the far corner. As the bar door opened, allowing in two more patrons, light illuminated a slender dark-skinned build, generous afro, and burgundy-painted lips. Nelle was intrigued.

"I don't think you do," Eve frowned. "I don't think you can. I know it sounds so trivial. I had a good life. Mama Ann raised me well. Why rock the boat?"

"Because you didn't place yourself in it to begin with," Nelle brought her attention fully back to her friend.

Eve nodded. "And not that it's your fault or anyone's for knowing their kinfolks, but—" She took another gulp of her beer. "—it's really hard when everyone around me casually throws around spending time with relatives. Dinner at parents' homes. Drinks with cousins. Visits to grandparents. Shit, I don't even know my daddy's name."

Eve finished her beer and glanced around the bar. "This wasn't half bad."

Nelle stood and placed her hands on Eve's shoulders. "You should go . . . to Georgia, I mean."

Eve's eyes flashed large. "Will you come with me?" The query tumbled from her lips without much thought, a holdover from their past effortless closeness. But once they were said, Eve did not regret the words. Her face reflected the struggle of their friend-ship—mouth set in stubborn firmness and eyes pleading for familiar connection.

"This is your journey, Every," Nelle's voice softened. "I got my own too, you know." Her focus drifted to an individual seated in the shadows of a small table in the corner.

"I wonder whether I'm quest-ready," Eve said.

Nelle smiled. "You've been asking questions all your wonky-ass life, Every. This is probably the only quest you're ready for."

Eve stood and surprised Nelle with a quick squeeze. "You still know how to say all the right things."

"Further proof that I haven't changed."

"I'm going," Eve declared.

"I know," Nelle grinned.

"Yeah, I mean I'm going—like, I'm leaving this charming bar to check on bus schedules and pack and tell Mama Ann and . . ." She sighed heavily.

Nelle grabbed Eve's hand in support. "Breathe, girl. You got this."

Eve nodded. "It's just I'm sure I'll be leaving in the next few days and we probably won't get a chance to see each other before I go, and even if we did, I'd be nervous that we'd backslide into weirdness."

Nelle drew her into an embrace. "Only forward from here on out."

"Promise?" Eve asked into her shoulder.

"Damn straight."

Eve pulled out of the hug. "Well, at least the intention is there."

Nelle watched Eve leave the bar, laughter plastered on both of their faces, when she turned to find the object of her previous attention standing beside her at the bar.

"It's not polite to stare and not say hello." The southern drawl revealed roots, but the husky voice belied no gender. "It's also not polite to ask."

Nelle was stunned and stammered, "What, what can I call you?"

"Jean, and the pleasure is mine." Jean extended a hand.

Nelle shook hands and glared. She opened her mouth but quickly clamped down the questions and comments that would demand the revelation of Jean's gender.

Jean smiled. "That's a good girl. Because you really don't."

"Don't?"

Jean drew closer to Nelle's ear and whispered, "Have to."

"To what?" Nelle's breath quickened.

"Know," Jean concluded. "You actually only need to know one thing."

"What's that?"

"That I drink gin or rum. They rhyme with all the best words," Jean giggled.

It was the start of a peculiarly intimate friendship that engulfed Nelle during the time Eve had given her to consider the trip. Jean coaxed Nelle into exploring bars and events outside the South Side's small Black lesbian enclave where she had joined a small community of brown women who liked brown women. They gathered in found spaces to dance, sing, talk, and laugh. Nelle wondered what it looked like to love a woman within the traditional confines of a relationship. This community gave her a lens to see Black lesbians beyond sociopolitical conversations. They talked about sharing homes and dreams. They discussed what to make for dinner, where to vacation, music that spoke to their lives.

They were an incestuous bunch in that friends became lovers, lovers became friends, and friends of lovers became lovers, so much so that it seemed to Nelle that everyone knew the taste of everyone else. She was hesitant to add her own flavor to the stew. Through Jean's various lovers, Nelle was introduced to the depths of queerness, beyond the dichotomy of gay and straight.

Nelle, still new to the community, admired the coalition building and camaraderie from the periphery. She attended their functions, usually before meeting Jean for drinks.

Jean never attended the concerts or poetry readings held in the rented church rooms. "They're separatists, you know," she confided after Nelle returned from an event particularly moved by the words of philosophy professor and Black lesbian activist Jackie Anderson.

"Oh, Jean, if you could have heard how impassioned she spoke about the need for Black women's spaces within lesbian spaces!"

"They don't much trust me because I'm not a lesbian." Jean disclosed as they sat in Jean's small studio apartment.

"They just don't know what you are," Nelle explained.

"You don't know what I am."

Nelle stood and refilled their drinks, pouring a healthy dose of rum into Jean's glass. She returned and planted a kiss on Jean's forehead. "I know who you are."

Nelle sat across from Jean, the person who had become her closest confidante in such a short time. She confided to Jean about the details she could not share with Eve, like leaving the bar one night, giddy with the gaiety of breathing in too deeply, too quickly the same-gender-loving spaces. High on acceptance, she failed to notice the tall figure approaching her on the sidewalk until he grabbed her purse and shoved her hard enough to send her tumbling backward.

"Dyke," he sneered before running off and disappearing down the nearest alley.

Before the last of her tears had dried, Jean was there to collect her from the bar patrons who nested around after the incident. As Nelle lifted her eyes from the line of bourbon shots purchased in her honor, a heavily made-up, evening-gown-wearing Jean parted the crowd. They retreated to Jean's apartment, where Jean tried to console Nelle.

"It's not even the theft, although that was fucked up," Nelle noted. "I don't even care that he called me a dyke."

"Oh, honey," Jean cooed and rubbed Nelle's back.

"I mean it," Nelle sniffled in spite of herself. "He was just a kid. Tall as a man, but that lanky run, and those wide eyes." She shook her head in disbelief.

"Big paws on a pup. That's what my daddy called it."

"The worst part, though—" Nelle shook with rage.

Jean placed a manicured hand on Nelle's shoulder. "Don't."

"I thought that she'd at least show up to see if I was okay." Nelle had recently been involved in a brief infatuation—in the ways that unreturned affections can be brief.

"That's not the way it works, love."

"I thought one-night stands were more mutually agreed upon."

Jean bellowed loudly, startling Nelle. "Chile, that's the funniest shit I've ever heard."

For her part, Nelle played nursemaid in the aftermath of Jean's many dalliances with male and female lovers. The boyfriends referred to Jean as "him." The girlfriends called Jean "her." Nelle stuck to Jean, foregoing all gendered pronoun usage. It was easy. Most of their interactions simply required Nelle to say "You."

In a matter of weeks, Nelle picked up the literal and figurative pieces of Jean's affairs. Jean and the lovers always fussed. They threw things. They never hit, but occasionally shards of some ill-aimed item would bounce off a wall and imbed themselves into the arm or leg of Jean or one of the lovers. Jean shared the guilt of the tirade, launching as many glasses as were dodged.

One evening—Nelle couldn't even recall whether it was a boyfriend or girlfriend—a fight had occurred. Nelle pressed a cold towel to Jean's head and remarked, "You know this ain't gay love."

Jean removed the towel. "I ain't gay."

Nelle gently pressed the towel back. "This ain't love at all, love."

In the adjacent bathroom, water ran into the tub. Their weekly ritual involved Jean in the bathtub while Nelle sat on a pillow leaning outside the door. They learned of each other's lives in this way. Nelle told Jean about the salt incident, Tuskegee, and her ebbing friendship with Eve. She shared her dreams of writing essays for Black lesbians in Black magazines, to which Jean laughed, "Can you imagine *Ebony* magazine putting lesbians on their cover?"

She told Jean about Professor Woodridge and the egg that she could no longer find. Apparently, it had gone the way of things lost along the way. Favorite T-shirts. Mates to socks in clothes dryers. Underwear stolen by jilted lovers clinging to those fortunate enough to have let go first. Somewhere in the packing of her dorm room and return to Chicago, the egg had simply vanished, along with any inhibitions she may have felt about her sexuality. Woodridge had called the egg her rebirth and a reminder of the ability of flight. Perhaps it had flown the coop. But eggs don't fly, and Nelle thought that, although beautiful, the analogy seemed a bit one-size-fits-all. Still, she wished that she had the egg to give to Jean.

"So, this egg . . . maybe it represents an ovary?" Jean offered.

"Well, that's biased," Nelle laughed. "Can't it be a testicle?"

Jean laughed. "You know that's not the way it works, right?"

"How would I know?" Nelle prodded. "How do you know?"

"I don't know," Jean teased. "Education? Books?"

Jean shared life growing up in Mississippi. "It was five of us, but my daddy loved me most of all. I had to leave though. It was killing him—me being me. He was a big Black country man, but he told me, 'Baby, you just be you.' Can you imagine that?"

Jean's voice was hollow as it reached Nelle's ears through the closed door.

"You were lucky," Nelle responded. "Not everybody got that." She choked down thoughts of June Bug.

Jean continued, "He was the strongest man I've ever known. Wanted to return every taunt and blow that they gave me. But some things you just can't serve back." Jean's voice trailed off before adding, "So he let me go."

Nelle could hear Jean shifting around in the water as it dripped from unimagined places.

Jean sighed. "No one knows what to do with me but you."

Nelle laughed. "I'm the only one who doesn't do anything with you."

"Exactly!" Jean's voice raised above the swishing water. "And it makes me so happy. Please always keep doing that." There was a silent pause, and then the splatter-tap of wet feet on linoleum. The bathroom lock disengaged, and the door creaked open.

Nelle scrambled around and was faced with the fluorescence of the bathroom light, the warmth of the steaming tub, and Jean— wet and nude.

Jean's eyes held Nelle's as Jean said, "I'm tired of talking through doors," before turning on heels and returning to the tub. Nelle looked at the bourbon in her glass, amazed that she hadn't upset it, and poured it down her throat. Slowly she rose and entered the bathroom, shutting the door behind her.

When Eve told Brother LeRoi about her plans to visit Macon County, he cautioned her to be careful. They sat in his office much like they had on their first meeting, with Brother LeRoi twirling the egg around in his pale palm and Eve perched on the edge of the chair across from him.

"I know that things are different in the South." Eve responded.

"It's not just that, Eve."

"I also know I'm a woman, and that comes with its own dangers—white people but also Black men as well." Eve remembered the warnings from Mama Ann, who issued just as many cautions against interactions with Black men as she did white people. *We love 'em, but they don't always love us.*

Eve liked to think that Brother LeRoi was different. He seemed kind and caring, but she'd known men who were like brothers to her while being the worst abusers to their wives. A childhood friend swore that if any man laid a hand on her, he'd unleash vengeance tenfold. Yet his own wife's heavy foundation and blush struggled to cover the bruises and crescent-shaped imprint on her cheek that matched her husband's ring.

"Yes, that's all true. But my warning is more about things . . . unanticipated," Brother LeRoi explained.

"Unanticipated? Like what?"

Brother LeRoi thought of his recent interactions with Amy. His half-sister's persistence in connecting with him and naive imaginings that he could ever access the lineage outside of his Blackness troubled him in advising Eve to go so willfully into the genealogical abyss.

"You're ready for the truth?" he asked.

"I've been waiting all my life."

"So then, you're ready for the horrible, painful truth of it all? The god-awful truth and reasons for the irrevocable lies that cover it?" He allowed the egg a spin on the desktop.

Without missing a beat, Eve replied, "I'm ready to be the one who determines what I get to do with it."

The egg slowly came to a halt, one end pointing at Brother LeRoi, the other at Eve. She left with a list of interview questions, the egg nestled snugly in her corduroy pocket, and a resolve to tell Mama Ann about her plans.

INTERLUDE
damnatio memoriae

(condemnation of memory)

Few women have ever served as Egyptian Pharaoh. At the time of Hatshepsut's rule around 1500 BCE, there didn't exist a word for female rulership in Egypt. Upon her death, her stepson-nephew ascended to the throne and obliterated Hatshepsut from history, chiseling his own name over her cartouches, removing her images, and destroying her statues. Hatshepsut was erased from history for 3,500 years. The struggle to wipe events and people from memory is equaled only by their reciprocal refusal to stay hidden. Perhaps there is a place for such erasures: a small Georgia town renamed and reestablished by two railroad executives; the burning away of an all-Black town in Florida; the same fate befalling the thriving economic community called Black Wall Street in Tulsa; the first Great Mississippi Flood that overtook New Orleans.

Ann could no more deny Eve's inquisition than Brother LeRoi could prevent Amy from disclosing the contents of his mother's letter. Taking Brother LeRoi's advice, Eve confronted her aunt with the photograph she had found, her own *damnatio memoriae*. Pulling

153

it from the rear pocket of her bell-bottom jeans, she placed it on the counter next to the dish rack one morning as Ann washed the breakfast dishes. Ann's eyes glanced toward it, but she continued to rinse the plate in her hand and placed it in the rack. Drops of water landed on the picture. Eve snatched it and pressed it against her shirt. "Careful!"

Ann continued to wash the dishes, but there was an added intensity to her scrubbing, as if every plate bore the hardened remains of dried food.

"Who are these people?" Eve inquired.

"It should say it on the back," Ann responded coolly.

"I mean who are they to you?"

"Dead."

"Well, they can't all be dead, can they?"

Ann dried her hands on a dishrag. "You're right. I'm still here. Have been all your life. The only family you know." She faced Eve. "And now that you all grown up and smellin' yo'self, I ain't enough."

"That's not true, Mama Ann. You know I love you and appreciate everything that you've done for me . . ."

"And this is how you show it? By rifling through my belongings?" Ann's lips pursed into a tight grimace, and Eve recognized it as a look that had shut down many conversations over the years. But she was not going to be deterred. "Well, who were they to me then?" Eve held the photograph between them and pointed. "I know that's you. And my mom. And Grandma Gertrude. But who's this man, Mama Ann?" Her aunt dropped her eyes and began to retreat into that silence where she stood guard over the secrets Eve was attempting to pry open.

"I don't understand how you can just . . . erase people, family even, from your mind." Eve's exasperation cracked through her voice.

Ann lifted her eyes in one final moment of defiance. "You have no idea who or what is in my mind."

"Then tell me."

But her aunt's mind held fast to her secrets, slamming the door against memory to ensure no one else found their way out of the *damnatio memoriae*, the metaphysical Alcatraz from which an Egyptian pharaohess had escaped and now escorted others. Hatshepsut, the Harriet Tubman of forgotten memories.

Ann untied the apron from around her waist. "I can't," she whispered and walked out of the kitchen. Eve called to her retreating form, but Ann continued to walk to her bedroom. Ann heard the words, heard her niece's threat to find out on her own.

"I've already looked it up, and it's a tiny town, Mama Ann!" The voice was muffled by the time it had traveled down the hallway and penetrated the closed door to reach Ann's ears. Ann sat on her bed enveloped in the greenness of her room and sighed. There were things she felt Eve should know, yet she was conflicted. She believed that it was not her duty to speak of them. She had raised her sister's child. She had even talked of difficult matters with her, as mother to child, woman to girl. She had educated her on bodily changes and hygiene and even sex, to the best of her sexually conservative nature. But there were some things that Ann could not speak of—undesirable things whose very description offended her sense of morality. Ann had tried at various times in the past to provide Eve with information about their family. But every answer she supplied only caused questions to spring tenfold from her niece. So Ann chose the silence and erased the undesirable elements until all that remained was herself and Eve, whose birth story gradually took on the characteristics of an immaculate conception.

But the presence of the photograph challenged the silence. In her bedroom, Ann wondered why she had even kept it only to have it resurface like Hatshepsut's obelisks from behind the concrete that concealed them. Ann felt her own walls crumbling, but she had known on some level that it would happen. In order to forget one, she had buried them all in the recesses of her mind. She could not discuss her sister, Eve's mother, without having to address the circumstances of her death and Eve's simultaneous birth. It was a terrible conundrum. She couldn't erase names from stories without it resulting in the dismantling of the story itself.

In the kitchen, Eve held the photograph, bringing it close to her face. She had the same high cheekbones, almond-shaped eyes, and full lips as the other women in her family. She had seen pictures of her aunt, mother, and grandmother before, but this was her first time seeing this man identified by name only in Ann's faded, curly script on the back of the picture.

Eve stared into the eyes of the solidly built, dark-skinned man. "Who the hell are you, Cornelius Gaines?" she whispered.

PART II

My great-grandmama told my grandmama the
part she lived through that my grandmama didn't
live through and my grandmama told my mama what they
both lived through and my mama told me what they all lived
through and we were suppose to pass it down like that from
generation to generation so we'd never forget.
—Gayl Jones, *Corregidora*

For if this story is to be told, we will have to put them
all back inside each other like Russian dolls.
—Zadie Smith, *White Teeth*

skin folk and kin folk

I've often thought that being a
light-skinned Black woman is like being
a well-dressed person who is also homeless.
—Zinzi Clemmons, *What We Lose*

If you are born in America with a black skin,
you're in prison.
—Malcolm X

Cornelius had achieved his own title of sorts when the photograph
was taken. They stood stoically. Eve's mother, Mercy, stood slightly
apart from the group. Unbeknownst to her, the tiny fetal forma-
tions of Eve were occurring within her stomach. It would be the
last picture in which Mercy would appear and, ultimately, their
final family picture. Before their mother, Gertrude, dreamed of
fish. Before they found out about the pregnancy. Before Mercy ran
off. Before Eve was born and Mercy died. The choices of everyone
in the picture had already set these events in motion by the time
the photographer pressed the button and the flashbulb popped.

Cornelius's own decisions, which would turn him into a ruler of sorts, began in 1920 when he was just a boy living with his grandmother. He suffered from trying to hang on to his own memories of the erased, often waking in the early-morning hours soaked in sweat and trying frantically to cling to the pale woman who disappeared with his dreams, leaving only her razor-sharp words: *Black nigga.* The dream occurred fairly frequently but irregularly. Sometimes it would stay away for months. Other times it hounded him nightly for weeks. He hadn't had it since the beginning of summer, and it was quickly approaching fall. But after rummaging around in the shed and finding a box crammed into a corner in the way of things meant to be forgotten, the dream beckoned.

Cornelius slept on a floor pallet in the one-and-a-half-room shanty he shared with his grandmother. Her own bed towered a few feet away. Against the wall, the fading embers of a wood-burning stove warmed the small space. His grandmother claimed that his mother hadn't left so much as a shoestring behind when she ran off with "that yella nigga from New Orleans," but the box told a different story. He slowly shifted his weight and turned slightly on his side, peeking at the sleeping mound just an arm's length away. Satisfied that his grandmother still slept, Cornelius slid his thin fingers into one of the large sacks that formed his mattress and snaked his hand through the hay inside until it closed around the smooth wooden handle. Keeping his eyes trained on the pallet across the floor, he carefully withdrew the brush from beneath him and laid it on his chest. He gingerly fingered the silken hairs still trapped within its bristles and absently reached up to pluck at the woolen mass atop his own head. The sun began to creep upward and enter the house through the small cracks in the roof. It lit the white bristles of the brush and the fine hairs it held. The colors of the quilt folded around him became alive, but the darkness of his hand did not go away. He didn't mind it, but his mother hadn't been able to get past it by the time he was three years old.

His mother Luella was a lighter complexion, and his grandmother Ida Mae, whom he called Grandmere, was lighter still. The moniker—French for grandmother—and her skin tone bore testament to the genealogy of Macon County and its various inhabitants. Language also migrated, and words like *grandmère* leapt into the mouths of African slaves taking refuge and intermarrying with Creek Indian tribes. Grandmere lost its accent on the tongues of Black Americans who would later fight for recognition from Native American leagues.

Ida Mae had always considered her complexion more trouble than it was worth. She did not like the attention it brought from men—Black and white alike—nor the distrust it instilled in women. She wore her long hair braided and wrapped into a tight bun at the base of her skull. She married the darkest man she could find and prayed to have Black baby boys. When her daughter Luella was born, she kept a careful watch over her and prayed that Luella could enjoy her childhood before male attention infringed upon it. But to Ida Mae's chagrin, something far worse occurred. Luella's own desire was ignited much earlier than anticipated. She welcomed the attention far too soon, and Ida Mae found herself to be a grandmere and raising Cornelius alone in 1920.

"'Nelius, if you wanna eat, then I spec' you best gits to dem eggs," she spoke from her bed into the stillness of the room.

"Yes'm," Cornelius muttered and shoved the brush back into the sack. Cornelius slid from the pallet and into a pair of overalls over his skivvies. Rubbing the sleep from his eyes, he shoved his feet into boots, grabbed the tin bucket by the door, and exited.

Outside he paused and sighed deeply before trudging through the mud-caked path toward the outhouse. Once he relieved himself, he continued on the path as the brush became slightly denser until he reached the well. He filled the bucket and enjoyed a cool drink before returning to the house.

The routine they shared was well established. He deposited the bucket inside the door and returned outside to collect eggs from the chicken coop. Ida Mae bathed in his absence and began preparing breakfast—usually fried ham, biscuits, and eggs upon his return. While she finished breakfast, he bathed. They completed their chores with their backs turned to one another, the only privacy the small shack afforded.

They usually ate in silence with the sporadic interruption of Ida Mae's humming. She hummed pieces of church music. Sometimes her speech was even punctuated with humming between sentences. There was much that Cornelius could ask her, but he'd learned years ago not to question her and still had the mark on his forehead from the cast-iron skillet that had ended his inquiries about his mother, unknown father, and absent grandfather. It was the only time she had struck him. She'd spent the hours afterward crying, rocking him in her arms, and praying for the two of them. Every night, she insisted that he speak his prayers aloud and that he include, word for word, his "crazy mammy and that no 'count, yella nigga that she run off with."

When the colored school was open—during the brief winter season, when the crops were withered and covered in frost—he attended to learn his numbers and letters. When it closed, during the planting and harvesting seasons, he continued to use what he'd learned in weighing their surplus goods and bartering them with neighbors or selling them in town to white folks, which he hated.

For them, the prices lowered, as well as his eyes. "Don't look 'em in the face," Ida Mae admonished.

"Why, Grandmere?"

"'Cuz dey always thinkin' we puttin' some kind of root on 'em," she tsked.

"*Can* we put one on them?"

"Hush yo' mouf, boy!" She gasped, but he had seen the small smile play on her lips.

There was no school now, not for the colored anyway. So after breakfast, Cornelius was allowed to run off into the woods.

"G'won git, boy. I don't know how you spec' to become a man in dis house watchin' me clean up after you," Ida Mae nudged him toward the door. "Check make sure dat mare ain't get out from the fence."

"Yes'm," he replied, flying out the door. In addition to raising Cornelius, Ida Mae's second-largest focus was on containing the mule. It was fairly large for its breed, the sterile offspring of a horse and donkey. She had named it after her daughter, Luella, and insisted that Cornelius check on it several times throughout the day.

Cornelius reached the small fenced area and slid to a halt. There was no mule in sight. The gate was slightly ajar, and Cornelius hoped that she hadn't gotten far. Following the trail of hoofprints perfectly preserved in the mud, he trotted again in the direction of the well.

"Lou!" he shouted for her, hoping that she would return on her own. Reaching the well, he faltered. The tracks grew dull where the ground hardened and brush took over. He scanned the area, his eyes stopped where the tree line began. There was a slight rustle. Cornelius shot toward it and was rewarded with a sight of the horse's rear end. But Lou was not alone. A figure was slung over her broad back.

"Hey!" Cornelius shouted. "What you doin' with my horse?"

Slowly the figure rose to a full sitting position and tugged gently at the reins encouraging Lou to a full stop. Cornelius heard a slight tongue click and saw the figure yank the reins to the left, turning the horse around to face him. His eyes widened, unsure of what to expect. He prayed that it wasn't a white horse thief. That would amount to one less horse, at the very least. He didn't want to think of what would happen in the worst instance. But the face that turned to him was just as dark as his own, and a lot harder. It was a hard-knock-life face, and the mouth was pulled into a tight grimace . . . or it could have been a weird smile. With a face like that, Cornelius couldn't tell.

"Hey there, lil man," the stranger said. "I found this ol' girl wandering around. Figured maybe she'd run off from home. But I ain't know where home was for her," he panted. "Guess it's a good thing you come along."

Cornelius remained silent as the man slid from Lou's back, which seemed to drain him of all energy. He stumbled and stabilized himself against Lou. "And," he continued, "dis ain't no horse, boy. It's a mule." He handed the reins to him.

"I know," Cornelius finally spoke, encouraged by his repossession of Lou. "Grandmere says she's an ass." At ten years old, he hadn't made the connection that the animal's name was an abbreviated version of his mother's. Had he been older, perhaps he would have been able to draw a parallel between Luella's running off and Ida Mae's near obsession with containing the mule.

The man laughed but stopped short and clutched his side. "Why don't you let me walk with you and this ass to get a drank from that well down yonder?"

Cornelius shrugged and began to walk, leading Lou and the man leaning heavily against her.

"So, you stay in that house down there, huh?" the man asked.

"Yessuh."

"With your grandma?"

"Yessuh," Cornelius repeated.

"You Luella's boy?" the stranger asked.

Cornelius stopped walking. This man knew his mother. He turned toward the man, full of questions. Before he could ask the first, the man collapsed. His face was covered in sweat. His jacket fell open to reveal a slit in his shirt and, beneath it, a slit in his side that was quickly soaking the rest of his garments.

Cornelius stepped back. The stranger's eyes were closed. Cornelius scratched his head and absently reached for Lou's reins. The stranger wasn't going anywhere. He could wait until Cornelius secured Lou in the yard and swiped some rags and things from the house.

After making sure that the gate was properly latched, Cornelius raced toward the house skidding to a halt just outside the door. Ida Mae did not allow running. He kicked off his boots and hopped across the threshold onto the wooden floor his grandfather had installed. It was the only thing Cornelius knew about the man—the house was built by him, and he had always been proud of the floors he had placed in them. It wasn't his grandfather's only construction. Impatient with the development of the water well, Ida Mae's husband had decided to construct his own. But wells are difficult to design and properly construct. Contaminants frequently were present, and the small community had voted to turn the Gaines construction into a dry well, a receptacle for water overflow. The dry well sat as a gaping mouth in the land, a parasitic twin to the prominent cemented structure that provided clean well water to the community.

"Boy, what's all that stompin' you doin' about on your grand-daddy's floors?" Ida Mae looked up from her quilting. But Cornelius was barely listening. He was busy watching her hands work with precision on the quilting squares and thinking of the stranger's gaping wound. Would it need to be sewn back together?

"'Nelius!"

"Ma'am?" he responded startled.

"Boy, where is your mind?"

"I . . . I found a . . ." he began, searching for a plausible expla-nation that would garner advice but not curiosity. Ida Mae was not one to help some strange man that had been stabbed. She'd be afraid that he was trouble. She certainly wouldn't want someone around that knew anything about his mother. He could say that he'd found a hurt possum. But ever the opportunist, his grand-mother would just want to add it to dinner. He could tell her Lou was hurt, but she'd insist on having a look for herself.

"Well?" Ida Mae demanded. "You found what?"

"A hurt dog," Cornelius sputtered.

"Hmph, and I suppose you want to bring the mongrel in here?"

"No, ma'am. I just wanted to see if I could patch him up."

Cornelius held his breath as Ida Mae took her time to answer. "You see about that mule?"

"Yes ma'am. She good. Even took her grazing by the well."

A worried look crossed Ida Mae's face. "Not that dry well." Cornelius shook his head.

"You stay away from that hole, boy. Ground's too loose. You liable to fall right in." Ida Mae paused. "Well, g'won then. Look in my needle box and get what you need. Nothing that looks new though!"

When he returned to the well, the stranger was still passed out. Cornelius drew water from the well and dipped a rag in it. He laid it on the stranger's head. After a brief pause and a sigh, he peeled back the man's shirt to reveal the wound, black around red edges. He took another wet rag and gently began to wipe around it. Once he finished, he sat looking at the needle and thread. Cornelius had never sewn anything in his life and was not sure how to go about stitching human skin. He picked up the needle and twirled it between his thumb and forefinger. Picking up the thread, he tried unsuccessfully to wind it through the eye of the needle.

"I'll take it from here," the stranger's raspy voice hissed.

Cornelius looked up, startled yet relieved. Silently, he handed over the needle and thread and busied himself picking at a callus on his hand while the stranger took three attempts before successfully threading the needle.

"You got a match?" the man asked.

"Huh?" Cornelius looked back down the path toward the house and shook his head.

"I s'pose your grandma don't know what you up to, huh?"

"Naw, suh," Cornelius admitted.

"Alright then. Guess I gotta do this the really old way," the stranger grinned. He placed the needle between his lips and gently drew it across, wetting it with his saliva. "It ain't exactly purifyin' by fire, but it's all we got."

"Is that really gonna help?" Cornelius asked.

"Well, we shole gonna see," the man answered. "But I guess if it don't . . ." he began and then extended his hand to Cornelius. "They call me Deuce."

Cornelius accepted the handshake. "I'm Cornelius."

"Lil C. I like that." Deuce grinned, or rather Cornelius thought that it was a grin again. "Guess y'all ain't got no dranking liquor down at the house neither, huh?" Cornelius shook his head.

"Alright then, Lil C. Here it goes." Deuce began to stitch the wound. He managed to get about halfway done before he passed out again.

Cornelius leaned toward Deuce, afraid to shake him should it undo the stitching. He gently tapped Deuce's forehead with his index finger. "Mr. Deuce?" There was no response. He looked at the needle, stuck mid pull between the two sections of skin. He thought about his grandmother and still could not bring himself to go get her for help, perhaps saving Deuce but definitely risking the chance of finding out more about his mother from him. He wondered if this was what his grandmother meant about going off into the woods learning to become a man. With new resolve, he firmly grasped the needle and slowly pulled it and the trailing thread through the skin. He tried not to focus on the blood collecting on the string or on the gentle resistance the skin supplied as the tension brought it together in what was appearing to be a very successful stitch.

He took his time and exhaled as he finished. Cornelius continued to hold the needle at the end of the stitch. He thought back to Ida Mae darning socks and repairing buttons, how she would bring the thread to her mouth and sever it from the needle with a quick bite. Deuce's blood coated the needle and thread. The sight of which caused Cornelius's stomach to churn. Whenever he tried to release the needle, the stitching grew slack, so he held on to it, maintaining the tension. Frantically, he looked around for a sharp rock, shard of glass, or anything that would cut the thread. Sliding his free hand across the ground, he found nothing. He wondered how long he had been outside. His grandmother would be cross, then worried, then come looking.

His palm was covered in dirt and the bloody fingers of his

other hand were beginning to cramp from pinching the needle so tightly. He roughly wiped the dusty hand on his overalls and then used his fingers to try to wipe some of the blood from the thread. But the more he wiped, even as he tried to be gentle, the more it tugged and caused additional bleeding. The sun seemed to be disappearing beyond the tree line. Cornelius took a deep breath, clenched his eyes shut, and swiftly brought the thread to his teeth and severed it near the eye of the needle. He spat several times until his mouth was free from the imagined taste of blood and dirt. Deuce still had not stirred. Cornelius tied a double knot near the wound and left the excess thread standing erect from the body. There was no way he was using his teeth again for that. Deuce could take care of that later.

"Mr. Deuce?" He gently nudged Deuce's shoulder and repeated his name until the man began to slowly regain consciousness. Deuce opened his eyes and winced. He licked his dry lips and Cornelius held a cup toward him.

Deuce drained it and cleared his throat. "Lil C, right?"

Cornelius nodded. "Mr. Deuce—"

"Just Deuce," Deuce interrupted.

"We gotta git you somewhere. You need me to fetch somebody for you?"

Deuce sat up quickly. It was the most alert Cornelius had seen him. "Nawl, Lil C. You ain't got to fetch nobody for me. I need to lay low for a while. Git myself together. Let's let folks think that ol' Deucey is outta the picture for a while."

Cornelius nodded unsure of what Deuce meant. "So, what you gonna do? Where you gonna go?" he asked, fearing the answer.

Deuce grimace-grinned wide and chuckled before grabbing his side. He looked down at the stitches. "Not bad, Lil C, not bad at all. You got ol' Deucey in yo' favor, and trust me, it's a good one to have. I just need one mo' thang."

Cornelius's small frame shook as he helped Deuce to his feet and then down the path to the chicken coop. He hoped that Grandmere didn't come out of the house and catch them or there would be holy hell to pay. As they slowly made their way, Deuce explained that he was a "bidnessman," which meant numbers runner. There had been a "disagreement" (fight) between Deuce and a "client" (gambler) over whether the client had bet on the number that hit. The client "got the best of" (stabbed) Deuce.

"But," Deuce said as he settled in the corner of the chicken coop, "dis will all blow over soon 'nuff. I got plans to expand my bidness, and I thank that I could use a lil soldier like you, Lil C." With great effort, Deuce dug into his pocket and retrieved a five-cent piece and handed it to Cornelius. "Whatcha thank 'bout that?"

Cornelius took the coin and smiled. Other than selling produce in town, he wasn't allowed to have any money. "What I gotta do?"

Deuce's eyelids began to droop. "We'll talk about it when you come by and feed these chickens. I know Ida Mae ain't gonna brang her hummin' ass out here and do it."

Cornelius's eyes widened. He wanted to know what else Deuce knew about Grandmere. Before he could say a word, Deuce was out again. Cornelius silently crept out of the coop. Ten-year-old Cornelius figured that he had time.

ELEVEN

hell on wheels

John Henry hammered on the right-hand side.
Steam drill kept driving on the left.
John Henry beat that steam drill down.
But he hammered his poor heart to death, Lord, Lord,
He hammered his poor heart to death.
—"The Ballad of John Henry"

The history of the railroad is analogous to the development of the country. By the time the Civil War began in 1861, there were thirty thousand miles of track. Chinese workers blasted through mountain rock in the west to create tunnels. Irish immigrants, former Confederate and Union soldiers, and ex-slaves worked side by side spiking down tracks. The Central Pacific Railroad Company moved from west to east while Union Pacific worked from east to west. Coal-fueled, the trains literally puffed as they advanced toward their goals. Wherever it went, people flocked and boomtowns—gambling houses, brothels, and saloons—sprang in its wake. These portable towns catered to the railroaders and sprouted and withered along with the railroad's arrival and departure. They were havens for outlaws and violence, which prompted a Massachusetts newspaper editor to label the towns "Hells on Wheels."

Railroad company names often included "Pacific" or "Western" to boldly imply their destination, although many never actually delivered on it. The Mobile and Gulf Railroad, a mere eleven-mile stretch, wasn't anywhere near Mobile or the Gulf. The Atlanta, Birmingham and Atlantic became AB&A, and eventually the "Bee Line." Although it may have begun as hundreds of separate companies, mergers from its inception well into the twentieth century saw the individual railroads drawn to each other like drops of mercury combining into one solid puddle: the Railroad. The Railroad revealed itself to be the Frankenstein-stitched seams of America, connecting land and corporate interests.

The Railroad named towns. Townspeople renamed railroads. Railroads renamed towns. In 1907 two AB&A executives stopped in a little town in Macon County, Georgia. One said to the other, "Now this is an ideal place for a railroad." The other replied, "I agree. I also think you've just named it." Ideal, Georgia, was christened, which is what happens to things, people, and places that have already been born but have yet to be accepted. In naming it, the Atlanta, Birmingham and Atlantic Railroad Company had literally placed Ideal on the map—a cartographic illustration of the value parceled out to tracts of land that have business interests tied to them. Specifically, Ideal was placed on the main line between Birmingham and Brunswick.

Unlike its western cousins, Ideal was no boomtown. Still, the Railroad imparted power. A town that had a depot had a portal to the rest of the world. This was of particular interest to those who needed to move large quantities of goods. To look closely at the seams of America is to see not only railroads as the stiches, but corporations, banks, and criminal enterprises as the inextricably twined filaments of the stitching thread. The Railroad delivered casks of liquor until Prohibition in January 1920, and America quickly learned that enacting a law and enforcing it were two violently different processes as big-city white mobsters found a more profitable, if risky, business venture.

Mobsters stole two freight cars' worth of alcohol from a Chicago rail yard and four casks of grain alcohol from a government warehouse. Prohibition agents became compromised. Violence was on the rise. And small-time racketeer Deuce learned that alcohol had become more currency than commodity when he was unable to pay back a debt in whiskey and was stabbed.

Seven years later, Italian mobsters like Al Capone could move Tennessee whiskey into Chicago via rail. Nucky Johnson illegally imported Irish whiskey into Atlantic City. But in 1927, seven years into Prohibition, local Black racketeers relied on a series of bootleggers and runners to manage small-scale local markets. Deuce had seventeen-year-old Cornelius.

The church service at the Holy Gethsemane Rock of Jesus Church of God in Christ began later than most. The choir started their first hymns just as other congregations in the area were filing out of the pews. In Ideal the roar of the trains drowned out chorus and message. Instead of competing, the church had pushed back the start of its morning service. The voice of God—via Bishop John St. Paul Delano Washington—could not compete with the roar of the coal-fired engine that shot through Ideal on Sunday mornings. Railroad time was precise. In fact, the Railroad had established standard time. How could a small-town church compete with that which gave the town life, name, and time itself?

Cornelius sat in the back pew of the church next to Deuce.

Cornelius had grown tall and wide, while Deuce seemed to have shrunk. They sat glaring at Bishop Washington as he sauntered across the small floor at the front of the church.

"To the gamblers!" he screeched at the small congregation, startling a timid man with his pointed finger, "dere is Jeeeeesus!"

"To the whoremongers!" Bishop pounced toward the row of elderly women clad in all white, "dere is Jeeeeeeeeesus!"

Cornelius and Deuce sat stoically, continuing to stare at Bishop and the five-member choir that swayed behind his every movement, singing exclamations of "Yes, Jesus!" The ten-pew church swayed, and Bishop danced. Cornelius could see Grandmere in the front pew with the rest of the mothers board, her white dress gleaming, her hat enormous. When Bishop slid to that side of the church, most of his massive body was obscured behind the hats of the mothers board.

Cornelius and Deuce were not there for Jesus. The good minister had some bad habits. A faint scar ran down his face like the Mississippi River. Slightly discolored, it squiggled diagonally across from his widow's peak, crossed the space between his left eye and nose, and hit the corner of his mouth before dropping off at the cliff of his chin. He had received the scar and his call to ministry during the same experience. But the scar more than likely preceded the calling.

"If you don't know Jeeeesus," Bishop continued, "then come know him through me!" Bishop was not a religious title. It was his first name. Years before and several towns away, it had saved his life. Throwing back his arms, Bishop lifted his head toward the wooden rafters. A quick motion of his hands started the choir singing, "Come to Jeeeesus . . . Come to Jesus . . . just now . . ."

"Come to Jesus," Bishop beckoned, and the congregation rose.

Entranced, they marched toward him. His new flock had replaced those previous associations of adulterous rendezvous. When he was caught dangling from a married woman's bedroom window, the husband mistook Bishop's name for a title. He spared what he thought was a wayward preacher's life but left the scar as a reminder. It couldn't have been any clearer to Bishop that it had been a sign.

As each person made their way in turn to Bishop, he blessed them, grasping their foreheads just long enough for the cold metal of his prominent pinky ring to press uncomfortably into the skin, and then nudging them headfirst toward the collection dish. They obliged by digging out coins and crumbled bills before making their way to the crowded exit to wait for Bishop, hoping to snatch a moment of additional time for counsel or a handshake.

Deuce's eyes opened slowly as if emerging from meditation. He rolled his head, allowing his neck to crack. He had mentored Cornelius closely over the years, and neither corrected anyone who mistook them for father and son. As they made their way in line toward Bishop, Deuce switched places with Cornelius pushing him in front. "This one's all you, Big C. Make it good."

Cornelius's stomach churned with excitement. He had been waiting for Deuce to give him the opportunity to step up. Already at seventeen, he had three young runners working under him. He had helped expand Deuce's "bidness," first serving as a runner and then as a collector for those who didn't have trouble settling their accounts. Now it seemed he was finally making his way to being muscle. He reached Bishop, and as the "hand of Jesus" reached toward his skull, he grabbed it and clasped his other hand to Bishop's shoulder drawing him close into a confidential hug. He dropped his shoulders to lend the appearance of one humbly seeking counsel, yet the words he whispered into Bishop's ear did not match his physical demeanor. When he pulled away and released Bishop's hand, fear was on the preacher's face. He and Deuce walked past the collection plate and out of the church. They climbed into the Model T and did not speak until they had made their way about a quarter of a mile down the road.

"Bishop John look like he was gonna shit hisself," Deuce laughed. "What you say to him?"

"I tole him he was gonna git to Jesus sooner than he liked if he ain't have that money by tonight," Cornelius chuckled, maneuvering the automobile on the small dirt road.

"Boy, you movin' up in the world. I knew you was good luck from when you stitched me up," Deuce's laugh became a hacking cough. He grabbed a handkerchief and spat, balling it up and shoving it into his pocket.

"Deuce—"

"Don't," Deuce warned. "I ain't dealin' wit no damn doctors. When it's my time to go, it's my time to go. And I ain't goin' jes yet."

"But I think you should—"

"Boy, when the hell I ever give rat's ass 'bout what you thank?" Deuce growled, silencing Cornelius. He sighed and lightened his tone. "You downright ornery, you know. Yo' mama could be the same way."

Cornelius's hands tensed on the wheel. He had asked Deuce many questions about his mother over the years but was scarcely rewarded with anything more than what he'd already known. Now, Deuce was volunteering information. "Tell me."

Deuce nodded. "Yeah, I guess it's 'bout time."

"You my daddy?" Cornelius asked. Fear crept into his stomach. It was the one question he hadn't previously been able to ask. He'd never wanted and not wanted anything so much. The not knowing, for him at least, strengthened their relationship. The possibility was stronger than any definitive answer, and Cornelius feared the loss of it.

Deuce chuckled. "I guess I got 'bout as much of a chance as anyone in dis county. But I 'spect you know that yo' mama was . . . friendly." Yet his mother, Luella, had not been friendly in the way that Deuce implied. She had been young and somewhat foolish for the times. But in the tradition of Romeo and Juliet, she had fallen for the wrong man.

Cornelius nodded, but he could not have understood the full ramifications. Luella was a young colored girl and the presence of the Railroad had provided a number of wrong men. But Luella's wrong man was a white foreman who had his sights set on her father's land. History rewrites conquests as love stories in the tradition of Thomas Jefferson and Sally Hemings. Who knows if the foreman loved Luella. What is true is that he courted her. He impregnated her. What is also true is that he continued to be with her even when it was clear that he would not get her father's land. And he remained in Ideal far longer than was required. He stayed through Luella's pregnancy, right up to the birth of Cornelius, the surprisingly dark child that shared his first name instead of his surname. When the child was born, he left for the evening train and did not return.

"But, nawl, I ain't yo' daddy. Probably been the closest thang you had to one though," Deuce continued. "She got knocked up wit you, and dere was some talk 'bout who the daddy might be, but when you come out all dark like you done . . . well, ain't nobody know nothin'. Yo' mama shole did thank the sun rose and set on them yella niggas."

Luella had waited for the pigment in her child to set. It was widely known that babies were born lighter and became darker. She had hoped that the opposite could be true. Having endured the whispers about her interracial affair, the birth of her child incited new rumors. It was a horrible offense to sleep with the enemy. It added salt to injury to sleep around as well. To the people of Ideal, Luella was not only a traitor but a whore. There was no need to place a scarlet letter on her bosom. The dark child she carted with her was the constant reminder. After three years of shame, she left Cornelius with his grandmother and fled to New Orleans with a man who made more promises than she could hold in mind at one time. Luella didn't care whether he could keep them. She just wanted out.

"Well then, who was around that coulda been it?" Cornelius pushed.

Deuce grew quiet and thoughtful. "Ain't nobody I know of."

Yet that hadn't stopped people from openly speculating. Wives accused husbands. Men mockingly teased their friends. And a few who had their intentions rebuked in the past by Luella, braggingly credited themselves. Small-town conspiracy theorists of the time even posited that her own father had taken advantage. It was this particular idea that caused Deuce's silence.

A surge reached into the pit of Cornelius's stomach and hurled up his next words. "I'm goin' to Nawlins."

"Sho you don't wanna save yo'self the trip and try talkin' to Ida Mae again?"

"Grandmere ain't talked about it this long. She goin' to the grave wit it, I guess."

Deuce lifted his left eyebrow but said nothing at first. "You even remember what she look like?"

Cornelius shook his head no.

Deuce clucked his tongue. "Well, I wouldn't go round there

messin' around wit any yella womin down there till I was sho. Zebras cain't change they stripes, boy." He strolled away, leaving a look of bewilderment on Cornelius's face.

When the AB&A pulled out of Ideal the next morning, Cornelius was on it. In LaGrange he transferred to the Louisville and Nashville's West Point line with its luxurious vestibule equipment. The Crescent Limited brochure boasted about the vestibule experience—movement between cars via enclosed vestibules. Passengers could move freely from one car to the next without exposure to high winds and the train's eighty-mile-per-hour speed. The addition of vestibules and intercar movement soon brought dining cars and parlors to the rail-travel experience. But Cornelius did not experience any of these features.

The arrangement of train cars reflected 1927's social hierarchy. The locomotive engine emitted large amounts of smoke and cinder, and privileged-class passengers were seated as far away from it as possible. After the locomotive engine was the mail and baggage car. Cornelius sat in the first passenger coach, the "Jim Crow car." Designed by the Pullman Company for short-distance travel, the basic car consisted of two rows of bench seats able to be reversed depending on the direction of travel. When used as a Jim Crow car by the Railroad, signs marked "Colored" were displayed at the entryways. Cornelius sat in the packed car and gazed at the sign.

Pressed next to him on the bench, a Pullman porter struggled to free his foil-wrapped lunch with minimum motion. The bench wasn't ideal for its two solidly built occupants. Despite his cautious movements, the porter periodically jabbed Cornelius with his elbow, smiling apologetically each time. As a peace offering, he held out a drumstick to Cornelius. Cornelius shook his head and muttered a thank you, but his growling stomach drowned it out. He accepted the chicken and quickly devoured it.

"Where you heading?" the porter asked, offering a biscuit and his extra bottle of Coca-Cola.

"Nawlins," Cornelius answered between bites.

The porter smiled. "'Fraid not, my friend."

"Don't this train go there?" Cornelius reached into the inside pocket of his jacket and retrieved the train schedule.

"Well, normally."

"What you mean?" Cornelius frowned.

"New Orleans is under water, son. Nothing's going in or out of there. And if you want my advice, from what I've seen, colored men need to stay far away."

"Well, from what I've seen," Cornelius responded, "there many places colored men need to stay away from."

The porter chuckled. "That's the God's truth."

"So, what's Nawlins doing to us now?"

The porter sighed, and his eyes grew heavy. "What you think? City's flooding and they standing on the backs of colored men, trying to stay afloat. They're snatching folk off the roads and forcing them to dig it out."

Cornelius's face fixed into a hard determination that the porter recognized. "Look here, son. You're young and you're strong. You think you can handle yourself, and I'm sure that most times you can. But right now, you're exactly what they're after down there."

Cornelius turned his head toward the window and stared. The porter sighed, cleared his lunch scraps, and rose. He'd return to his duties in the sleeping car section. While Cornelius would be turning over in his mind where he was going, the porter would be turning down seating into sleepers, brushing off his charge's coats, and finding a small space to wrap himself in the blue-dyed blanket that was issued to porters after a lifetime of warming white patrons.

Hours later, he'd be relieved to see Cornelius exit in the small town of Pascagoula, Mississippi.

Cornelius exited the train depot and walked toward a small storefront where several colored men sat shaded from the summer heat. They were older, perhaps Deuce's age, give or take a few years. One was thin; another wore a hat pulled low over his face and appeared to be sleeping. He made sure to make eye contact with each as he nodded and spoke clearly, "G'afternoon, y'all. It's a hot one, ain't it?"

The slender one grinned, revealing two gaps in the space where his front teeth should have been. Cornelius pretended not to notice.

"Boy, dis is *Mis'sippi*. Dey all hot ones!" Snaggletooth laughed, not bothering to wipe at the sweat that was slowly dragging down his face. "Where you comin' from?"

"Macon County, suh."

"Aw, well hell, you ought to know 'bout heat." Snaggletooth paused and took a long sip from a bottle of Coca-Cola. "Where you headed?"

"Nawlins, suh."

"Nawl, you ain't," one of the others broke his silence. "Nawlins is under water. Been that way for a couple of months now."

Cornelius directed his attention toward the speaker. "I ain't scared of no damn water."

"Shoot, son, if da *Mis'sippi* take up in its mind to let loose like it done, it could do it anywhere from way 'yond Chicago all way past Nawlins."

"And dat jes what it done too!" Snaggletooth chimed in. "This ain't jes some water you can wade in yo' swim trunks."

"So you ain't gonna make it. Can't nobody git cross dat Ponchatrain." Sleeping Hat concluded, finally lifting it to look Cornelius square in the face. "But that's the least of yo' worries, boy."

"It ain't safe for no Negroes to cross," the final porch dweller added. "I hear it's back to slavery times over dere. Dey roundin' up as many of us as dey can and makin' them dig Nawlins out of mud!"

"And you don't wanna muss up yo' fancy clothes!" Snaggletooth laughed, sending the rest of the porch howling.

Cornelius plopped down on the store's porch and slapped his handkerchief against his thigh. He no longer cared about the Sunday suit he had worn especially for this trip, which began in his mind as a search for his mother but had evolved with each passing mile into an introduction to big-city living, a place from which he could return as someone who knew of things outside Macon County. He had enjoyed it when Deuce called him Big C and wanted to live up to the persona the name insinuated.

"So, what's so special in Nawlins?"

Cornelius exhaled. He didn't know who the question came from this time. It no longer mattered. They seemed to speak as a single unit, filling in parts of the same story. "I'm looking for . . ." He paused, unsure of how much to divulge.

"A woman?" Snaggletooth interjected. "Dressed like that you gots to be lookin' for some tail." The porch erupted in laughter again.

This time Cornelius smiled. "Well, suh, actually I—I am," he stammered. "Not for tail, I mean—a woman. I'm lookin' up some kinfolk I got down dere."

Sleeping Hat sucked his teeth, his eyes were once again concealed by the wide brim. "Lot of dem folk up here now. You might want to stick around for a few days. Dangerous for a young Negro to be movin' around."

The quieter of the three spoke again: "Who dat you say you lookin' for?"

"Her name Luella. Luella Gaines." Cornelius anxiously searched their faces. There was a scratch of a chin, an adjustment of a hat, and a last drain of Coca-Cola, but nothing that looked like recognition.

"We don't know all dey names, the ones that come up here, but most night dey over dere at one of dem juke joints . . ."

Snaggletooth interrupted the quiet one, "Aw, you should go to Junior's!"

"Junior's?"

"Yeah, Junior's Bait Shop. Dey got a fish fry tomorrow. Every Friday."

"Alright," Cornelius responded. "What's the other one?"

"The other place," Sleeping Hat said.

"Yeah," Cornelius answered. "What's it called?"

Snaggletooth laughed, "That *is* what it's called . . . The Other Place." More laughter from the porch. Cornelius joined in. Snaggletooth finally wiped the sweat from his neck. "So, you gon' stick around then?"

"Look like it."

"Well, in dat case . . . me an' da missus run us a little board-inghouse—nothin' fancy, but clean. Um . . . you got any money?"

Cornelius had quite a bit of money, but he was no fool. "I got a little." He sat straighter, working to communicate that his youth told nothing of his strength.

Snaggletooth grinned. "Aw, don't go swellin' up, young buck. I jes wanna make sho you can pay somethin'."

"How much?"

"Five dollars a week."

Cornelius pretended to think. Then he slipped his hand in his pocket and pretended to count. After waiting a few seconds, hoping that Snaggletooth got the impression he was short on money, he responded, "Well, alright. I shouldn't be here no longer than that, I reckon."

Snaggletooth grinned, "Well, c'mon then. Let me show you."

———————

Junior's was indeed a bait-and-tackle shop, at least in part. The rear section of the building, with its haphazardly built room additions, lent a spacious area where a three-man band played blues. As Cornelius' eyes adjusted to the darkened room, he realized why Snaggletooth had recommended the place.

"Welcome to Junior's!" Snaggletooth embraced Cornelius and clapped him on the back. "I'm Junior." He continued to hold Cornelius's elbow and guided him to a table in the corner. "Set right here and you can see e'rybody."

Cornelius settled into the rickety chair and scanned the room. Junior was right: it was a great view of the entire place, and of the door. He had learned from Deuce to never sit with his back to a door and to always keep it in clear view. Cornelius took another look, this time slowly taking in each person. He searched the faces of the women, keenly aware that he no longer remembered his mother's face. His suit began to feel tight on his body. He slid a finger into his collar in an attempt to loosen it. Although he wore the same suit, he had changed shirts and shined his shoes. Looking at the scattering of men, he felt appropriately dressed.

Junior appeared, slapping down a mason jar filled with clear liquid. "Here, son, try some of this shine." Moonshine is strong enough to power an automobile, and everyone makes theirs differently. Some distill it from corn, others from potatoes. Just as Cornelius reached for the glass, four red-painted nails curled around it. He followed the hand up the slender, golden-brown arm to the face. The woman smiled before gulping half of the glass down. She seductively licked her full lips. "It ain't half bad, shug."

Junior gave his trademarked toothless grin. "Wish I could say the same 'bout you." He looked at Cornelius, "G'on finish dat, and watch out for dis lady. She'll drank you under the table."

Cornelius looked at his tablemate and examined her face. She was older, maybe younger than his mama, but maybe not. He hadn't had much experience with women and was set on heeding Deuce's advice. "They call me Big C."

"Mmm," she murmured. "Why dey call you dat?"

Cornelius smiled. "Maybe later. What can I call you?"

"You can call me whatever you want. But buy me a drink first."

Junior, seemingly privy to some private joke, arrived unsummoned with another jar of shine. Glancing at Cornelius's glass, he slid the lipstick-rimmed glass in front of the woman and placed the new glass in front of Cornelius. "Baby Girl, at least let the man have a drank to hisself." He disappeared before she could respond. Once again, Cornelius stared into her face.

"Baby, you keep looking at me like that and you'll go blind."

He tried a different approach. "So, where you from?"

"Oh, round about. You?"

Cornelius took a sip of the shine and clenched his jaw shut as it burned his throat and stomach. When he could speak again, he answered in a voice that had been scratched and deepened by alcoholic conflagration. "Macon County."

"Is that right? I got some people up that way."

"Yeah? Who? I might know 'em."

"Aw, shug, they probably long gone by now. I mean, maybe not that long ago . . . I'm still young, you know." She winked.

Cornelius continued to sip and began to feel the burning give way to another, more pleasant sensation in his chest. "Anyone can see that." And suddenly, he could see youth beyond the rouge and eye shadow, and perhaps a few years past, but he was starting to see it. She reached across the table and stroked his hand. Cornelius recoiled.

"Aw, don't worry, shug. I can go slow."

His lips felt dry. He licked them, sipped the shine, and stretched his neck to clear his vision. He looked at the woman and cleared his throat. "What's your name?"

"You still stuck on that, shug?"

Slowly, at first, then quickly he saw her spin around him, still seated. He shook his head trying to stop it. When that didn't work, he reached out and clutched her arm. "Who are you?"

The woman yanked her arm back, knocking over his glass in the process. "Turn loose my goddamned arm! Look, I was just trying to make nice, knowing you was new in town, but you ain't got to be grabbing me." She stood and left him steadying himself against the table.

Junior was at his side in seconds. "Son, sometimes it's jes a slow-hand, easy touch, know what I'm sayin'? You really pissed Josephine off good."

"Josephine?" Cornelius muttered.

"Yeah, Josephine. She's a tough little gal, but still a woman, you know what I'm sayin'. Uh, soft-like. You cain't be too rough on 'em."

"Josephine . . ." Cornelius repeated and weaved his way toward the exit.

Junior grabbed his shoulder. "You alright there, son?"

Cornelius stopped and turned to face Junior, "You my daddy now?" he slurred.

"Huh? Boy, you gotta speak up! The band getting started again." Junior shouted in his ear. Cornelius nodded but continued to shuffle out the door.

Cornelius spent the rest of the week sitting at the depot watching the trains pass. They were always timely. The 1401 hit Pascagoula precisely at 12:40 in the afternoon, Central Standard Time, as established by the Railroad in 1883. The Railroad insinuated itself into America's landscape and is often mistaken as a permanent fixture. But in truth, the Railroad is movement, a series of departures. Cornelius thought that he could board the same train and end up in the same place as Luella. But the Railroad is like a wormhole. Once boarded, it's not always clear where one may end up. Simply put, the Railroad moves, and some are just left behind.

TWELVE

birth of a mann

It's a long old road, but
I know I'm gonna find the end.
—Bessie Smith, "Long Old Road"

Johnita's Inn, a quaint two-story Georgian in the middle of Back Street, had been a boardinghouse and juke joint in a previous life and proudly listed in the *Negro Motorist Green Book* until about eight years prior to Eve's stay. Eve hadn't spoken much to Johnita after her initial arrival, and she gave only a cursory wave to the woman on her exit to meet Deuce. Eve flew out the door, propelled by a hunger for food and a thirst for whatever information Deuce could share about her family.

Much to the delight of Deuce and his wife, Evelyn, Eve ate ravenously, and as he and Eve sat on the large wraparound porch afterward, Deuce felt the intensity of her gaze and knew that he could no longer foil her questions with dinnertime pleasantries.

"Mr. Deuce, what can you tell me about my grandfather?" Eve once again extended the photo.

Deuce hesitated before taking it in his withered hand and

smiled at the memory of Cornelius addressing him in the same way so long ago. He wondered if there existed a best way to share information with one who is entitled to know it while respecting the privacies of those who had lived it. He glanced at Evelyn, and upon receiving a barely perceptible nod of approval, answered, "I can tell you that that ain't him." He pointed to Cornelius, allowing his index finger to linger slightly before returning the photograph. "Your granddaddy name was Hezekiah Mann. He come up this way as a boy from Flawda—that town the white folks burn down back in '23."

Eve's face twisted in confusion. "This is not my grandfather?"

Before Deuce could respond, Evelyn chimed in, "Nawl. That's somebody else."

Questions flew through her mind at lightspeed. Who was the man? Why wasn't her grandfather pictured? But as Deuce began to speak, the slow tenor of his voice lulled her into a calm. As storytelling goes, there were some omissions. There were some things that he didn't know. But in small southern towns, too many people know too much of what they shouldn't about others, anyway. But there were also other things that Deuce just didn't feel comfortable telling. In recounting Hezekiah's story, omissions occurred quite naturally on several levels—at the intersection of an elder addressing a younger person, a man addressing a woman, and a southerner addressing an outsider.

———

Deuce told Eve that her grandfather was a proud man who loved his family, especially his children. He did not share that Hezekiah also loved to drink and gamble. Hezekiah Mann mostly loved to

189

do everything on a large scale. His passion for women other than his wife had made things difficult at home. But it wasn't entirely his fault. Gertrude's passion was reserved for the Lord, and there hadn't seemed to be anything left over for Hezekiah. One opinion on the matter, mostly held by Hezekiah, was that it was Gertrude who was cheating on him, and it didn't matter that the receiver of her affections was Mr. Jesus H. Christ. Of course, it hadn't always been that way. But this was well beyond the scope of Deuce's knowledge and the range of his interest. It was Deuce's wife Evelyn who provided an additional layer of information regarding Hezekiah's courtship, which contained its own omissions. Had Evelyn known them, she wouldn't have approved or shared. Had Deuce known, he would have simply seen it as a rite of manhood, a man learning the things that men need to know before marriage and that women wait to learn through marriage.

Hezekiah spent a year courting Gertrude in the summer of 1932. He would have proposed marriage the first day they met, he later boasted to friends. It was Gertrude who needed the time to fall in love with him. He enjoyed the challenge of exercising restraint in his courtship.

Hezekiah's courtship of Gertrude was an enviable fairytale that, if one must view it as a trope, had to end tragically. Hezekiah's wooing was worthy of folklore.

During their initial walks, he never made a move to touch Gertrude. He walked close enough that their shoulders nearly touched, and his eyes sparkled when he looked at her, but it was Gertrude who initiated hand contact, reaching for his as they strolled among the tree-covered area east of town. He gently squeezed her fingers and continued to point out the different varieties of trees to which neither paid much notice. The heated sensation pulsating within their clasped hands crept up their arms, making it difficult for each to concentrate. Yet they pretended to be unaffected and trudged on past the spot where the old dry well lay broken and exposed, a gaping hole in the earth. Holding hands became a permanent component of their daily walks. Sometimes they would swing their arms as children. Other times, their arms hung rigid at their sides, fingers entwined.

They had managed to lengthen their walks by incorporating basket lunches. Hezekiah would carry the wicker basket that Gertrude filled with thick chunks of ham between slices of bread, fresh fruit, and jugs of lemonade. They would carefully wind their way to the dry well, where they would spread a blanket and relax into conversation between bites of food. When they were done, Hezekiah would toss the remains into the depths of the well and recline to feel the sun's warmth on his face. It was during one of these times that Gertrude leaned over and planted a soft kiss on his lips. Hezekiah opened his eyes and slowly returned the kiss.

Gertrude never took Hezekiah seriously whenever he talked about the large house he was building in an area near the place where they walked. To her surprise, Hezekiah's wagon stopped at the large house that was indeed constructed for their union. It was an impressive two-story home with a fresh coat of gleaming white paint.

Gertrude prepared a feast for their first meal as man and wife. When Hezekiah saw the spread of fried catfish, smoked ham, collard greens, sweet potatoes, biscuits, ho' cakes, and sweet potato pie he remarked, "Trudy, who gon' eat all dis food? We ain't even started workin' on young'ns yet."

Gertrude blushed and responded, "I guess I gots to git in practice."

Hezekiah smiled, hoping to comfort her apparent nervousness.

She seemed to be waiting for the impending deed of all honeymoons. Surely women have spoken to her about it, Hezekiah thought. But she didn't have to worry with him. He didn't want Gertrude cringing in pain when they joined. Hezekiah wanted her to feel the ecstasy that he would experience.

When they joined, Gertrude could not stop her body from moving in a way that was foreign to her mind. She was certain that it had never performed such a dance, yet her hips rolled of their own accord. She was no longer in control of her body. Hezekiah was a puppeteer manipulating her with his hands and mouth. She could only hold onto his shoulders as she cried out for Jesus in a way that had never happened in church. There was a final burst of electricity that jolted through her body, and her throat went hoarse from utterings she could not later remember speaking. They lay spent in each other's arms.

"Wuz dat how you thought it wuz gon' be?" he asked, still nuzzled in the hollow of her neck.

"No. Ain't nobody ever said nothin' like what I felt," she answered, absently stroking his thigh. "I ain't neva felt so wonderful, Hezekiah."

But along with sexual satisfaction brewed guilt. Gertrude had been raised like all southern girls to remain chaste until marriage, unleash the pent-up energy for procreation, and then repackage it to be rationed out and scheduled like weekly pot roast meals. Gertrude was unable to reconcile her elation and her shame. She became equally eager and nervous to go to bed. At dinner, she fidgeted with the cornbread crumbs that had escaped her plate onto the table.

Noticing her preoccupation, Hezekiah grabbed her hand. "What's the matter, Trudy? You ain't happy?"

She lifted her eyes to meet his. "I . . . I'm . . ." She could not find the words to describe the ecstatic nights that overshadowed her mundane days. Hezekiah waited patiently. Taking a deep breath, she continued, "I'm so happy with you that I don't know how to be by myself."

Hezekiah grinned. "You jes needs a hobby . . . somethin' to do when um workin'." He continued to stroke her hand.

Gertrude felt heat rising from his touch. "Maybe I can help out at church."

"That's a good idea! Dey always tryin' to git folks up dere to be on committees and such." Hezekiah's fingers traveled up her arm, causing Gertrude to shiver in response. "You feelin' tired?"

"No!" she answered more forcibly than she had intended, but she did not want to miss out on any of the night's activities.

Hezekiah smiled. "Well, I guess you wanna stay up a while then?"

Gertrude's jaw dropped. She didn't want to stay up either. "No," she responded softly, lowering her eyes.

Hezekiah chuckled. He was playing with her.

Boldly she returned her gaze to his eyes. "Take me to bed, Hezekiah."

Three years, two children, and one church-volunteer job later, Gertrude's opinion had changed. She began to distrust the rapturous feelings of the physical intimacy. Waiting in the house for Hezekiah felt more wrong than right. She spent her days repenting the night's activities. Her nighttime prayers were frequently interrupted when Hezekiah knelt beside her, then behind her. She clutched the small thin cross at her neck, and it became unclear to whom her whispers of "sweet Jeezus" were directed. Eventually, Jesus the Christ won, and Hezekiah began his transformation into the man that Deuce struggled to describe to Eve decades later. But what neither Deuce nor his wife, Evelyn, could bring themselves to share with Eve was what she wanted to know most: what happened to her grandfather.

Hezekiah moved two towns over, to Montezuma, and kept company with the women of Macon County, who were just as neglected as he. Men who were too busy with their work, their gambling, and their own indiscretions urged their wives to "go to Mann" to fix broken chairs, holes in chicken coops, and leaky roofs; and Hezekiah Mann made those repairs and found himself also mending broken hearts, renewing self-confidence, and scratching incessant itches. Much can be said about gossiping housewives, but among the women of Ideal, not one uttered a word to their husbands or to Gertrude, who called many of them friends.

Every weekend, Hezekiah traveled the ten miles from Montezuma to Ideal to work the plot of land on which Gertrude's house sat. It was this land that fed them while most others were either starving or leaving by the busload to the North. Hezekiah worked, and his wife continued to beg him to return to their home and the church for good. For Gertrude, everything could be solved in the church. She was certain that all Hezekiah need do was give testimony in church and let everyone know that he had seen the error of his heathen ways and was ready to repent. In his mind, he would repent as soon as she was ready to do the same.

When Hezekiah did return a while later, it had nothing to do with repenting his heathen ways. Times were always hard for colored folk, but now even white folks were feeling the squeeze, which meant that it could only get worse. People were starting to steal anything they could lay their hands on. Hezekiah worried about Gertrude and their two small girls. Hezekiah loved both of his children, but he had a tender spot for Mercy. It was after her birth, the last of his children with Gertrude, that Hezekiah had felt the presence of God.

Holding that tiny brown form in his hands caused him to fill with so much energy that Hezekiah could not help but feel and believe in the presence of God. Gertrude attended church several days a week, and Hezekiah acknowledged that it was good for her. Anything that lifted the spirit was a good thing. Gertrude had the church, and Hezekiah had his own devices for elevating the spirit. With the birth of Mercy, he had one more to add to his pile. Hezekiah imagined that if Gertrude felt in church even half of what he felt around Mercy, he could understand her unwavering attendance.

It was these thoughts that kept him company on his return to Ideal. Hezekiah wanted to bring the girls some candy. He also thought that it would be appropriate to enter their house with money. Gertrude would probably need some things for the house. People could say much about Hezekiah, but no one could ever call him a man that did not support his family, even if he hadn't been living with them. Hezekiah didn't have much money with him, but he knew exactly where he could find more.

Before it became Johnita's Inn, where Eve lodged, Johnita's Place was a local boardinghouse frequented by her grandfather. Hezekiah and Johnita had at one time been very close before he met and married her cousin Gertrude. Since then, he had managed to frequent every other gambling spot in town, and there weren't many others from which to choose. Still, he reckoned that Johnita knew that what they had in the past was nothing more than a glorified friendship. It had been many years since he had lain in Johnita's bed. Yet when he entered the boardinghouse, she greeted him as if it had been not more than a week's passing. Hezekiah merely tipped his hat toward her and maneuvered his muscular frame past her with surprising agility. He ambled down the dark staircase toward the meandering cigar smoke and syncopated sounds of "Twelfth Street

Rag" competing against the hoots and hollers of the basement crowd.

"Hezekiah!" Johnita shouted at the quickly retreating figure. Hezekiah continued his downward stroll, oblivious to her calls. His mind was fixed on money, his girls, and whether Gertrude would be in a loving mood. They were still man and wife after all. That line of reasoning had served as adequate justification for their past couplings, but lately Gertrude had become more and more hesitant. Hezekiah considered her increasing aversion as cause to find sexual release from more willing participants. But now that he would be moving back, Gertrude would have to open up to compromise.

When Hezekiah walked into the basement, men greeted him with handshakes and women planted red lip marks on his face. He floated around leaving smiles on faces even as he glided away from poker tables with collections of money that would never make it to the landlords or grocers for which they were intended. Hezekiah was a gambler with an enviable streak of luck, and he loved to gamble, win or lose. As he eased past the crammed tables overflowing with cards, liquor, and chicken dinners, a pair of arms encircled his broad shoulders. Soft breasts pressed against his spine, and the scent of jasmine tickled his nostrils. Hezekiah took a moment to compose himself as he pulled away from the embrace and faced his smiling assailant.

"Claudette, ain't you got nothin' betta to do than try to get me kilt?" He could not help returning the smile as his gaze waltzed over the voluptuous frame snuggly housed in a bright red dress that matched her generous lips.

Claudette returned the gaze appreciatively and stroked Hezekiah's arm. "Well, shuga, least you git a taste of heaven 'fore you go."

Hezekiah shifted backward to place some distance between them. "I'm fo' real, woman. What you wanna play around wit me fo' when you got a big important man like Big C?"

"Well, maybe Big C ain't so big," Claudette responded, closing the gap that once was between them.

"Shh. Why you gotta be so loud and . . . and . . ." He glanced around.

"And sexy?" she supplied.

"I was gonna say wanton," Hezekiah finished. The crowded space seemed to facilitate Claudette's intention to get closer to him, and he could feel her hips pureeing against him. He placed his hands firmly on her waist and shoved her away. "Woman, thou art loose."

"Since when did you start quotin' scripture, sinner?" Claudette teased.

"Since the devil sent his concubine in here wearin' a red dress." Hezekiah countered.

Claudette pointed a red-tipped finger at her chest and feigned a look of surprise. "I know you ain't talkin' 'bout me, is you, Hezekiah?" Her voice was rising slightly, and he could smell the gin wafting through her ruby lips.

Hezekiah took hold of her elbow and guided her through the noisy crowd into a storage closet. He closed the door behind them. Claudette threw her arms around his neck. "Hezekiah, I thought you'd never—"

Hezekiah shoved her away. His jaw was locked in tension and his brows were furrowed. "Look, Claudette, you all woman. You know that. You got a lot of . . ." Hezekiah struggled for the words that would compliment yet discourage further advances. "You got a lot of gifts, Claudette."

"You don't know the half of it." She smiled and sauntered toward him.

"But I'm a married man." Hezekiah continued.

"That never stopped you before." Claudette grazed his chest with her palm. "E'ryone know that you like other women's . . . gifts. You layin' up with half the menfolks' women in here! So why not with me, Hezekiah?"

"Claudette, you know better than me." Hezekiah leaned on a shelf that held a variety of preserved fruits in mason jars. Each was clearly labeled in a script he recognized as belonging to Johnita. Yet Claudette's words rang true. He was a man whose demons had been out of control. With the return home, Hezekiah hoped that a change would come.

"Why you scared of Big C?" Claudette hissed at him. "Is he the only real man out there that want a real woman like me?"

The reality of her womanhood was that there wasn't a place for it in this world of racketeers, womanizers, and God-fearing women. Hezekiah was correct. Claudette was wanton, but it was a wantonness that defied the neat packaging of sexual desire. Claudette wanted more than she could have, more than there existed for her to have. She wanted more. She wanted forbidden love. In her eyes, she and Hezekiah were the same—two people trapped by other people's expectations.

"Yeah. I suppose that's why he called Big C." Hezekiah turned to exit.

"Don't you walk out on me, Hezekiah!" Claudette screamed at his back, pained by his lack of understanding and distraught by his inability to conceive of sex as comradery.

"Bye, Claudette."

"Hezekiah, wait."

Hezekiah paused as Claudette moved closer and placed her hand on his chest, tilted her lips to his ear and whispered, "Please. Take me with you tonight."

Looking into her eyes, Hezekiah saw fear, but he chose not to investigate further. He had his own family to tend to. "Just . . . just be a man about it, Claude."

Claudette recoiled with a sharp intake. "And you're supposed to be one of the good ones."

With a lowered head, Hezekiah quietly removed her hands and exited the pantry directly into the path of Big C.

"Hey, Big C." Hezekiah tried to think of something else to say, but it didn't matter. Big C tightened his lips around a cigar. He took a long pull and slowly exhaled the smoke into Hezekiah's face, then turned and walked away.

Hezekiah no longer felt the electric jolt of excitement to gamble. It had been replaced by an inexplicable sadness and a longing to see his family. That closet contained more than a contemptuous vixen. It held Truth. Hezekiah had come face-to-face with himself through Claudette's accusations. She had mirrored the licentious fiend within him. Hezekiah stayed a while longer, but his concentration had been broken and he quickly lost the money he had won earlier. The room was gradually emptying as the hour grew from late to early.

As was custom at the end of the night, Claudette took to the makeshift stage area and serenaded the late-night departure of drunkards and the house cleaning. Her presence commanded the full attention of remaining patrons. It had only been a week since she'd stumbled to the very stage, plied by gin and heartache from a frequent argument with Johnita.

"Johnny, please let's just leave this God-forsaken town! There are places where we can go. Bigger places that won't take notice . . ." she pleaded.

199

Johnita silenced her with a raised palm. "Claude, you don't have no attachments here, but I do! I have a business. Do you know how hard it is for a Negro woman to have a business? One that ain't washing white folks' drawls or cleaning they toilets?"

Their private arguments spread out to others like small rivers feeding into larger lakes. Johnita pressed against Hezekiah upon his arrival, and the previous week Claudette, intoxicated and impassioned, had taken the stage.

"It's not time yet, Claudette," the drummer hissed through bites of fried chicken.

"Just follow my lead, boys." Claudette's ruby lips glistened beneath the single light illuminating the stage. She wrapped her arms around the bassist's neck, loosened his necktie, and smoothly removed it. She placed the tie around her own neck, where it hung loosely against her bare neckline as she turned and faced her audience. Unlike at the end of the night, the room was filled to capacity.

Her voice rang clear and loud, slicing through the room. "Manly man!" She sang and shimmied around the stage. "A manly man wasn't enough for me."

The audience cheered and hooted as Claudette's invocation of the manly man became deeper. "My manly man cheated on me." They were drawn into her confessional as coconspirators and clapped and stomped their feet as the band found the rhythm.

"It seems the manly man I sought was me!" Claudette's song declared before inquiring toward a man at one of the card tables, "What do manly men do to deserve the soft touch of a woman?"

He responded lewdly with his tongue. Claudette smirked and pushed him back into his chair. The audience howled at the rebuff as she sauntered toward the back of the room, where Johnita stood, face stiffened with a mix of disbelief and fear.

"And if I must add tough to my womanhood in order to partake of that sweetness . . ." Claudette crooned.

Johnita shook her head and silently pleaded with her eyes for Claudette to end the song but to no avail.

Claudette's voice dropped and scratched as if coated in gravel. "Then call me daddy!" She swaggered back toward the stage. "Call me Claude! Call me, lover, and let me bulldagger on!"

The night rode the fervor, and Johnita's Place pulsated with the energy of a living, breathing organism complete with heart and blood but also a malignant mass within its walls. In a corner of the room, apart from the gyrating bodies, sat Big C with piercing eyes that never left Claudette's form.

A week later, he watched from the same seat. His eyes scanned the crowd and landed on Hezekiah faltering on the staircase before returning to a seat and training his eyes on Claudette on the stage. He followed Claudette's gaze past Hezekiah to Johnita slowly drawing on a cigarette at the back of the room.

Everyone moved in slow motion, breathing through the smoke and silence, waiting for Claudette's song. Wondering if it would resemble the boldness of the raunchy "Manly Man" or the usual sadness of a dying night yielding to the impending morning.

Claudette's eyes sopped up the sadness in the room and sought Johnita. Her voice caressed the lyrics, layering the refrain "this bitter earth" in beautiful despair.

> *This bitter earth / Well, what a fruit it bears*
> *What good is love / Mmm, that no one shares?*

And if my life is like the dust / Ooh, that hides the
glow of a rose
What good am I? / Heaven only knows

Hezekiah watched her, entranced. He would go home. He would spend more time with Ann, his older daughter. She was Gertrude's child in every way. A daughter that any father would be proud of, yet next to Mercy, Ann appeared so rigid. She obeyed Gertrude without question while Mercy questioned everything. He loved it! He felt more secure about Mercy growing into womanhood. She would be able to discern the types of men that could be trusted from . . . He hesitated in his thoughts as the honest completion to his sentence came to him. Mercy would be able to distinguish well-intentioned men from men who were like him.

Hezekiah was anxious to reach the warm shelter of home. His steps squished as his feet made contact with the mud-caked road. Sniffing the air, he surmised that the day's earlier rain was a mere sample of what was yet to come. The night sky growled its concurrence, and lightning briefly illuminated the horizon just enough for him to see the faint silhouette of the house as he trod toward it. He barely heard the approaching motorcar. He froze in his steps. A motorcar meant one of two things: white folks or Big C.

The Ford rolled alongside Hezekiah as a face loomed from the obscurity of its interior. The passenger door opened, and Hezekiah remained fixed. From the depths emerged the pinstripe-clad, 250-pound frame of Cornelius Gaines.

Hezekiah allowed himself to breathe but was still guarded. "I wouldn't spec' you out dis late, Big C."

"I ain't neva had no set bedtime, Hezekiah." Cornelius's voice was rolling thunder. A smile lit his dark countenance.

"I mean out the juke joints." Hezekiah's laughter allowed him to relax.

"Business don't sleep either." The smile disappeared from Cornelius's face, silencing Hezekiah.

"We got business, Big C?"

"'Fraid so, Hezekiah."

A glance toward the automobile revealed two more people. In the driver's seat sat Deuce. Stoic in the back seat, was Claudette. Hezekiah looked toward the road. He could just make out the stream of smoke from Gertrude's chimney. Big C moved closer and wrapped a large arm around his shoulder almost comfortingly. "Don't worry, Hezekiah." He soothed. "I'll take care of 'em."

Hezekiah struggled to think of the words that would inspire Cornelius to let him go. "I neva touched her, Big C."

Surprisingly, Cornelius laughed. "I know. But it's somethin' bigger than you and me. You know what dat is?" Hezekiah remained silent as he continued. "Big C is what dat is. Hell, we just men, Hezekiah. But it's the name, my name, dat's got bigger than even me. I got to protect it. It's all I got."

"I got family, Big C . . ." Hezekiah began. He looked pleadingly at Deuce who lowered his own eyes.

"Then you lucky!" Cornelius growled. "I got a wicked woman that—" he momentarily lost himself in the memory of Claudette sauntering the stage in a necktie before continuing, "a wicked woman that would see a man kilt than accept that he don't want her."

"But—"

"And . . ." He continued. "I got a name that so big round here that I gotta kill a man too dumb to know dat chickens always come home to roost and it don't matter whose chicken it is." Cornelius nodded toward Deuce and the car began to move away from them. They watched it a while in silence.

It was true that Hezekiah had not touched Claudette, but he was guilty just the same for the many women that he had touched. It didn't matter whose chickens; they always came home to roost. Cornelius's blade slid quickly beneath Hezekiah's rib cage, stealing his breath mid gasp. Hezekiah struggled to take one more breath as he slumped against the massive frame of his assailant. Cornelius caught him and held him gently. "I'll make sho yo' family eat and yo' girls be safe."

Hezekiah heard the words, but he was far more captivated by how bright the sky had gotten. His final thoughts were of his girls. He struggled to say their names one final time, Ann and Mercy, yet what he managed sounded instead like "Have Mercy . . ."

Cornelius nodded and made the sign of the cross over him. "Right. Lawd ha'mercy on yo' poor soul and mines." He continued his confession to the dying. His grandmother had taught him that it was one of the surest ways to achieve absolution. "And Claudette be finished in dis town. I worked hard for dis name. Ain't no way imma let some gal use it, spittin' venom round town and put me in a situation like dis." He paused and looked down into the staring eyes, open but no longer seeing. Cornelius's large palm gently closed them. "I gots a special place fo' dat gal."

The car returned and picked up its cargo, leaving only a small collection of blood to blend into the red clay dirt. Inside, Claudette sat nervously next to Cornelius. Her constant chatter grated on his nerves. A few miles up the road, Deuce pulled over.

"Where we goin', baby?" Claudette purred. Her thoughts were on returning to Johnita's. She was tired of her role and the play of keeping men so enticed that they'd dig no deeper than she allowed. She just needed to talk to Johnita and hoped that was where Cornelius was taking them. All she had wanted was for Hezekiah to walk her outside. The rumor mill would have taken care of the rest. She'd be called a whore and harlot and all manner of insults, but those would keep her and Johnita safe from what happens to women who choose each other over men.

"You and me goin' fo' a walk by the ol' dry well," he answered stoically.

"The well, baby? But no . . ." She stroked his arm, but he did not look at her.

Claudette was a wildcat, clawing and scratching. It had taken both men to remove her from the car and carry her into the woods. Deuce more than once suggested that they first silence her to make their work simpler, but Cornelius wanted to see the fear in her eyes for as long as possible. He wanted her to feel every moment, knowing her fate. Hezekiah deserved that much. Yet fear had not been a part of Claudette for a long time, and it made no presence on her countenance. Her face only projected hatred even as she struggled to breathe in the vice grip of Cornelius's last embrace.

A tear and a barely perceptible "Johnny" rode her final exhale, so faint that Cornelius couldn't be sure he'd heard anything at all.

Deuce and Cornelius stood for what seemed like an eternity at the edge of the dry well. "I ain't hear her hit bottom," Deuce said. "How long you figure it is to the end?"

"Ain't no end," Cornelius answered. "Grandmere always said dis ol' well go straight to hell."

———

If the dry well was the portal to hell, it had become a very busy thoroughfare for forgotten souls. Perhaps it was the reason that it took so long for stories to be resurrected.

Still, Eve would never know the particular details of her grandfather's demise, and she was too amazed and happy to have learned the little that Deuce and Evelyn shared to pry too much further.

When she asked, "How did Grandfather Hezekiah die?" Deuce and Evelyn shared a sideways glance. Deuce stared off across the yard, and Evelyn answered for him. "He fell down a well."

the wives' tales

There is a strange emptiness to life without myths.
—N. K. Jemisin, "Dreaming Awake"

Ancient Egyptians are credited with creating the first urine-based pregnancy test. According to a papyrus document dating back to 1350 BCE, pregnancy and gender could be determined by a woman urinating on wheat and barley seeds over several days. If the barley grew, then the child would be male—female if the wheat grew. If neither seed sprouted, the woman was not pregnant. A 1963 test of this theory found it to be 70 percent accurate.

The Mayans believed that the gender of an unborn child could be determined by taking the age of the mother and the year of conception and comparing the numbers. If both were odd or both were even, then the child was a girl. If one number was odd and the other even, then the child would be a boy.

The ancient Chinese used the mother's birthdate and the date of conception to determine the sex of the child.

Much later in other parts of the world, it came to be believed that if a woman carried the child high in her stomach, she would have a girl. If she carried low, then the child was a boy.

A ring tied on a string and held over the pregnant woman's stomach is said to reveal the child's gender by the way it moves. If it swings from side to side like a pendulum, it is a girl. It moves in a circle for a boy.

If a pregnant woman picks up a single key by the wide end, she is having a girl; the narrow end means she's having a boy.

If a toddler boy shows interest in a pregnant woman, then she will have a girl. If he shows no interest, then she's having a boy.

Perhaps one of the most troubling methods of all involves mixing the woman's urine with Drano. The Drano-urine mixture emits fumes that may be harmful.

In the rural south, during both the time of Eve's conception and her investigation into it twenty-two years later, the prevailing belief was that a dream about fish was the harbinger of pregnancy for a close personal acquaintance. Not quite satisfied with the information she had received, Eve made a second visit to Deuce and Evelyn's house, hoping that she could spend more time with Evelyn. There had been a sparkle in Evelyn's eye, a twinkle, as if she were holding on to something in her mind. Eve felt the connection with the older woman and tried to soften her own eyes to encourage sharing. She'd soon find that the only encouragement Evelyn required was a little cup of liquid courage or what she referred to as her "nip."

Evelyn didn't drink around Deuce. Growing older, he had "retired" from the early days of criminal activity and completely changed his lifestyle. This included getting himself a bona fide churchwoman and getting into the kingdom of heaven by marriage. He wanted to cover all the bases. It's not to say that he didn't love Evelyn. He had fallen in love with her very quickly. But certainly, her religious background had played a part. He had desired her chasteness, not as one who wanted to break it or own it, but as his very own vessel to God. In his mind, Evelyn had done all the grunt work toward salvation. Marriage to her, coupled with relinquishing his past endeavors, should land him on the right side of the rapture when Gabriel's trumpets blew. Quite naturally, as Deuce was coming into his awareness of spiritual development, Evelyn was realizing, after a lifelong devotion to Christian dogma, that one's purpose was not to ignore the physical or to avoid engaging in it, rather it was to be *in* it but not *of* it.

They had debated the issue. Deuce scornfully watching Evelyn pour two fingers of Old Fitzgerald whiskey into her water glass and admonishing that it was the devil's playground. Evelyn, raising a defiant eyebrow, responded, "If the devil was in this likker, then you wouldn't have ever gotten to where you are now."

Deuce credited his turnaround to "the power of the Lord."

Evelyn's frequent retort, "If the Lord is so powerful, then what's the risk?"

To which sometimes Deuce shook his head and said, "Woman, you don't know I been there in a handbasket."

Evelyn replied, "Husband, I been where you tryin' to git to. And I can tell ya that the color of the grass don't even matter."

They eventually settled into a typical compromise of the married: to agree to disagree. Most evenings Deuce settled on the front porch with an after-dinner pipe, while Evelyn headed to the back porch with an empty glass to join the bottle of "Old Fitz" that she kept on a rickety bookshelf next to her white wicker armchair.

This is where Eve found her when she returned for her second visit. After greeting Deuce, she had been unceremoniously waved toward the rear of the house, where she found Evelyn. Her gray hair was as neatly pressed as at their first meeting, and she wore a 1950s-era house dress with kitten heels. To Eve, she looked like a brown-skinned, pleasantly plump model from an older *Ebony* magazine.

"I remember you." Lubricated by her first sip of Old Fitz, Evelyn's smile eased toward her eyes.

Eve's eyes furrowed. "Yes, Ms. Evelyn, I was here yesterday."

"Don't be flip, gal. I ain't that old. At least not as old as my husband, you know." She giggled. "I remember you 'fo you even got here." Evelyn gestured for Eve to sit in the matching chair across from her.

Eve complied, taking a gaze at the older woman as she refilled her glass and offered one to Eve. Evelyn was younger than Deuce in a classic May-December romance manner. Eve's thoughts were just grasping at the importance of such a detail yet couldn't fully uncover its implications. She accepted the glass but didn't drink from it.

"I was there when your grandmama dreamed of fish." Evelyn smirked, and slowly clarity began to enter Eve's mind.

1950

Gertrude had dreamed of fish last night and it had thrown off her entire day. She couldn't concentrate on cooking, cleaning, or any of her church duties. She sat next to the charred brick that was Sister Evelyn's pound cake and stared at the fierce woman who trembled with anger in front of her.

"What de devil, Trudy! All I asked was for you to watch it. Now look at it!" Evelyn grasped in vain at the scarf tightly bound to her head. "What on God's earth is goin' on in yo' head?"

Gertrude opened her mouth to speak, but the words escaped her. All day she had searched the faces and mannerisms of each woman with whom she had come into contact. They all appeared the same. No one had made any changes. Still, Gertrude had dreamed of fish, and it only meant one thing. If there was a woman who reflected some change in her body, then it was someone in her own home. She dreaded going back there.

Evelyn's tirade lost steam. She sighed and plopped onto the bench next to Gertrude. "Trudy, what is it?"

Gertrude focused on her friend. They had been as close as two peas in the church pod. Gertrude had taken Hezekiah's advice and began volunteering at the church to give her a sense of purpose while he was away at work. She found such comfort in the place. Polishing the wooden pews felt like dusting her own furniture, and she sat with such pride in them every Sunday morning. She beamed at the other parishioners, knowing that the seat of their salvation contained her sweat and work. Yes, church was home to Gertrude. More home than home itself.

Pastor Reid's thunderous voice was the vessel of God. Its cadence rumbled inside of her. When it spoke, she listened. What it said, she obeyed. She had tried to get Hezekiah involved, but he wanted no part of it. He seemed to revel in his heathen ways. Gertrude felt that it was her duty as a Christian and a wife to help him to salvation, but when he refused and denounced the pastor as a two-bit hustler, she knew that she would have to save herself alone.

After Hezekiah was killed, Pastor Reid and the church were lifesavers to Gertrude. It still seemed like yesterday when she was awakened in the early morning by the intent rapping on her door. It could be no one but Hezekiah. She snatched her housecoat from its perch on the bedroom door and checked on the girls before making her way to the front door. She sighed. She would make him wait a while. She would feign anger when she saw him, but the truth was that she missed her husband. She missed his presence and his touch. Most of the time, her body belonged to the Lord, but Hezekiah had a way of borrowing it now and then. She blushed with the thought as she yanked open the door.

Cornelius stood before her, filling the frame with his mass. He removed his hat. "Gertrude . . ." She began to shake. Cornelius Gaines had never been the harbinger of good news, and he was usually the cause of whatever devastation he reported.

Evelyn stayed by Gertrude's side night and day for months until she was able to get herself together. The years passed, and time brought about a very odd construction of family in a way that only small communities can incubate. The cement that hardened Gertrude's insides against Cornelius gradually melted until it was a mere stone at the center of her heart. He provided for her family financially. She tolerated him. He became a father figure for the girls. She cared for him. He never made any advances toward her, and she began to accept the strangeness of this fictive kinship and allowed herself to admit that she now had with Cornelius what she had tried so hard to shape with Hezekiah.

Her heart battled with the realization. She told herself that the price was too great. The price of Hezekiah was not worth the life she had with Cornelius. Yet Hezekiah had been a spiritual test with his every visit. He was the last temptation that she could not overcome. Eventually she reconciled that the Lord had known her struggle and had removed Hezekiah, casting him away and giving her the angel of death, who did not tempt her physically yet cared for her girls. Was not the biblical Job blessed with a replacement family once God and the devil were done playing chess with his life?

When Mercy and Ann began to call him Uncle Cornelius, Gertrude did not correct them. It was a Faustian exchange: a life for a particular lifestyle, with the payment made up front. Normalcy settled like a scab over a wound, visible yet allowing continuity and function. But a scab removed too soon may reopen the wound. And when Gertrude dreamed of fish, it ripped her world apart.

Gertrude thought again of her dream as she gazed at her daughters. Her eyes fell on Mercy. At fifteen, Mercy exhibited the changes of a girl becoming woman. Her hips were rounding, her bosom expanding, but where her face should have narrowed in the transition from mahogany cherub cheeks to firmer raised cheekbones, something was awry. There was a fullness to her face. Her nose had widened. Gertrude examined her youngest daughter with her eyes. Mercy had indeed changed—changed in a way that only a mother knows. She stared until Mercy dropped her eyes.

"You wit chile." It was more a statement than question.

"I don't . . ." Mercy began. Know? But she did know. Understand? She had understood. A part of her had probably even hoped.

"Who the devil is it?" Gertrude demanded. Devil was right. For Gertrude had made a deal with the devil and foolishly thought that the debt had been prepaid.

As if mocking her mother's feared transgression, Mercy replied, "It's the Lord's."

"Don't you get smart with me, Mercy! Don't you dare blaspheme God with some lil bastard!"

Mercy folded her hands across her chest.

Her sister Ann stood across from them at the stove, silent but listening. It would serve Mercy right. Did she think that she could have everything and everyone? She smirked at Mercy.

"Why cain't it be God's will?" Mercy shot back.

"Because God's will is marriage, not opening yo' legs for anybody at any time!" Gertrude shouted.

"But God's will is also murder, ain't it?"

"What you talkin' 'bout, girl?"

"It was God's will for Cornelius to kill Daddy . . ." Mercy's eyes were full of anger.

Gertrude interrupted, "Don't you talk 'bout things you too young to know!"

"You sit here and take care of him! The man that killed your own husband! I guess that's fine with God though."

The slap was not surprising. Not to Mercy, who didn't even flinch upon its impact. Not to Ann, who was riveted by the drama. And not to Gertrude, who had been suppressing the impulse since she saw the prenatal spread of her daughter's body. Truthfully, she had wanted to do much more harm, and it had scared her. The slap served as a compromise. Now, confused by the turmoil of her actions, she didn't want to take it back but had an impulse to grab Mercy into a hug that was tight enough to be both love and hate. But she didn't. Her arms stood limp at her sides. Her feet remained planted on the floorboards.

1972

Evelyn had neared the end of her glass. Eve's remained untouched in her clenched hand. "Who was the . . . Who's my father?" she asked.

Evelyn sighed. "Well, you got to understand how different things was twenty years ago. Small town. Everybody was always up in everybody else business 'cause we ain't have all the distractions you young folk got now."

"Who was he?" Eve repeated.

"Well, your mama never did say. But . . ." Evelyn drained the last swallow of whiskey.

"Ms. Evelyn, please."

Evelyn nodded. "They say it was Cornelius. He denied it, of course." Evelyn glanced cautiously toward the door and lowered her voice. "Don't even think about asking Deuce. He practically raised Cornelius, and he won't hear no parts of it. Say ain't no way Cornelius done that."

"What do you think?" Eve asked.

"I think Cornelius was complicated. He done some bad things, and he done good things. We like to think that men are simple. Feed 'em and love 'em, and that's all they need. But they more complicated than that. They do some great things and then turn round and commit some of the worst sins ever thought of."

"Did he . . . Was she forced?"

"She never said one way or 'nother. Never said who the daddy was or wasn't. And if it wasn't Cornelius, then Lord help us all, 'cause he went to his grave claiming it wasn't him. Spent that whole time before your mama took off pleading with her to tell the truth."

Eve finally sipped her whiskey. The shock of the information overpowered the burn of the liquid making its way down her throat. "Is there anyone else who'd know anything?"

"Maybe Geneva. She and your mama was thick as thieves, if I remember."

"So . . . my sort of step-grandfather may have been my father too?" Eve looked at Evelyn. Evelyn peered out into the darkness beyond the porch. Somewhere in her storytelling, the floodgates had opened, and lines between what should and shouldn't be told had blurred. She had not shared the circumstances of Hezekiah's death, perhaps out of some allegiance to Deuce. Perhaps as a last-minute reprieve to Cornelius, whose kindness to Gertrude she had witnessed. More than likely, it was because of what happens when large chunks of lived experience and relationships are abridged into answers to single-sentence inquiries like Eve's question. Years of love and pain become trivialized into story lines that resemble soap opera plots—tales for housewives, with which Evelyn had become familiar. She had been a faithful viewer, like most who could manage to steal a break during work hours, of *One Life to Live* ever since Ellen Holly graced the screen as the first Black soap opera actress. The series saw a spike in its African American viewership, even among men, who were not part of its target audience. To Evelyn, Eve's summation sounded like something straight out of her morning stories, and she was reminded why no one wanted to go back down this particular road.

FOURTEEN

unfixable things

> I believe that to know the essence of a thing
> requires returning as closely as possible to the
> origin of that thing. The passage of time tends
> to quietly erode meaning and enthusiasm. The farther
> you move away from the sun, the colder it gets.
> —Wynton Marsalis, *Moving to Higher Ground*

The past is an unfixable thing. It cannot be mended. Its deeds are always irreparable. The past is read-only. It does not allow for revisions. Yet it remains tethered to the present, waiting for visitors who can only watch it replay itself. Its most salient lesson is not that past wrongs can be made right, but rather that they do not have to be repeated. The past says to remedy seekers, "Look upon me and learn, but do not seek to change me." It stares at daughters from their mothers' eyes and is as implicit in the handshakes of strangers as it is in the burial of secrets.

James wasn't much of a drinking man. Over the years, he had tried, knowing that those who imbibed on a regular basis had some nominal success in keeping the past at bay. But James didn't have the constitution for it, and the only taste he could develop was for light potables like sweet-flavored wines and sherry. He generally kept a small bottle of something hidden in his shed as most of his friends did in their private spaces. After rushing out of the back door just as Eve entered the front, James now settled himself in his shed and fumbled to pull open the rusted metal drawer that concealed a bottle of port.

The shed was filled with an accumulation of unfixable things: telephones, lamps, and other items that Geneva had insisted he throw away but that never quite managed to make it to the trash. James liked to tinker with them. He took them apart, performing electrical autopsies that sometimes uncovered the cause of their dysfunction. He could put them back together fairly efficiently, but that was the limit of his skill set. So the broken things were dissected and pieced back together without repair. James enjoyed having an intimate knowledge of the parts of things. But he was unconcerned with their function as a whole.

Shed time did not solve the problems of the day, but it did calm most of its turbulence. He could tinker with a "new" item or reflect on tinkering with old ones. James took a swig of the port and gently placed the avocado-green toaster he had purchased less than a month ago on his worktable. Geneva had spent four months begging him to buy it and had taken only one month to break it. He didn't know the details of its untimely demise, only that it had arrived at his shed soaking wet. James had long ago resigned himself to the fact that his wife seemed to enjoy breaking things as much as he enjoyed tinkering with them once they were broken.

He blamed the magazine subscriptions that Geneva convinced him to purchase. Her weekly visits to the hairdresser had become marred with despondency. She complained about not being current on events. When he suggested that she read the newspaper as he did, she became enraged, pacing and flailing about until she almost knocked over the recently purchased Mr. Coffee percolator that he'd driven nearly fifty miles and exhaustingly stood in line for at the Sears, Roebuck and Company. Once the magazines began to arrive, James realized that it wasn't so much about current events as it was current fashion, household appliances, and gossip. *Essence* magazine encouraged them to "subscribe to Blackness," but James found that what he had actually subscribed to were appliance manufacturers, various makeup and hair-care companies, and other people's ideas about his daily life. It was a monthly bombardment of advertisements that fed Geneva's thirst for the "new," and James was sorry he had ever caved in to her pleadings.

Another swig of port, and he placed his hands on the toaster. He would have personally preferred the copper tone, but Geneva had insisted on the green as it matched the Frigidaire. James picked up the screwdriver and carefully removed the screws from the bottom panel. He pushed the toaster aside and exhaled deeply. His head wasn't in it. Before his departure from the house, he had seen Eve's eyes, and they were the same as his own. James had always known, but seeing was a different type of knowing. Now he wanted to push it back into the recesses of his mind, where it had been secured for over twenty years. Even then, he'd thought that the knowledge was too close for comfort. Yet compared to now, with the physical evidence drinking iced tea in his kitchen with his wife, what he felt before had been a cakewalk. Grabbing the port, he chugged as much of it as he could. James willed his heartbeat to slow from the frantic pace that had begun earlier in the day when Geneva received a phone call from Evelyn Johnston. He'd only caught one phrase, *Mercy's child*, but it had set his heart racing. He hadn't known that he would flee the house upon her arrival. In fact, he'd planned to stay and open the long-buried conversation. But when he glanced the spitting image of Mercy approaching up the walkway, he was out the back door and into the shed before Eve had pressed the doorbell.

When Geneva opened the door, she was taken aback by the resemblance of Eve to her girlhood friend. Eve was a little curvier than her mother had been. Her bell-bottom jeans and matching denim jacket would not have been Mercy's style even had she lived to see the changing fashions of the seventies with women wearing trousers. Geneva pulled Eve into a startling embrace. "Oh my God, child. If you don't look like your mother."

Eve stepped back. "I guess I never realized it till now . . . down here. My aunt doesn't really say much about her."

Geneva guided Eve into the sitting room. "Nawl, I guess she wouldn't. They didn't get along. Those two were water and oil if I ever did see it."

Eve sat perched on the edge of the sofa. She'd been a bloodhound on the trail of finding whatever she could about her mother. Now it seemed that all that energy and the implications of this newfound knowledge were suffocating her. Geneva was the same age—late thirties—that her mother would have been. Sitting there talking, Eve was struck by how close in age she would have been to her mother. Her mother had been a pregnant child. She hadn't really thought of it that way before. They would have grown up together.

Geneva was the youngest person Eve had spoken with in Ideal. It had given her the impression that the town was old. Although Geneva didn't look old. Her hair was styled in a fashionable bob, she wore green polyester pants and matching loafers. Geneva may have looked youthful, but she, too, felt aged in the way that southerners appear to their northern counterparts. Perhaps it's due to their unhurried nature. It had taken hours for Eve to get stories from Deuce and Evelyn, and it seemed that information was not going to pour from Geneva any quicker.

Yet, they wanted to share. All of them had. Deuce, Evelyn, and now Geneva had invited Eve into their homes, offered her food and drink, and had every intention of sharing everything they knew about her family. But when they thought of where to begin and flashed back through all the events from effect to cause, they became stifled. Trapped between what should be known and what couldn't be told.

"Your mother and I were the best of friends. We did everything together," Geneva told Eve. And she shared with Eve stories of her adventures with Mercy. Stories that were limited to schoolyard tales and pranks on Ann. Stories that were strangely bereft of schoolboy crushes.

Eve's thoughts naturally drifted toward her lifelong friendship with Nelle. She wondered what, if any, rift had occurred between her mother and Geneva. Had Mercy died before it could be sorted out?

Eve relaxed into the sofa and reached toward her mother through the retellings. Still, she was not deterred from seeking the obvious missing information. At some point in those young-girl shenanigans, Mercy had ended up pregnant. "Ms. Geneva, I don't know who my father is."

Geneva paused and walked to the mantel and retrieved a photo album. "She wouldn't even tell me who it was. We had . . . grown apart in those months." Geneva suspected the cause, but fearing self-incrimination, she remained silent. She couldn't tell Eve why Mercy had withdrawn from her that spring of 1950, after Ann had spotted them kissing in the shack.

Spring 1950, Macon County

Geneva and Mercy hadn't worried about Ann, but perhaps they should have. One evening the sisters were helping their mother clean up after dinner. Gertrude was in an unusually talkative mood. "What you girls gon' git into today?"

Ann was silent, but Mercy replied, "Me an' Geneva thought we'd see how that plum tree comin' around."

Ann snorted to herself. Gertrude glanced at her before responding to Mercy. "Your sistuh's right. That ol' thang ain't neva gon' bear no fruit. I don't know why y'all even waste your time on it."

Mercy chuckled and put away the last of the dishes she was cleaning. "If you have but the faith of a mustard seed, Mama."

Gertrude laughed. "Well, I'll be! Somebody's been reading the Bible."

"I know all the good parts by heart." Mercy grinned and rushed out the door, leaving her mother to shake her head.

Mercy's departure freed Ann's tongue. "Mama, don't you think that she spend too much time with Geneva?"

Gertrude faced Ann. "You wanna spend more time with yo' sistuh?"

Ann frowned. "Nothin' like that, Mama. I jes think . . ." She paused as she tried to figure out the best way to tell her mother, a woman who in her mind walked with God, that her daughter was a sodomite.

"You think what?"

Ann couldn't do it. But there were other options. She decided to choose a path that she felt was righteously silent. Her mother had already lost a husband to sin. Ann wasn't about to tell her that she'd lost a daughter as well.

Gertrude mistook the silence. "You wanna know what I thank?

I thank that maybe you could use a close girlfriend yo'self. Then you ain't got to be jealous of yo' sistuh."

Ann spun on her heels. "I ain't jealous of her. I hate her!"

"That's enough! I ain't gonna stand here and let you spit evil in my house. Hatred against yo' own flesh and blood. I ain't raised you that way."

Ann closed her mouth on the thought that her mother would be surprised at what she had raised. They worked in silence until Gertrude left for evening prayer, a much-needed one due to the evening's activities. Ann looked out of the kitchen window at her sister, who was picking dandelions in the yard. If prayer saves, then in that moment Ann plotted her sister's salvation. She retrieved her small Bible from the room they shared and joined Mercy outside.

The first day, she read Romans. "For this cause God gave them up unto vile affections: for even their women did change the natural use into that which is against nature . . ." Mercy continued to pluck dandelions and ignored Ann, who continued, "And likewise also the men, leaving the natural use of the woman, burned in their lust toward one another . . ."

Mercy cast a glance at Ann and began walking away, with Ann in pursuit. ". . . Men with men working that which is unseemly, and receiving in themselves that recompence of their error which was meet." Mercy trotted away at a quicker pace. Finding it too difficult to read and walk, Ann returned to the house with a sly grin.

The next day, Mercy awoke to 1 Corinthians in the form of Ann's withering voice. "Know ye not that the unrighteous shall not inherit the kingdom of God? Be not deceived . . ." Mercy covered her face with the pillow and turned her back toward Ann's side of the room.

It took two days for Ann to find additional passages, but she was pleased to catch Mercy on her way to visit Geneva. She had memorized the short verse in Leviticus and was able to keep up with Mercy as they tramped through the brush toward the shack. "Thou shalt not lie with mankind as with womankind. It's a 'bomination." Mercy faltered in her steps, and Ann smiled before delivering the final blow. "And if a man also lie with mankind as he lieth with a woman, both of them have committed a 'bomination. They shall surely be put to death. Their blood shall be upon them."

Mercy ran into the shack and slammed the door. Ann waited outside and was rewarded minutes later when a stunned Geneva emerged with tear-streaked cheeks. She stumbled past Ann as if she didn't see her. It was this memory that Geneva withheld from Eve decades later: that whatever happened to her mother, Ann had set it in motion. But no one could extricate themselves from it. Not Ann. Not Geneva. And not her husband, James.

James loved Mercy, but it earned him no favor with her. She looked right through him as if searching for something better on the other side. But Ideal was a small town, and matches were made in church houses, woodshed groping sessions, and shotgun wedding ceremonies. James knew that unless some stranger came to town and whisked her away, Mercy didn't have much of a choice other than him. Small-town colored girls dreamed of small-town colored boys, and those that didn't did not have the mobility to find their fate elsewhere.

It seemed to James that Mercy was coming into this awareness amid frequent arguments with her mother and sister. She was becoming a woman; he had certainly noticed it. Time, he thought, for Mercy to spend less time with Geneva and more time being courted. Everything required timing, and James was just working up the nerve to approach Big C for permission to court Mercy when she sought him out. He was surprised, to say the least. It had seemed that a great deal of her existence was predicated on avoiding him, so when she came around one afternoon to the funeral home while he was making up the recently departed elder Hughes, his first thought was that something had gone so terribly wrong that she had been forced to seek him out. Perhaps as the last man in Ideal.

He placed the cinnamon-hued foundation on the table and rushed to escort Mercy out of the preparation room. Sliding the doors closed behind him, he turned to Mercy. "Everythang alright, Mercy?"

Mercy nodded. "You wanna take a walk?"

Afraid to speak lest his voice squeak and reveal his nervousness, James managed to grunt his consent. They walked down the recently paved road until it returned to its former dirt. Mercy paused at the old dry well, running her hand across the jagged concrete edges. She knelt to sit, and James rushed to her side. He wanted to do something chivalrous like spread out a blanket for her, but he had nothing save the shirt on his back. He stripped off his shirt and grandly placed it on the ground. He was rewarded by Mercy's laugh, which seemed to emerge from her throat in spite of herself, and she clasped her hand to her mouth in a delayed effort to contain it. James knew he had to say something to try to make the most of each moment with her. He was the man, after all, and it was fully expected of him to take charge of things.

"Mercy—" he began.

"You ever think this ol' well ever worked?" Mercy interrupted.

James knew the stories of the well. Everyone did. He knew that one of those stories belonged to Mercy's father, Hezekiah. He knew enough to remain silent, as silence had earned him this walk and Mercy's companionship for an undisclosed amount of time.

Mercy sighed. "I think it's always been just what it is . . . a graveyard." She turned and peered over the edge into its darkness. "But even graveyards got endings, don't they?" Without waiting for a response, she continued, "I don't think this . . . thing ever end."

James was confused as to what role he was playing in this discussion. Clearly, his input was unnecessary. He wondered why he was here. Why had Mercy specifically sought him out for reflections that seemed too personal to share with anyone? Before he could fully process the thought, the words tumbled from his mouth: "I could go down there." He immediately wanted to recall the words. What was he saying? No one goes down there, not alive anyway. But Mercy's eyes shone as she seemed to actually see James. He noticed that she was looking directly at him.

Bolstered by this attention, James continued, "I'd do it for you, Mercy. I'd do anything for you."

She smiled and placed her hand against his cheek. "You're sweet . . ."

James felt the rebuttal but resolved to press on. Years of repressed feelings surged as he grabbed her hand and placed it on his bare chest. "You know I have loved you from the time we was little . . ."

"Well, that's just a crush, James . . ."

"It's not a crush, Mercy!" He paused, searching for an entrance into the place where she held things most dear. "I'll do whatever it is you want. I'll give you whatever you want. Just tell me what it is."

"I don't know what it is, James."

His heart pounded beneath her palm still pressed to his chest. Mercy looked at her hand, brown like nutmeg against his pecan chest. The hairs bristled between her fingers, and she caressed the smooth skin, allowing her hand to trail downward to his stomach.

James inhaled sharply but kept quiet and still as she continued to explore his torso and arms. Her gaze and touch were coordinated as she felt his biceps and shoulders. He watched her, fascinated by her exploration. Although he ached to touch her, his arms remained at his sides.

Mercy gently pushed him onto his back and lay beside him with her ear to his chest, tapping out his heartbeat with her index finger.

James wrapped an arm around her, and they lay in this way until his heart rate slowed considerably. He wanted to stay this way forever, feeling like Mercy belonged to him. As he watched the clouds drift lazily across the sky, he felt his trousers being unzipped. Every muscle immediately stiffened and his jaw clenched. She freed him from his pants, and he lay exposed to the warmth of the sun and intensity of her gaze.

James was too surprised to be self-conscious or feel much of anything beyond arousal. Her hand was soft on him, and her eyes watched her handiwork. When his breathing intensified, she watched his face, correlating her actions to his responses. A smile played at the corner of her lips, and her own breathing increased. With her free hand she unbuttoned her dress, pausing her caresses just long enough to disrobe. She returned to his side and pressed against him, resuming her touch. Mercy grabbed his arm and placed it around her. James looked into her eyes, and she planted soft lips against his own. It was all the invitation he needed. He gently placed his weight atop her and allowed her to guide him inside her.

They lay naked, with the breeze drying their sweat. James thought of how they would announce their courtship. Would Mercy want him to speak to Big C and Gertrude first? He propped himself against the well. "I been saving up a little. In 'bout another six months or so, I should have enough to make a real nice start for us . . ."

"James . . ."

"I don't 'tend to be workin' in my daddy's funeral parlor all my life, Mercy. It's a 'spectable profession, but . . ." James faltered looking at his hands. They were well manicured. He trimmed and cleaned them obsessively. They were smooth, free from calluses because he always wore gloves when working with them. Still, they were dead hands. Jealous of his family's large home and the other comforts afforded by having the only funeral home in Ideal, that was the nickname given to him by his peers: Dead Hands. But when he was with Mercy, they felt alive.

"I cain't be wit you, James."

"I don't understand. You jes—you jes did. I mean, you was jes wit me, Mercy," he stammered.

"I guess I'm still lookin' for what it is I want," she explained. "I jes don't see it being this."

"But you got to give it another try. It ain't 'posed to feel good the first time. Did I hurt you? I'm sorry."

"Nawl, James. You ain't hurt me. It was . . . it was nice."

"Then what's the problem?" He took her hand, but it felt limp in his. "This was yo' first time, right?"

"Don't matter none, James. I guess I jes wanted to . . . not . . . feel something. I cain't be wit you, and that's all there is to it." Mercy rose and placed his crumpled shirt in his lap. She slid into her dress and left him propped against the well.

There is magic in love lost. Spirit in unrequited love binds souls. Had Mercy stayed, the story would have been different, as stories are when the what-ifs in life are explored. They mentally play themselves out to resolution. In James's mind he could imagine courtship and marriage, but before children came, a fuzziness clouded things. It would not facilitate his imaginings. They violated its own reality, and so James was not allowed to "see" what could have been, because it was not a possibility in any realm. He was unaware, but this is exactly how Mercy saw her existence in his world, in the world as it was at the time. She simply could not see herself in any of the available roles.

————

1972

Twenty-two years later, James sat in his shed, hidden away with port wine and broken appliances, reflecting on Mercy's desire to not feel. He still didn't understand how she could not feel something—or anything—especially while she was physically feeling him move inside of her. This was, he knew, his prideful reason for pushing those thoughts back into the past.

James was not fixated on Mercy. It had been first love, sometimes called puppy love—not to trivialize it. Nothing compares to it. It is the first, and as such, it is the only. No matter how brief, it remains a constant yardstick for its successors. First kisses establish kissing protocol. First highs are always chased and never recaptured. It's never as good as the first time. That didn't mean James didn't love Geneva or wasn't in love with her. It simply meant that he would never forget Mercy. It meant that she would creep into his thoughts throughout the years. Briefly taking him unawares during his courtship of Geneva, at uncomfortable moments on their honeymoon, and now, mostly in his shed as he tinkered with things that were not so much beyond repair as uninterested in it. Sometimes he could replace every part of a vacuum or clock and it would still refuse to operate, as if its essence had vacated.

This process was a type of grieving. After the moving on. After the death of the relationship. Left with the lifelong mourning of living. Living with and without. James was not fixated because there was nothing in his dealings with Mercy to have been fixed. Dead hands could not fix dead things. The shed was a mausoleum of memories.

When James heard farewells, he emerged from the shed and crossed the yard to the back door of the house. He entered the kitchen, where Geneva was placing meatloaf, mashed potatoes, and creamed peas on two plates.

"She didn't want to stay for dinner." Geneva placed the plates at the small kitchen table. There were four chairs crammed around it, yet they rarely needed more than two of them. Although they had tried, they hadn't been able to conceive children. James sat at the table and waited for Geneva to join him. She sat across from him. "After all this time, how could you not even want to share space with her?"

He lifted his eyes to meet hers. Geneva held his gaze unblinkingly. Of course she had known within five minutes of looking at the girl. Geneva had recognized the eyes as well. They were the same as the ones she had gazed into every night for the past twenty years. They were placed in a face that mirrored one that she had spent years dreaming about so long ago. The eyes that she had stared into belonged to lips that she had kissed until it had been disrupted by the pestering of a lover's sibling, as is often the case. But her kiss bore added weight. It hadn't been a smooch behind a house with a local boy. It had been a passionate lip embrace with another girl. With Mercy.

Mercy and Geneva never discussed the "it" between them. Small town idioms made room for intimate relationships between girls. They were two peas in a pod, peanut butter and jelly, molasses and biscuits. It was perfectly acceptable for girls to walk hand in hand, play with each other's hair, and whisper in each other's ear. This behavior was expected and encouraged because the alternative boy-girl intimacies appeared far more dangerous by comparison. So Geneva and Mercy's affections lived within the loopholes of social decorum—their public displays appeared no different from those of girls who pined for boys instead of each other.

It had been so natural that they had to remind themselves it was wrong, to take caution against the excitement, to leash their souls and stifle their spirits, which lunged for each other every time they were near. Natural is what they told themselves in the confines of the wood shack. They took to each other like fish to water and calf to teat. They had been drawn to one another without exposure to anything that would have encouraged such behavior. It had been uncharted territory, yet they had responded to this land as if born to it, already fluent in its language and culture. The foreign land had been Geneva's marriage to James. She, too, grieved.

James said nothing at first. His shoulders slumped slightly, and his hand trembled as he sliced into the meatloaf with his fork. They sat in silence for a moment, each with their thoughts on Mercy. Each thinking of her lips, soft and moist. Her hair in plaits brushing against them. Her smile. Her laugh, so easy in spite of their illicit activities, as if she knew what they would only later come to realize: That nothing compares. That some things will always be unfixable, so enjoy them while they work. While they function. While no one is there to judge.

James lowered his fork. "I 'spect you ain't share your . . . closeness to Mercy either?"

Geneva's eyes widened. "What?"

"Geneva, we been married nigh on twenty years. You think you the only one get to learn somethin' in it?"

Geneva gently slid her plate away. "It don't do anybody any good to go speculating . . ."

James waved her off. "If I talk to her . . . it'll never be just about me. It'll lead to you. To Big C."

"That poor man. My God, James . . . what we allowed happen to him." Geneva shook her head.

James slid her plate toward her. "Eat, baby. Just eat for now."

So Geneva ate dinner with her husband and thought of Mercy. Her fork slid a little slower in her mouth, depositing the meatloaf a little gentler. She chewed a little slower. Savored.

And James did the same, allowing his tongue to encourage the food to the roof of his mouth and down his throat. He closed his eyes and felt every spice and every texture.

And they ate dinner. And memories. And Mercy.

FIFTEEN

desiderata, or how to build a well

> Go placidly amid the noise and the haste,
> and remember what peace there may be in silence.
> —Max Ehrmann, "Desiderata"

Before Cornelius Gaines set off to find his mother, Luella. Before he returned as Big C and killed Hezekiah. Before he was accused of impregnating Mercy. There was the well. The dry well had been a miscarried attempt at prosperity for the Gaines family. It had the misfortune of conflicting with the interests of the Railroad. It had been conceived under the mistaken belief that all men were created equal even as its birth occurred by digging through remnants of those whose deaths proved otherwise. The land was cursed, but this is an oversimplification.

The dry well tunneled through the space-time continuum of a multiply colonized land. Its primary facade consisted of an overlay of bone fragments from those later described as Native Americans. Water is life, and the purpose of the well was to bring it forth, but a well dug in death cannot produce life. Even before the Railroad sought to poison it to prevent its use by Cornelius's grandfather, the elder Mr. Gaines, the dry well was cursed by consequence.

The Gaines family worked hard to move from sharecropping to ownership. Hard work would have meant the same amount of nothingness to them as it did to their hardworking neighbors had not the elder Gaines set his sights on barren land. No one could make it yield any crop. No one white could make it yield any crop. The land had been overused and exhausted of its resources like many surrounding areas. Like all of its abused workers.

They let him have it, amused by his temerity but unaware of his knowledge. In 1906 the Daughters of the Confederacy were erecting a statue in Tuskegee while one of Tuskegee Normal School's premiere instructors was changing the understanding of agriculture. They called him the Peanut Man because George Washington Carver traveled the rural countryside advocating to Black farmers the planting of peanuts as a way of rejuvenating their land. Carver, a *castrato*, was born in slavery. Some later historians would describe his castration as cosmetic, a way to secure a privileged slave position. Carver himself told people that it was due to a childhood incident that he could not take a wife. Both are *a posteriori* retellings of the white physician—or perhaps veterinarian (it was chattel slavery)—that had taken in hand the prepubescent testicles of one of the greatest minds in science and sliced them off for the purpose of ensuring a more docile house slave. Carver could not desire women—white or otherwise. He could not reproduce his Blackness, or his gen(i)us.

Carver's renowned high-pitched voice, withered yet sharp, pleaded a case for the peanut. And they derided him—not for the voice but for the suggestion. No one could live on the peanut. So the man without testicles produced a multitude of products from nuts. He began to be taken a little more seriously, especially by the elder Gaines, who leveraged the unfair wages from sharecropping by saving the seeds of the harvest. Farmers couldn't afford to waste seasons planting anything other than cash crops—cotton, tobacco, vegetables. Mr. Gaines planted the peanuts on the barren land, successfully wagering that no one would want it or the peanuts. By the time he purchased the land and built his family home, the soil was vibrant and waiting. Ida Mae was his beautiful wife, and Luella was his blossoming daughter. At a time when others cursed the birth of a daughter as trouble, Mr. Gaines secured the future of his with his own wealth. She would be courted by only the worthiest colored gentlemen.

Luella showed up pregnant the day Mr. Gaines found out that the Railroad had been poisoning his well. He had survived poverty and sharecropping and servitude only to be bested by the Trojan horse of his daughter carrying the seed of a white railroad manager. Mr. Gaines saw it as a casualty of war between men. Even the race war was couched in the opposing narratives of men. He refused to hear his daughter's pleas that she had fallen in love. But she could not have fallen in love. She could only have fallen down the well of illusion to think that consent could exist between a white man and a colored girl in 1909. And further, that, even if this were possible, her desire as a colored woman could matter to the economic interests of her father and a suitor. If her mother, Ida Mae, had worried about Luella's interest in men, she was in utter despair over her daughter's ignorance about them.

When the rumors started about the parentage, the family kept silent. They lingered on Mr. Gaines, who counseled Ida Mae as he carved details into the wooden crib, "The world always prepared to believe the worst of a Negro man. This won't be my legacy."

Mr. Gaines was surprisingly calm during the pregnancy and the rumors. He walked with an air of superiority even as his neighbors jeered behind his steps referring to him as "Daddy Grand," a bastardized version of granddaddy that hinted at incestuous impropriety.

The baby's birth brought the biological father and his hopes that maybe Luella and the child would be passable enough to journey to New Orleans where miscegenation was more flexible. But the child was born with the mark of Cain, and Mr. Gaines watched the man's face carefully as the baby was brought to him and the blanket slowly removed. He watched the man nervously assure his daughter that he would secure passage for them all on the train in a few weeks. He watched the man falter when Luella insisted on giving the child his name. And when Luella called out, "Cornelius?" he watched the man pretend not to hear, as if she were talking to the child instead, and take his leave.

———————

Eve felt overwhelmed with the amount of information uncovered. She sat in her room, flipping through notes and family charts that she'd begun to sketch out from her conversations. Tired of looking at her own handwriting, she wandered around her lodging until she returned to the framed photographs on the staircase. She'd been so taken by the picture of Claudette when she first arrived that she had neglected to pay closer attention to the other photographs. In one, she could see the large form of Cornelius hovering in the background while a man and two women sat cloistered at a small table in the foreground. Glasses of various degrees of emptiness and half-pint bottles crammed its surface.

Cornelius wasn't her grandfather, but he had been responsible for taking care of her mother. She needed to know what happened to him.

"I knew your granddaddy." Johnita's words startled Eve.

"Pardon?" Eve looked at the woman who had silently appeared at her side.

"I guess you could say we had relations," Johnita continued. "I'm not 'shamed to say it. Everybody know it and has throwed it in my face here and there."

"My grandfather?" Eve asked. "You mean Hezekiah or Cornelius?"

"Hezekiah"—Johnita tapped the picture of the man seated at the table—"was your grandfather, chile. What's wrong with you?" Johnita lit a cigarette and eyed Eve skeptically.

"That's Hezekiah?" Eve lifted the photo from the wall and brought it close to her face. It was the first time she'd seen a picture of him. She searched his features for some connection to her own. She saw it in the fullness of her lips and high pitch of her forehead. "He was very handsome. So, you and Hezekiah . . . And this was before Grandmother Gertrude?" Eve struggled to dig for information while relating it to her new source.

Johnita's eyes shifted quickly from left to right. "Yeah, nearabouts. Anyway, you like on a treasure hunt? For information?" She dragged on her cigarette and exhaled. "Thought you'd eventually get to me, being your cousin and all—you know, your grandma's cousin—but the way folks always flappin' off at the jawbones, I guess they must've scared you away. Your grandaddy was here the night he died."

It took the force of the world to keep Eve rooted on the staircase. "With you? Hezekiah was with you that night?"

"Nawl, honey." Johnita chuckled. "I know this place don't look like much now, but it was one of the liveliest juke joints in Macon County. Your granddaddy shole loved to play him some cards. He was a lucky sumbitch too."

———————

Johnita watched as Claudette pressed herself against Hezekiah and they retreated into her pantry. She tried to follow, but every step brought an inquiry from a patron. They wanted their credit extended or to know why the kitchen was slow in serving their chicken dinner order. *Why the gizzards small as crumbs? Why turnip greens instead of collards?*

By the time Johnita was able to glance toward the pantry again, she saw Claudette dash out as Hezekiah bumped into Big C. Ignoring one last plea for credit extension, she caught up with Claudette and they moved to an unoccupied corner.

"What do you think you're doing, Claudette?" Johnita still firmly held her wrist.

"The same as you, Johnny," Claudette responded, her voice still filled with venom yet unsure as to whom it was directed.

"Really, Claude? That was years ago!"

"You sure about that?" Claudette glanced toward the stairs where earlier Hezekiah had squeezed past Johnita.

Johnita loosened her grip on Claudette's wrist and gently rubbed it. "Yes, Claude. But what ain't years ago is Big C. And that stunt you pulled last week! You attacked that man's manhood and sangin' about bulldaggerin'! You cain't be playin' around with the likes of him."

Claudette rolled her eyes and smirked. "Everybody sanging about bulldaggers, Johnny, in the big cities. We can go—"

Johnita gently squeezed her wrist again. "I'm serious, Claude. That man is dangerous."

"I got this, Johnny." Claudette slowly pulled away from Johnita. "Time to close up shop. Let me do us a song." She sauntered to the stage as Johnita grabbed the broom and began to sweep at the feet of her lingering patrons, waking those who had fallen into a drunken slumber at their tables. Yet it was Claudette's voice that raised them all like Lazarus and intoxicated everyone within hearing.

> *And if my life is like the dust / Ooh, that hides the*
> *glow of a rose*
> *What good am I? / Heaven only knows*

Words soaked with longing and gin poured from her, past Hezekiah, and hovered on Johnita, her intended.

> *Lord, this bitter earth / Yes, can it be so cold?*
> *Today you're young / Too soon you're old.*

Claudette's eyes closed, and she allowed the song to take over and use her. Tears slowly crept down her smiling cheeks as the hymn played her as an instrument—diaphragm to vocal cords.

> *But while a voice within me cries / I'm sure some-*
> *one may answer my call*
> *And this bitter earth / Ooh, may not, oh, be so*
> *bitter after all.*

Opening her eyes, she strode by Johnita and gave her a reassuring smile. "What good am I?" she sang softly and added, "I'll see you tonight." But she did not. She saw the interior of Big C's Ford before her descent down the seven circles of hell. She saw Big C's white father, his bones muddled with those of disappeared persons. She saw Native remains by the hundreds, layered in accordance with American land acquisitions. She saw nothingness and then the realization that she had not been seeing at all. She had not been at all.

———————

Johnita's face hardened as she left the staircase and opened a credenza in the sitting room. She extracted a glass decanter of whiskey and poured two glasses, taking one and sitting in one of the wingback chairs. "We ain't stupid or powerless like y'all up north think. We know how to take care of our own. Your mama was our own. Wasn't right what Big C done."

"You mean Cornelius?" Eve slowly followed and grabbed the remaining glass, her movements measured and breath restrained for fear any shift in the wind might disrupt Johnita's revelation.

"Mmm-hmm. That's the muthafucka."

Eve was nearly out of air but continued to ration her breathing, sipping the whiskey to steady her voice. "You think he was my father?"

"Chile, hell nawl. Everybody know he couldn't get it up. That ain't the point. Claudette was my—" Johnita's voice cracked, and she swallowed a healthy gulp of her whiskey. "And he just throwed her down some dark hell where she couldn't even be buried proper. That muthafucka."

Eve nodded, overwhelmed by it all. She remembered Brother LeRoi's warning to her about uncovering buried truths. At the moment, it was all so exhilarating. It was as if the photographs she had seen were becoming more vivid. At first, hearing about her mother from Geneva and Hezekiah from Deuce was like reading stories in a book. But the more she heard, the more the book sounded like a biography of real people living real lives connected to her own. It's what she said she wanted. Still, it felt so incomplete. "And what about Hezekiah?" she asked.

"Hezekiah was kind. Nice. He was a whore though, ain't no doubt about it," Johnita bellowed a whiskey-coated chuckle, and she looked youthful for a moment before her face crumpled into sadness and age. "But she . . ." She closed her eyes before continuing, "Claudette was like breathing when you ain't even know you couldn't."

Eve struggled to breathe through it. Cornelius. Hezekiah. And now Johnita lamenting the thirty-year lost love of a woman. She couldn't help but think of Nelle through Johnita's narrative. Had she truly been condemning her friend to choose between a life lived and one unlived with her insistence that Nelle choose men over women? "You really loved her?" she asked Johnita, but her query drifted to Nelle.

"I really did," Johnita smiled. "And I know they say it's wrong, but I never felt so right. And I haven't felt so since."

They sipped in silence after that. Each with their thoughts on love lost. Johnita's on Claudette, who once told her, "Men ain't stupid, Johnny, but they shole is foolish." Johnita smiled at the memory.

"Men's foolishness is dangerous, Claude," she'd warned in response only to elicit a throaty laugh from Claudette.

Eve's thoughts went to Nelle. She wondered what it would be like to see Nelle with another woman. Would there be any place for her if Nelle had a woman who could be a lover as well as a friend? She shook away the inquiry, imagining Nelle's response: *That's a foolish question, Every.* Eve lifted her glass to her lips only to realize that she'd emptied it while lost in thought. Glancing over to Johnita, she saw the older woman was snoring softly, still grasping her own empty glass. Quietly, Eve rose and gently removed the glass from Johnita's hand. Her gaze lingered on the woman's face, observing the youthfulness that returns in slumber. Relaxed creases erased the previous moment's worries, and Claudette and Cornelius disappeared into the recesses of the past. But not for Eve.

Eve left Johnita's. She walked by memory the small town's layout, allowing her mind to examine her surroundings in light of the new information she had been acquiring. Meandering the streets past the old train depot, she followed the street names casually dropped by Geneva and Evelyn until she reached a modest wooden home.

"This is it," she said aloud as she stared at her mother's birth home. It looked inhabited and well cared for. The small lawn that surrounded it was manicured and a wooden flowerbed lined the porch. Eve walked up the porch stairs and rested a hand on the wooden swing that swayed slightly in the breeze.

The front door opened, startling her, and she gasped.

"May I help you?" A dark-skinned woman about her own age peered out of the screen door.

"Hi—hi, um . . ." Eve stammered. "I'm sorry. I'm told this was my grandmother's house. I just wanted to see it."

The woman smiled and opened the door fully, revealing a small infant on her hip. "You must mean Mother Gertrude. Come on in."

Eve hesitated briefly, but the lure of seeing the interior of the house propelled her forward. She barely heard the homeowner's chatter as she stepped across the threshold and was overcome with a rush of emotion that left her breathless.

"Are you alright?" the woman asked. "Have a sit-down." She whisked away and quickly returned with a tall glass of the most refreshing-looking lemonade Eve had ever seen.

Eve obediently sat and accepted the lemonade. "Yes, I'm sorry. I just didn't know my grandmother . . . Gertrude." She sipped from the glass. "This is amazing!"

"I'm Paulette, and this little one is Josie."

"Eve."

"Well, Eve," Paulette sat and placed Josie on her lap more comfortably, "Mother Gertrude passed when I was still young. I don't recall much about her. She left this house to the church, and when I fell in a bad way, they rented it to me."

Eve scanned the small, tidy living room. "Do you know if it's changed much, the house?" She needed to know that if she walked the floors and touched the walls, they were the same as they'd been when Mercy had done it.

"I don't reckon it has," Paulette answered thoughtfully. "The furniture came from the church, but I haven't painted or anything."

"Do you mind if I look around?"

Paulette shrugged and reclined the baby in her arms as she lifted her shirt. "It's time for Josie to eat. Make yourself at home."

Eve left them, infant gorging on her mother's breast, and made her way through the small house. The kitchen and bathroom were immediately off the living room. She peered toward them but passed uninterestedly and continued down a short hallway until she came to two bedrooms. Eve drifted into the sparsely furnished one decorated in the vibrant colors of childhood. A small crib, rocking chair, and dresser of mismatched wood lined three of the walls. Eve sat in the chair, inhaling the scent of baby powder. Her gaze rested on the walls, and she rose from the rocker and ran her hand along the textured paint. These were Mercy and Ann's walls.

Along the wooden baseboards, she noticed small scratches in one corner. Eve knelt and crawled toward it. She gently rubbed a finger across them and realized that they were etchings of letters, difficult to decipher.

———————

1950

"What are you doing?" Ann directed to her sister's backside as Mercy crouched in the corner of their shared room.

Mercy turned wearily toward Ann and sat pressed against the wall, clutching a small knife. "Praying."

"With that?" Ann pointed toward the knife.

"We clearly pray in different ways." Mercy frowned.

"Didn't think you prayed at all," Ann responded and turned on her heels, exiting the room.

Alone, Mercy turned back to her task, deeply carving an M into the wooden baseboard.

———————

"What are you doing?" Paulette asked from the doorway.

Eve turned quickly, clutching her chest. "You scared me." She slowly stood up. "Sorry, I thought I saw something." She dusted her hands on her jeans. "Thank you for letting me look around, Paulette. I'm going to go now."

Paulette, with Josie joined at her hip, accompanied Eve to the door and watched as she trudged down the stairs. "It's M heart G," she called after Eve.

"What?" Eve stopped and turned.

"What's carved in the wood on the floor. It's the letter M, a heart, and the letter G." Paulette replied.

Eve nodded and continued down the path. Who was G? Cornelius didn't start with a G. Who was this mystery person, and did no one appear to know him? Eve didn't know where her feet were carrying her until she arrived at Deuce's home. She walked around to the back porch and caught Evelyn lighting a wooden pipe. "Ms. Evelyn?" she gasped.

Evelyn inhaled, unperturbed. "Yes?"

"What is that?" Eve asked incredulously.

"Reefer. And whatever you say, don't ruin my relaxation."

"Ms. Evelyn, what happened to Cornelius?"

"Didn't I just say . . ." she sighed and thought better of it and took a prolonged puff. Her glassy eyes peered through Eve. "Men leave, and women are left to take care of things. Sometimes they take things when they go. Pieces of us." She inhaled again, holding the smoke deep within her before releasing the rest of her narration. "Sometimes they leave things. Pieces of them. Sometimes it's not romance or love. Just their leavings."

Eve grew impatient. Although they were more forthcoming with information than her aunt, they definitely shared the same lack of urgency. The feeling of dangling on the precipice of knowledge, awaiting one more piece of information, was maddening. "What did you do, Ms. Evelyn?"

Evelyn smiled. "Chile, men don't understand that we carry the risk . . . the burden of their lust."

"What . . . did . . . you . . . do, Ms. Evelyn? Please."

"We killed a monster."

"How do you kill a monster?"

"By feeding it to a bigger monster," Evelyn answered matter-of-factly.

———————

The Ideal Sewing Circle had no seamstresses. Their first meeting was about mending human materials as opposed to cloth. They gathered in the summer of 1950 at Johnita's Place—the juke owner, the churchwoman, and the widow. All defined by their relationship or service to the men of Ideal. They were not rebel women or rabble-rousers for feminists causes. Even if they had wanted to, their race prevented their entry into women's rights factions, and their gender barred them from serious service to civil rights caucuses. Yet these women enacted their activism and manipulated their occupancy within the concentric confines of multiple oppressions for one fatal cause. Johnita, Evelyn, and Gertrude killed a monster that summer.

Mercy's pregnancy and departure were the talk of Ideal. The chatter always circled around Cornelius, fueled by an awareness of Mercy's contempt for him.

Johnita looked at Gertrude. "Did he do it?"

Gertrude had been asked the question so many times by so many people—those whom she welcomed in her life and others who had previously barely been able to manage a passing greeting to her. All felt entitled to ask whether her youngest child had been made an adult before her time. Their eyes questioned her parenting, having allowed her husband's murderer such closeness and access to her home. She looked at Johnita. "I don't know," she answered honestly.

Johnita pressed. "Do you think he could or would?"

Gertrude shrugged. "I never would have . . ." She trailed off. She never would have thought it of Cornelius. He was a hard man but always gentle within the walls of her home. No one believed that their relationship was purely platonic. She didn't expect them to extend any benefit of doubt with regard to Mercy's pregnancy. "I don't think so."

Johnita planted her hands firmly on the kitchen table, around which they all sat. "Well, I think he killed your husband. I think he tossed Claudette down that well. He is a killer."

Gertrude returned Johnita's gaze. "Yeah, but that don't make him this. Not all men—"

Johnita cut through the sentence with her eyes and a heavy snort. "Why else wouldn't Mercy talk then? She's scared."

Gertrude thought of her headstrong youngest child. "That child don't know fear. He's the one scared. I don't think he did it."

Evelyn broke her silence. "I don't think it matters. He's done plenty. Hezekiah . . ." She reached and squeezed Gertrude's hand. "And Claudette." She glanced at Johnita, whose lip quivered briefly in response. "It's not enough to have white folks cutting down our every breath but we gotta have our own menfolk preying on us too? Even if he did do it, what would happen to him? Everybody think he did it, and ain't nothing happened. They'll be buying him cigars and clapping him on the back come winter."

Gertrude nodded. "So, what do we do?"

The founding members of the Ideal Sewing Circle spent their inaugural meeting discussing the problem of white folks and Black men on Black women. Johnita poured them glasses of the good whiskey she kept locked in her private cabinet. They were quite drunk when the obvious solution came to them through the barrel-aged bourbon. Big C was a monster, and white folks were a bigger monster. Evelyn, new to the seduction of alcohol, summed it up as she slurred, "Feed the lil'n to the big'n."

Twenty-two years later, Evelyn—high on Old Fitzgerald and marijuana, with a long-standing familiarity with both—spoke clearly to Eve. "White folks were always on the hunt for colored men for something or another." She thought of the great lengths to which the community went to shield boys and men from rabid lynch mobs. It had taken the Ideal Sewing Circle very little effort at all to do the opposite for Cornelius. They had simply refused to shield him from any white allegations. They did not act on his behalf. They did not beg or plead his innocence regarding any floating allegations. They did not do what Black women were expected to do. They did not point any fingers, but that was not necessary. Their inaction was enough. If there was any doubt as to the importance of Black women in Black communities, then the death of Cornelius Gaines served as a testament to it, an example of what happened when those women ceased to involve themselves. There was no fury to compare to that of hell. They simply stopped, and a man died.

Eve poured herself a glass of water from a pitcher on the small porch table. She recalled the imposing image of Cornelius from the photograph she discovered in her Chicago basement. Even in her mind he was intimidating. Yet Gertrude had not believed that he'd harmed Mercy, and even though her grandmother made questionable decisions regarding Cornelius, Eve chose to believe as she had—that Cornelius was not her father. He was a murderer who they allowed to be taken.

"Do you feel bad about that, Ms. Evelyn?" Eve asked.

"Killin' the man that killed your granddaddy? Nawl." Evelyn stared at the horizon. "'Course, I don't feel *nothin'* bad at the moment." She pulled on her pipe.

SIXTEEN

warmth of other suns

I was leaving the South to fling myself into the unknown . . .
I was taking a part of the South to transplant in alien soil,
to see if it could grow differently, if it could drink of new
and cool rains, bend in strange winds, respond to the warmth
of other suns, and, perhaps, to bloom.
—Richard Wright, *Black Boy*

Between the time of World War I and the early 1970s, nearly six million African Americans left the South. Spreading northward and westward, they sought to escape the severe racial oppression of the South and searched for better opportunities. They left in droves by bus, rail, car, and even on foot in what is now called the Great Migration. Writer Richard Wright left the Mississippi plantation of his birth for Chicago, for, as he coined it, "the warmth of other suns." Within this pipeline of leaving were women who sought to escape oppressions within their communities. The abused wife, who was smuggled not north but to a neighboring town; the daughters who feared being married off so that there'd be fewer mouths to feed; the sisters who whored themselves to neighboring farm men so that their own land could be worked—they, too, sought the warmth of other suns.

In 1913 Luella Gaines boarded the AB&A train out of Ideal. She chased a dream of reconnecting with the white father of her three-year-old son, Cornelius, his namesake. She'd heard that he had gone to New Orleans and hoped that the nuanced racial politics of the Creoles would provide refuge for a light-colored woman, her white lover, and their dark child. She may have been right in that assumption, but Luella would never find the white Cornelius, just as her son would never find her when he boarded the same train fourteen years later. It had taken Luella three years of bearing the town's shame to decide to leave. Yet her own father had acted much sooner. The elder Gaines had seen the Railroad try to take his land, declare his well defunct, and defile his daughter. Luella rode that train unaware that Gaines had shot white Cornelius three years prior and tossed the body into the freshly constructed dry well.

———

In 1950 Mercy Mann boarded the AB&A train out of Ideal. She carried only a small suitcase in her hand and, even smaller, the growing fetus in her stomach. Mercy hadn't wanted to leave home, but it had ceased to be a place of comfort. She was bombarded with questions from those closest to her and stares from those who weren't. Spite kept her from denouncing the rumors that Cornelius was the father of her child. He had murdered her own father without repercussion. Fear prevented her from claiming James as the father. She could not tie herself to that life. She hoped to find other women like herself in Chicago. Wild women who shunned the social expectations of the times. She was right, of course. She would have found a haven on Chicago's south side, where Blacks, the red-light district, and queers were making peace with being cramped into the same area. But Mercy never found this utopian nugget. She shared a one-bedroom tenement apartment with cousins who were so distant that they were no longer related. She worked twelve-hour days cleaning until the pregnancy prevented it and bore the scornful looks from her cousins as she remained on bed rest. It had been clear for many hours during her labor that things were not going as they should; still, the cousins waited too long before getting her to the hospital.

She had felt encased in light, and perhaps this was the other sun to which she was destined. The bedsheets were soaked with her blood, while everything else was soaked in clarity for Mercy. She felt the connection of all things so clearly—all people drenched in the same light. Some know it as God, but in that moment, Mercy was aware that it was so much more than the constructions of God that she was taught, more than the scriptures that her sister had once hurled at her, more than what was preached from the pulpit. What she felt, everyone and everything was part of it. Seamlessly so. In an effort to impart this epiphany to those around her, she murmured, "Every man is a child of God." Confused, the nurses only heard "every man." Knowing Mann to be her last name, they mistook this final sentence as a naming rite.

In 1972 Every Mann waited for the Greyhound bus out of Ideal. She had received a ride to the Quick Mart from Deuce, who stood beside her, hands at his sides and uncertain of what to do, so he waited with her for the bus's arrival. It arrived at the same time

James pulled his pickup into the parking lot. Deuce tipped his hat toward Eve and left her wondering if he knew of his wife's hand in the death of the man who was like a son to him. Ideal was a time capsule of information that Eve could barely process. It overwhelmed her and these new memories rushed over her in waves as one recovering from amnesia. She had not changed, but this new knowledge gave her the feeling of a new life, one with a history. Unaccustomed to it, she had no idea what one did with a history. She had longed for it but was now uncomfortably aware of how it differed from a past. A past was unique and individual; a history was deep and shared.

James carried a brown paper sack and walked hesitantly toward her. Eve vaguely recognized him from the pictures at Geneva's house and was relieved when he spoke first.

"My wife, you know Geneva, didn't want you to get off half-starved." He thrust the sack into her hands.

Eve smiled. "I appreciate it."

James swiped imaginary dust from his pants and shifted from one leg to the other. "I, uh . . . I was close friends with your people growing up." He had caught Eve's attention. The driver began loading passenger luggage into the undercarriage of the bus.

James and Eve stared at each other in the way of those who want to make a full study of it but can only afford a series of glances strung together in the hope of creating a lingering picture. They stood side by side in silence. Eve did not receive any divine last-minute knowledge that she was a breath away from her father. James did not get hit with an urge to confess his relationship to her. Southern decorum dictated the pacing of such things, and surprise revelations were best left in the realm of soap opera dramas.

There were some physical similarities between the two, but

nothing particularly noticeable. Only someone who had made a serious study of them would do a double take at the father and daughter in passing. They had the same ears, but no one notices ears unless they are unusual. Eve had her mother's hands, which James would appreciate, still having issues with his own. They had the same eyes, unremarkable except to those who fell in love with them. When Eve's gaze darted furtively and caught James, she rested on his eyes and felt a peace that she wouldn't recognize until a later time. Her mouth, full and well-shaped, was Mercy's, and when she smiled, James felt a hint of the fatherhood pride he had never known in his life.

Eve boarded the Greyhound, mirroring James's one-handed farewell as the bus pulled out of the only Ideal city in Georgia. She thought of Nelle, the one person with whom she wanted to unpack her experience. For some reason, Eve felt more grounded and less threatened by Nelle. Perhaps her biggest issue with her friend was that she had possessed a history, a treasure, and barely paid it any attention. Not that Eve knew what one did with a history, but she was sure that Nelle was misusing her own. Now she was beginning to grasp that part of one's birthright was in deciding what one would do with history. It was just as much her prerogative to uncover it as it was her aunt's to bury it. She'd spent most of her life fighting to learn who she was and lumping together Mama Ann, Nelle, and classroom bullies, and now she'd have to extricate each of them and reexamine her relationship to them.

She thought of Brother LeRoi and his funny little egg. A beginning, he had called it. Her history was a beginning from which she emerged. Her own fragile but resilient egg. Brother LeRoi, and Woodridge before him, held on to the egg. They brought it out for an occasional examination that had more to do with themselves than the object. Sometimes they held onto it for too long, and guilt crept in. Sometimes they thought of discarding it, but obligation prevented them. Woodridge passed it down, bequeathing it to those he deemed worthy. For LeRoi, the egg and his mother's letter would remain untampered with.

Eve would be a couple of hours into her journey before she opened the paper bag stuffed with oranges, pecans, potato chips, and the fried chicken that had been wrapped in foil straight out of the grease pan. "It'll stay hot longer that way," Geneva had told James. It had remained hot, but it had also leaked. The fruit had a greasy film, and at the bottom of the bag, a grease-stained envelope with Eve's name scrawled on the outside had absorbed the remaining oil. Geneva and James had written the letter together, filling in only a few more of the gaps in Eve's quest for information.

It had taken them the better part of the night and had involved lots of tears and silences followed by cathartic confessions. They absolved each other for loving Mercy and comforted each other for losing her.

"We were just kids." Geneva dabbed at her eyes, remembering the shed and scorning her inability to not make martyrs of each kiss she and Mercy had shared.

"Don't make it no less real, baby." James patted her hand. "We were all kids. And that girl—Mercy and me . . . we still did that. We still—" His voice cracked.

Geneva embraced her husband. "She's a beautiful young lady."

He nodded and pressed himself to her as if he were trying to hide his large body in his wife's smaller form.

Geneva continued to hold him and stroke his back. "She's called Eve."

"That's beautiful," James murmured into her chest.

255

"Says it's short for Every," she added and felt James stiffen.

He gazed up at her. "What's that?"

Geneva sighed. "Every Mann." James slowly shook his head. The name confounded them both, and their combined pity inspired the letter writing.

By the time Eve would open their letter, the hodgepodge of smudges and stains would resemble the redacted narrative she already possessed.

But she would know the one thing that would change her existence. Eve would know her name.

acknowledgments

My mother was the head librarian at Avalon Branch Library on Chicago's south side, so my childhood was filled with books and well-read Black folk (mostly women) whose literary knowledge could rival Google. They were the internet before there was an internet. I learned how to ride my bike in the library after hours, when Charles Freeney Jr. (perhaps the greatest curator this world has known) popped popcorn and played Scott Joplin's "The Entertainer" on the record player. I was raised by librarians, and I must express my gratitude to that community and my early introduction to it by my mother, Jerri Conner, and her sister-friend circle (the Divas), my honorary aunts: Mary Williams, Faye Hardiman, Eloise Smith, Frances Littlejohn (RIP), and Marie Smith (RIP).

My parents are southerners who relocated to Chicago during the Great Migration. The South has always been an adjacent home space for me, nurtured by summers with my grandmother Sudie Mae Wright in Memphis. *everyman* parallels the Great Migration and also takes 1920, the year of my grandmother's birth, as its chronological beginning.

This story coalesced from my previously mentioned beginnings, my mother's genealogical research of our family, and my experiences teaching in Chicago Public Schools—specifically, when I attempted to start genealogy projects with my students. It took form during my study at the University of Illinois at Chicago's (UIC) Program for Writers and was refined over many years (about a decade). Thank you to my dissertation committee: Cris Mazza, Jennie Brier, Madhu Dubey, Chris Grimes, and Natasha Barnes.

After UIC, I delved more into the spaces and eras depicted in *everyman*, and I would like to extend a heartfelt thanks to Dr. Loretta Burns and Dana Chandler (Tuskegee University) and Jackie Anderson (RIP, a great lesbian mentor).

I cannot stress enough the importance of Black books by Black writers. My literary forefolk: Zora Neale Hurston's storytelling and curation of Black life; Toni Morrison's linguistic ingenuity; Alice Walker's queer narratives; James Baldwin's fire within; Isabelle Wilkerson's *The Warmth of Other Suns*; and Edward P. Jones, because it was *The Known World* that made me set aside the first incarnation of *everyman* and start applying to grad school.

everyman took a lot of noes. Its first yes came from my superstar agent, Beth Marshea at Ladderbird Agency. Thank you for always advocating on my behalf and for introducing me to my wonderful editor, Marita Golden. Thank you to Blackstone Publishing for all the yeses.

Finally (because if I started here, I wouldn't have mentioned anyone else), my love, partner, support, wife, and mermaid, Tiffany. You've seen how emotionally draining this work can be, and you reinvigorate me.

To my friends (Chicago and beyond) and family that are too many to name: Thank you all. I love you.